Had he really se[...] [...]e imagined it?

The smell of dea[...]

Yes, that was the [...]d been reaching his no[...] [...]thing—something big—had died up ahead.

Could it be related to the flash of color he had seen a moment or two ago?

With a sense of foreboding, the peddler increased his speed as much as he could without actually running. And now that he was close, he had an awful premonition that he knew what the object might be.

Not man-made, after all. But not an animal either. It was human hair, red orange as flame, blowing softly as the wind wafted it and attached to a body that had once belonged to a young girl, a pretty girl.

Praise for Clyde Linsley's *Death Spiral*:

DEATH
OF A MILL GIRL

Clyde Linsley

BERKLEY PRIME CRIME, NEW YORK

To Nancy
Thirty-three years and counting

DEATH OF A MILL GIRL

A Berkley Prime Crime Book / published by arrangement with the author

PRINTING HISTORY
Berkley Prime Crime mass-market edition / November 2002

Copyright © 2002 by Clyde Linsley.
Cover art by Craig Nelson.
Cover design by Rita Frangie.
Text design by Julie Rogers.

Visit our website at
www.penguinputnam.com

ISBN: 0-425-18713-6

Berkley Prime Crime Books are published
by The Berkley Publishing Group,
a division of Penguin Putnam Inc.,
375 Hudson Street, New York, New York 10014.
The name BERKLEY PRIME CRIME and
the BERKLEY PRIME CRIME design
are trademarks belonging to Penguin Putnam Inc.

PRINTED IN THE UNITED STATES OF AMERICA

10 9 8 7 6 5 4 3 2 1

Chapter 1

There. Up ahead.

The peddler squinted again at the tall grass by the side of the road, just below the crest of the hill. The flash of color that he had seen before was gone. He shook his head to clear the image from his mind and began trudging forward, the twin peddler's chests balanced precariously on his shoulders.

Had he really seen something in the grass, or had he imagined it? When the cold November winds began to blow, they sometimes blurred his vision and made it difficult to see distant objects clearly.

And the winds were certainly blowing now. They swept off the Green Mountains to the west and rushed headlong easterly toward the ocean, chilling everything in their path. This was the way of autumn in New Hampshire, and anyone who lived here learned to adapt.

The peddler was a young man, not yet twenty, but

he had been on the road for two years and was gradually building his wealth. In another two years, or perhaps three, he would have enough saved to take up permanent lodgings in a sizable town and open a store.

He had his eye on Portsmouth, a bustling seaport city blessed in the summer with cool ocean breezes and the tang of salt in the air. In Portsmouth there would be cultivated people with a taste for finer things—European fashions and exotic spices—and a willingness to pay for them. Not like these backwoods farmers and their sullen wives, who haggled over the meager price of every piece of tinware and then, like as not, would insist on paying in rags or eggs. The eggs would be rotten, and the rags would be a bundle of worn-out linsey-woolsey wrapped loosely around a handful of straw or lint. Once he had poked through such a bundle only to discover that it was filled with rocks—easily New Hampshire's cheapest and most available commodity. And they had the nerve to say that peddlers drove a hard bargain.

The peddler understood hard bargaining and even sympathized with it, because he, too, had come from a backwoods farmstead much like these. He knew full well the tricks to which a man will resort when he is hanging on to his livelihood by his fingernails, and the smell of death is at the door.

The smell of death.

Yes, that was the name of the sour-sweet odor that had been reaching his nostrils these last few minutes. Something—something big, judging by the odor—had died up ahead.

Could it be related to the flash of color he had seen a moment or two ago?

The odor came back as the wind caught it and brought it to him. He glanced ahead once more, searching the grass by the roadside for another flash of color.

Then he saw the crow rise rapidly from the ground less than a hundred yards ahead of him. If there was one crow, no doubt there were more to be found in the grass. Something had indeed died, and the scavengers had arrived.

The peddler began to walk faster, his eagerness for excitement warring with the fear that was now growing in the pit of his stomach.

Something big, but too small to be a horse or an ox. Something too colorful to survive in the deep woods, where animals tended toward browns and grays.

With a sense of foreboding, the peddler increased his speed as much as he could without actually running. The odor was stronger now, and the peddler peered closely as he approached the patch of grass.

The snatch of color was there again, although it was deeper into the grass than he had remembered. And now that he was closer, he had an awful premonition that he knew what the object might be.

Not man-made, after all. But not an animal, either. It was human hair, red orange as flame, blowing softly as the wind wafted it, and attached to a body that had once belonged to a young girl, a pretty girl. She was no longer pretty. And if she lay so quietly in this out-of-the-way place, and smelled so bad, as the crows picked at her and the maggots swarmed, she must be beyond caring.

But what a face it had been, in life. He remembered her smile, especially, and the memory brought him closer to tears than he had come in many years. The tears were put aside, however, by the overpowering stench and the horror that lay before him.

He reached the body and stood over the lifeless

form, staring stupidly at the bloated corpse, while the revulsion swept over him. The stench rose again in his nostrils, and he could feel the gorge rising in his throat.

He turned and vomited twice in the yellow grass.

Chapter 2

The letter from the vice president of the United States arrived on the coach from Boston shortly after noon on a bleak Thursday in mid-November. Samuel Skinner, the postmaster of Warrensboro, New Hampshire, was not altogether surprised to see it, for it seemed to confirm what the town had long suspected: that the recipient of the letter had not completely severed his ties with Washington City and the national government.

Skinner, unlike many of his fellow townsmen, was pleased to have been correct in his assumptions, for he—like most postmasters—was a Jackson man himself, and something of an admirer of Mr. Van Buren, as well. He was also, if it came to that, an admirer of Josiah Beede, the man to whom the vice president had written such a voluminous missive.

Skinner placed the letter behind the counter of his store and sent his eldest child out to the old Rice farm-

stead to inform the recipient of its arrival. It was, of
course, not the Rice farmstead anymore—not since
young Asa Rice had moved out to the Illinois Territory, selling his 140-acre legacy in order to raise a
small stake on which to start anew. Thank the lord old
Ezekiel had died too soon to see his son dispose of the
family property, although perhaps even the old man
would have understood the logic of trading old, worn-
out land in New England for fresh, new land in the
West.

Skinner's boy soon returned, not with Beede, but
with his Negro hired man, Randolph.

"Mr. Beede is in Concord. The superior court is in
session until tomorrow," the hired man said. "I'm certain he'd want to receive the letter promptly, however.
Can you send it on to him there?"

The letter rode the next stage south and arrived
on the following day not long after the court had
adjourned. The Concord postmaster, recognizing
the name of the addressee, decided to close his store
an hour early and personally deliver this particular
letter to the famous advisor to the president and
boy hero of New Orleans. The opportunity to meet a
personal friend of Old Hickory was too good to pass
up.

Crossing the common, brown and bare from autumn, the postmaster studied the letter for signs of
greatness, not really expecting to see them. It was not
Jackson, after all, but his all-but-certain successor, the
little Dutchman from New York, who exercised this
call on Mr. Beede's attention, and the letter itself, having traveled more than 600 miles by coach, was far
from prepossessing.

The tavern keeper pointed Beede out to the postmaster. Old Hickory's man was sitting at a table in a
far corner of the taproom, a tall, solid man who ap-

peared to be in his midthirties, with a long face and dark hair that was going to gray, looking a bit like dirty pewter. The hero of the Battle of New Orleans—he hardly seemed old enough to have acquired such an honor—was sitting by himself, nursing a tankard of ale.

The postmaster approached quietly and stood at a discreet distance in a position where Beede would see him if he looked up from the table. Presently, Beede did so.

"Are you waiting to see me, sir?" Beede asked with a smile.

"I believe, sir, that you are Josiah Beede?" the postmaster said, waiting for Beede to nod before continuing. "A letter has come for you. It was forwarded yesterday from Warrensboro, and I thought that I should deliver it to you personally."

"I'm grateful, Mr. . . ."

"Bunyan," said the postmaster, blushing like a maiden at the unexpected show of recognition. "Peter Bunyan. I'm the postmaster, here." He handed the letter to Beede, who glanced at the name of the addressee and paid the postage, but, to Bunyan's dismay, did not break the seal.

"Please join me, Mr. Bunyan, if you are freed from your duties for a moment."

Having closed his business for the day, the postmaster had no compunction about joining Beede at the tavern, which, in truth, was exactly where he had planned to spend much of his evening. He accepted the seat Beede offered him and signaled to the publican for a pint.

"You're here in Concord for the court session, I gather," he said as he seated himself.

"That is correct," said Beede. "I'm a farmer now, as

you may know, but my legal practice offers some remuneration and makes farming a bit more comfortable than it might otherwise be."

"I believe you are acquainted with Mr. Amos Kendall, the new postmaster general, are you not?" Bunyan said. "He speaks most highly of you."

"Indeed I am. We worked together in what is often called the president's kitchen cabinet. I have the utmost respect for his wisdom and prudence."

"I have known him since we were boys together in Massachusetts," Bunyan said. "We still correspond regularly, after all these years, even after he moved to the West to start a new life in Kentucky. He has had quite complimentary things to say about you. In particular, he wrote enthusiastically about your ability to resolve puzzling mysteries concerning criminal acts. There was a murder in Washington City, he said, as well as one or two in New Orleans during your years in that city. I remember reading about your exploits in the newspapers. Your fame precedes you."

"I seem to have a certain aptitude that I wouldn't have expected if the need for it hadn't arisen," Beede said.

"A useful skill, indeed."

"I suppose so," Beede said. "I doubt, however, that it will be all that useful now that I am home again in New England. Crime here is an altogether simpler, more straightforward affair."

That evening, after his companion had left, Josiah Beede sat alone at his table in the taproom and opened the letter from Vice President Van Buren. He smiled at the florid hand, which so resembled the round little New York squire himself. The letter was a personal invitation for Beede to return to Washington City in March, in the event of Van Buren's election, to take part in his inauguration.

"As a symbol of national unity in this transition of power, it would be constructive to demonstrate that my administration has the blessings and support of those who so effectively served my predecessor," Van Buren had written. "Your presence on this occasion would be politically valuable in this time of difficulty."

Under his signature, Van Buren had hastily scribbled an addendum:

"It would also be personally gratifying to me to renew our old acquaintance. Please consider my invitation seriously."

The letter continued for several pages, discussing Van Buren's plans for his own administration and hinting that Beede might wish to become a part of it. "However, I know how great is your desire to make your life in New Hampshire. I will not insist, but you will always be welcome."

Beede smiled as he closed the letter. It would be pleasant to see Van Buren again and to say his farewells to Jackson before he returned to Tennessee. He thought of Washington City, wearing its great aspirations on its sleeve despite its muddy streets, empty vista, and ramshackle boardinghouses. He did not regret his years in the capital, and the urge to return—for a brief time only—was strong.

But it would be a difficult trip. It would take nearly a week, at best: two days to Boston, two more to New York, at least two more days to Washington, if the roads were passable at all after a hard winter. And March was the season for sugaring off and for preparing equipment and tools for the spring planting.

Well, he could think about it, even if he concluded that the journey was not possible. He folded the letter carefully and put it in his pocket before climbing the stairs to his room for the night.

Chapter 3

Early the next morning, Josiah Beede packed his green bag and had the inn's stableman saddle his horse for the ride home. After a breakfast of ale and bread, he settled his accounts and was on the road just as the sky was beginning to lighten.

The road took him westward, out of the river valley and up to higher ground. Here the systematic clearing of land for cultivation was less evident. The unfortunate farmers who had preceded him had learned well the futility of plowing the steep slopes in the hope of scratching a living from such boulder-strewn land. For several miles, the woods closed in on him from either side, and several times he saw white-tailed deer grazing the low-growing bushes.

Down the hill on the other side, skirting a marsh, up another hill—little more than a drumlin, really—and down again. Beede rode slowly, not prolonging the trip but not rushing it, either. He was content to enjoy the quiet melding of autumn into winter. The scent of woodsmoke was in the air; somewhere, over that ridge or around the next bend, another farm family was already busy at the hard, everyday work of living. Even without seeing the farmhouse, Beede could imagine the chores that occupied them—chores he had himself performed so many times that they were now second nature.

Once he had feared that he had been away too long, that the everyday tasks of the farm would be foreign to him after the years spent in Washington City and elsewhere, pursuing the demands of public life.

"After all," Jackson had said, "you've been away for nearly twenty years. You've been living soft, here in Washington. I tell myself that I can do anything I could do when I was eighteen, but I know it ain't true. Some days it's hard just gettin' out of bed in the morning."

"I know, General," he had replied. "Maybe you're right, but I know I have to try. I have the money now; there's nothing I need work for here. And the memories are painful here."

"My offer stands, you know."

Beede turned to face the man who had taken him into his home, many years before. It was painful, indeed, to see a vital, ramrod of a man now bowed and worn by age and care and the pressures of office.

"Thank you, General," he said, after a moment. "I appreciate that, but there's nothing left for me in Tennessee, either."

"I need you, Josiah," President Jackson said. "When I am finally permitted to pack up my belongings and leave this godforsaken city, I will need someone capable of managing my affairs."

"With respect, sir, your estate runs well enough that

there's nothing I can do to improve it," Beede replied. "You already have a good manager and overseer. I cannot contribute anything that they can't do better than I."

"I need a man to be my legs and eyes," Jackson said. "I'm not the man I was before God and the voters put me in this place. I'm old, and tired."

"An old, tired Andrew Jackson," Beede said, "is worth ten ordinary men."

"Then come with me for friendship's sake," Jackson said. "A trusted friend is worth more than all the overseers I can hire."

Beede looked out the window of the president's house, over the expanse of green and black—the new grasses of spring melded inextricably with the new mud of spring—to the marshlands beyond. What an abysmal city, he thought. In reality, hardly a city at all, with only a few thousand people and a handful of decrepit wood-frame houses and broad, visionary avenues, pockmarked and pitted with mud and ruts. No, not a city, and hardly a village, either. He glanced up the street to the hill in the distance where the still-unfinished Capitol stood in its state of perpetual undress. Less like a city than a pasture, he thought, a pasture with pretensions.

"General," he said, at last. "I appreciate the offer. I really do. I will always be your friend. And you know there's almost nothing I wouldn't do for you. But . . ."

"But not this."

"You don't need me, General. You may need a clerk, or a secretary, or an overseer, but I'm none of that; I'm . . ."

Jackson smiled grimly. "Yes," he said. "And what are you, Josiah?"

Beede thought a moment

"I'm a farmer," he said, finally.

"What else?"

"And a lawyer."

"Yes," said Jackson. "Go on. And what else?"

"A Yankee," Beede said, astonished even as he said it. "By God, I'm a Yankee."

Old Hickory shook his head in mock sorrow.

"You're a damn fool, Josiah," he said. "But my prayers will go with you."

He had had no reason to fear, for the rhythms of the farm had returned as naturally as the seasons: planting, tilling, harvest, and then resting through the bleak winter for the cycle to begin again. And if the work was harder than he had remembered—and it was—he had Randolph, and there were always hired men who passed through for a while and then went on their way. Between his farm and his legal work, he even managed a small profit.

The route Beede took on his way home skirted the turnpike and was, in fact, little more than a cattle trail. Although many travelers found it advantageous to leave the turnpike before they reached the toll booth and then rejoin it on the far side, it was not through penuriousness that he took the less-trodden path. He enjoyed the slower pace and the solitude of the trail, free from the clatter of the mail coach and the clanging of iron pots in the peddlers' carts. Here, an occasional stray sheep was his only companion. Soon, the weather would be too cold even for sheep, and soon after that, the early snows would come. And then this path over the flank of the hill would be buried deep, not to reappear until after the spring thaws. May, perhaps, or early June.

The trail climbed not quite to the top of the hill before beginning to descend again. At the foot of the hill, it joined the turnpike, and Beede dutifully paid his toll

for the brief ride to the Warrensboro turnoff. He would
not be required to go all the way to the village, for his
farm lay on the near side of it. The turnoff told him he
was practically home.

An hour later, with the sun well into the sky, he
topped the last hill before heading down to Warrensboro. Below him, at the edge of his farthest fallow pasture, a knot of men was gathered at the side of the
road. Something fluttered in the tall, dry grass near
where they stood: something blue, and something else,
which was red and orange.

His horse whinnied in impatience to be home, and
one of the men turned at the sound. The man waved
urgently to Beede and shouted something that he could
not make out.

"Come on, Peter," Beede said. He urged him forward, and the horse eased its way down the rutted
slope.

A sickly, sweetish smell reached his nostrils. It was
an odor he had smelled too often before, and it caused
his heart to sink. Memories of the battlefield outside
New Orleans, when he was barely in his teens, washed
over him. He could see in his mind's eye the dead
British soldiers lying where they had fallen, abandoned by their comrades in their headlong retreat.

Two men detached themselves from the party by
the side of the road and began to walk in his direction:
a thin man of middle height and a shorter, rounded
man. Beede recognized the lanky one as his closest
neighbor, Jacob Wolf, and the shorter man as Israel
Tomkins, gentleman farmer, selectman, justice of the
peace. And hovering uncertainly on the fringe of the
crowd, that was Stephen Huff, the constable.

"Josiah," said Wolf. "Something terrible has happened."

Tomkins overrode him. Standing fiercely in the

center of the road, hands on hips, he glared up at Beede.

"Is this not your land, sir?" Tomkins asked.

"You know that it is," Beede said. "Have you not attempted to buy it from me more than once?"

"You do not deny it?"

"How could I do so? The transaction is on record."

"Then, sir, I do not doubt that you can explain this," Tomkins said. He turned to the knot of men by the roadside and motioned to them to move apart. They did so, exposing the body lying brokenly in the tall grass—clearly young, quite probably, at one time, pretty.

"She's dead, I gather," Beede said.

"And can you determine that without even dismounting?" Tomkins said, his eyes sharp and in accusation as he stared up at Beede. "You must have keen eyes, indeed. Can you also tell us her name?"

"I have not seen the girl's face," said Beede, forcing back the angry retort that first came to mind. "My eyes are not as acute as they were when I was younger, but there's nothing wrong with my nose. I know the smell of putrefaction."

Beede dismounted and handed the reins to Wolf. The horse shivered slightly and whinnied nervously as the odor reached its nostrils. Beede picked his way cautiously through the grass beside the road. The girl lay on her back, her face puffed and bloated, the flesh darkening like leather.

"So young," said one of the men nearby. "So young." The speaker was Nathaniel Gray, pastor of the Congregational church. It was natural that someone would have thought to bring a man of God to the scene of untimely death.

"Young, yes," Beede said after a moment. "Perhaps

eighteen? Probably no older. It's difficult to determine, considering how long she has been here in the open."

"How long ago did she die?" Gray asked. The question hung in the air a moment, and everyone seemed to be looking at Beede.

Beede bent down for a closer inspection. "I can only guess," Beede said after a moment's inspection. "Perhaps two to three days. Not much longer than that, I think, or else the deterioration would be much more severe. The days have been cold and clear, fortunately."

"Surely she did not die naturally? So young?"

"She was strangled, I believe," Beede said. "Notice the bruises on her neck, perhaps the fingers of a strong man. There was a young mulatto girl in New Orleans with marks like this. But, first, I think, she was violated."

"Why do you think so?" said Gray. He was a man of nervous disposition, putting it charitably, and Beede thought he would be of little help today.

"Look at her torn clothing. See the blackened blood, here under the fingernails. She fought someone as she died, I think. And underneath . . ."

He reached down and swiftly pulled up the skirts and shifts before a gasp of protest could be uttered. Beneath were only the long white leggings, now tattered like the dress, though not from wind and rain.

"As I suspected, bruises on the inside of her limbs, particularly along the thighs. And signs of bleeding between. There was a rape, gentlemen, or at least an attempt."

"You seem quite knowledgeable about rape and murder," said Tomkins, his suspicions clearly returning.

"I have seen both before," Beede said quietly. "In New Orleans, and in Washington City, as well."

He bent again over the darkened, swollen body and smoothed the girl's hair where the wind had blown it. He could do nothing about the tongue, which protruded grotesquely from the mouth. And even now, with the eyelids shut, the eyes bulged behind them. He raised one lid with his index finger.

"Deep blue eyes and flame-colored hair," Beede said. "And a dress to match the eyes. It's difficult to believe, seeing her in this condition, but she must have been pretty. And vain."

"Not a farm girl," said Gray.

"No," Beede agreed. "The dress is finely woven cotton, not homespun. And what farm family could afford the indigo needed to dye her dress this shade of blue?"

Beede felt she had died with her eyes open. Someone, perhaps her murderer, had shut the lids after death. An attack of guilt brought about by an accusatory stare? The sight of those protruding and unblinking eyes, which had continued to glare at him after death, might have mocked the passion of the moment and caused her killer to close her eyes in a feeble attempt to hide from himself the reality of his deed.

But guilt did not explain the careful attempts to smooth her skirts and petticoats and to arrange her hands so carefully and peacefully in her lap. It suggested that the girl had known her attacker, and that he, for it was almost certainly a man who had done this, had, in some strange fashion, felt some compassion for her—after the deed, if not before.

"Who found her body?" Beede asked.

"A peddler," said Tomkins. "He was traveling toward Concord and happened to see her hair fluttering in the weeds beside the road. The color attracted his eye. Or so he says." The old squire now seemed to have abandoned the idea of Beede as a suspect and to have pinned his suspicions on the stranger.

"Where is he now? Someone should question him."

"He is locked in a storage room at Sam Skinner's store. We could not let him go on his way with this matter unsettled."

Beede straightened and turned to look the older man in the eye. He realized, for the first time, that Tomkins was an inch or more shorter than he.

"Do you think the peddler murdered her?"

Tomkins shrugged. "He's a stranger. She was a stranger. It has nothing to do with us."

"Perhaps," Beede said, "although it seems unlikely he would have reported the body if he is the one who killed her. In any event, we have a duty toward this poor girl."

Arrangements were made to remove the girl's body. Tomkins reluctantly agreed to permit the use of his barn until she could be prepared for burial. It would not do to bring her into the house, as the body had been too long exposed to the elements, and decomposition had proceeded too far.

Tomkins had a house full of daughters, and Deborah, his eldest, would be enlisted to help make the body ready. Beede volunteered the assistance of Mrs. Shelton, a widow who he had hired as a housekeeper and who often was called upon to serve as a midwife in the community.

So the somber little party began to break up. A wagon was sent for and soon arrived, trundling behind a pair of ancient oxen. As the wagon pulled away with its desolate cargo, Stephen Huff fell in beside Beede and motioned to him with his head. The two men walked in companionable silence a short distance away from the others.

"An unfortunate business," the constable said finally.

"Especially unfortunate for you," Beede agreed. "Apprehending the man who committed such an act will not be an easy task, I fear."

"Indeed," said Huff. They walked on a few paces more, and Huff said, "I hope that I might persuade you to assist me in this matter."

"In what way?"

"I have no experience with crime, as you have," Huff said. "You have already been useful. You saw readily enough that a murder had been committed here. I confess I had not known what to think, but murder was far from my mind."

There was the ring of truth to that, Beede thought. Those who held the office of constable in rural New England, like the office of road surveyor or selectman, were appointed each year by the town meeting. The qualification for such an office would be minimal, at best. Often, the less attractive offices were parceled out to those unfortunate enough to arrive late to the town meeting. In an area where violent acts were not commonplace occurrences and, when they happened, were usually obvious, it would be an unusual constable who had had to deal with murder within his jurisdiction. It was not surprising that Huff would not think of murder.

"I am still a newcomer to Warrensboro," Beede said, thinking of his farm, which he had neglected during his weeks in the courtroom.

"That is true," Huff said. "However, you have earned the respect of nearly everyone in town through your knowledge and your industrious nature."

"Except, perhaps, for Mr. Tomkins."

"Even Mr. Tomkins," Huff said. "Your disagreements are personal and political, but he would admit, if pressed, that you're an honorable man. And you have acquired an impressive record for bringing criminals to justice."

Beede considered this. While he had, indeed, been away from his farm, he knew that it was in good hands with Randolph. And in fact the work of the farm was largely done by this time of year. That was the reason court sessions were scheduled for the fall season, after harvest was mostly completed.

What would he lose by helping with an investigation? Some reading time perhaps. But that was a selfish consideration, which should not overshadow the needs of the community.

"What would you have me do?" he asked.

"We have a man in custody," Huff said. "The young peddler who claims to have found the body. Perhaps you could accompany me when I question him. I have heard his story, but you may sense the things he does *not* say."

"Then we should talk to him while the matter is still fresh in our minds," Beede said.

They returned to the place where the body was found. The little band of spectators was dissipating, but Wolf readily agreed to ride Beede's horse back to Beede's farm and to inform Beede's household that he had returned.

"This is truly a tragic affair," Wolf said as he mounted. "Who is she, do you suppose?"

"I have no idea," Beede said grimly. "But I intend to find out."

"It's probably beyond hope that her murderer can be identified," Wolf said. "The murderer would have had three days to make his escape. He could be in Boston by now, or Canada."

"Perhaps. We must make every attempt, however."

• • •

Samuel Skinner's storeroom had no windows, and the young man had not been provided with a candle. The constable led him out, blinking, into the dim sunlight that filtered through the windows.

"What's your name, boy?" asked Huff, not unkindly.

"Albert," the boy said. "Albert Sanborn."

"And where do you live?"

"On the road. I was born in Massachusetts, but I've not been back for two, nearly three years."

"Sit down here, Albert, and tell us what you know of this affair," Huff said, pointing the youth to a stool that had been moved out from behind the counter.

The peddler was young, as Beede had been told, with blond hair reaching almost to his shoulders. Beede studied him carefully, noting the thin, straight nose on the triangular face, the cobalt-blue eyes, and the smile that alternately appeared and disappeared as the boy fought to control his anxiety. Slender almost to the point of emaciation, he seemed to Beede an unlikely candidate for the role of murderer of young ladies.

"I've already told you all I know," the youth said. "I ain't hiding nothing."

"Tell us again, if you please," Beede said gently. "I haven't heard it yet."

The boy turned, startled, at the new voice.

"Go ahead, boy," Huff said. "This is Josiah Beede, one of our leading citizens. He's a fair-minded man. If you're innocent, you have nothing to fear by telling him your tale."

"*If* I'm innocent," the boy snorted, emphasizing the word *if*.

"You must admit it's a bit unusual to stumble upon a body the way you did," Huff said. "Two strangers in Warrensboro on the same day, and one of them cruelly violated and murdered. Who would you suspect, if you were me?"

"I didn't kill her," the boy said. "I found her, but I didn't kill her."

"Tell us how you found her," Beede said.

"But first, sit down," Huff added.

The boy glared defiantly at the two men for a moment, then slowly settled on the stool.

"I was on my way to East Warrensboro," the boy said. "She was lying in the grass by the side of the road."

"How did you happen to see her?" Beede asked.

"I noticed the hair, first. But then there was the odor, too. The smell was horrible, like rotting meat."

"How was she lying when you saw her?"

"On her back. Her eyes were closed, but her face was darkened and her features cruelly distorted."

"Where were her hands?" Beede asked. The boy pondered the question.

"Her hands were folded in her lap," he said, finally. "She looked almost peaceful, as if she had simply gone to sleep by the side of the road. Except, of course, for that horrible expression on her face."

"What did you do then?" Huff asked.

"I walked farther down the road, looking for a house. When I came to one, I knocked on the door until someone came, and I told the man what I had seen."

"You walked?" Huff said. "You should have run for help."

"I have two heavy chests, which I must balance on my shoulders," the boy said, contemptuously. "I'd like to see you run with such a burden. And it was clear that the girl was beyond help. There was no reason to hurry."

"And what time was this?"

"The sun was high. Near midday, I think."

"Who did you ask to help you?" Beede asked.

"I did not ask his name. An older man, long and thin. A farmer."

"Jacob Wolf came to see me while I was at dinner," Huff said. "The time would be consistent with this young man's account."

"Then we had better talk to Jacob, as well," Beede said before returning his attention to the young man.

"Mr. Sanborn, you must travel these roads frequently," Beede said to the peddler. "Have you ever seen this young lady before?"

"No, sir, I have not," the peddler said. The hesitation was almost, but not quite, unnoticeable.

The young peddler was taken back to his storeroom. After he was gone, Skinner approached the two men.

"That young man must be moved from here," he said. "I must make use of that room, and it is exceedingly difficult with a prisoner occupying it."

"We can't let him go," Huff said. "Josiah, could you put him up for a few days, until this matter is settled?"

"I believe so. Give me an hour or two to break the news to Mrs. Shelton. Then bring him out to the farm. With Randolph and Mrs. Shelton always present, he will be unable to go far."

They took their leave of Skinner and began walking toward the town common. At Woolard's tavern, they prepared to go their separate ways, Huff to the taproom and Beede to his farm.

"Do you think the young peddler is our murderer?" Huff asked.

"I do not know," Beede said. "If he's guilty of this crime, the guilt does not appear on his face or in his manner. He was not entirely forthcoming with us, however. Did you note how he hesitated before denying that he had ever seen the girl before? He knows something that he does not care to tell us."

"How could a man commit such a crime and not show it in his face?" Huff asked, pausing at the tavern door. "I think such guilt would follow a man to his grave."

"Certain men are capable of greater subtlety than most of us can imagine," Beede replied. "And I believe some men have no sense of guilt for their actions, no matter how heinous."

He took his leave of the constable and began the walk home.

Chapter 4

The sun was low in a sky the color of musket barrels, and it cast long, cold shadows across the village common. Beede walked the three miles back to his farm as quickly as possible, and in less than an hour he saw his clapboard house dozing in the afternoon sun beside the kitchen garden.

Winter was not far away. Beede anticipated the winter with pleasure. Winter offered opportunities for reading and study that often had to be forgone during the growing season. He had gone to Boston the previous March and had returned after a week, saddlebags bulging with books that could not be obtained in New Hampshire: histories, books of political discourse, almanacs, and agricultural treatises. The long nights of December and January would enable him to immerse himself in those books.

Adrienne had not understood about his books. Her English had been serviceable, at best, and she was

barely literate even in her native French. She had
found no pleasure in reading and envied the pleasure
he took for himself. Not for the first time, he allowed
himself a moment of guilt for the five years in which
they had coexisted in an uneasy truce.

Five uncomfortable years, two strangers sharing
pleasurable intimacies and unexpected tensions. Five
years, and then she had died, taking with her their stillborn son. He remembered the accusation burning in
her eyes in the moment before the life ebbed from
them.

A frightened rabbit darted across the rocky path,
startling him out of his reverie. He watched it vanish
into the underbrush, and he became aware of the squir-
rels all around, scampering noisily over the forest
floor in desperate search for winter forage.

He had, he knew, spent too much of his life alone
with his thoughts. Now they were familiar acquaintances that often took liberties with his hospitality and
came to him unbidden—occasionally at inappropriate
times.

In the yawning opening of the barn, a dark hulk of
a man was pitching manure onto a waiting oxcart.
Catching sight of Beede on the path, the man lay aside
the fork and strode in his direction.

Adrienne's man Randolph was Beede's constant re-
minder of that short, unhappy marriage. Two years of
farm work in the watery New England sunshine had
lightened Randolph's walnut exterior slightly and had
added perhaps twenty pounds of dense muscle to his
tall frame, Beede noted approvingly. But the traces of
Louisiana and Washington City lingered in Randolph's brisk walk and cheerful demeanor. He had not
yet acquired the lumbering, taciturn ways of a Yankee
farmer—a manner that strangers sometimes mistook
for sullenness. That, and the precision with which he

spoke, often confused those who assumed that all Negroes were slovenly and uneducated. Randolph, however, had been taught to read as a boy by a mistress
who had taken an interest in his education. That early
training, coupled with a quick wit and keen powers of
observation, had prepared him well for freedom.
Beede was happy that he had been able to provide it.

"Mr. Beede, welcome home, sir." The walnut face
was wreathed in a grin that seemed genuine and wel-
coming.

"Thank you, Randolph," Beede said. "I confess I
have been thinking of home for more than a week
while I sat and dozed in that courtroom. It's good to be
back."

"Mrs. Shelton will be overjoyed to see you, as well,
sir. After three weeks with only two mouths to feed, I
fear she is feeling unappreciated."

"And how are you and Mrs. Shelton faring?" Beede
asked. His housekeeper's feelings toward Negroes
was not something she kept hidden.

"We are reaching an accommodation," Randolph
said. "She did not refuse to feed me, but she did so
with minimal civility."

"That, at least, is an improvement, is it not?"

"Indeed, sir. And I have hope of further improvement to come."

"Do you require my intervention?"

"Not at present. I relish the challenge of winning
her over."

They had reached the edge of the barnyard now,
and Beede looked around with approval. Randolph
had attacked farm work with the same diligence with
which he had always undertaken new tasks, and he had
mastered it as he had mastered everything else. The
life of a black man—even a free black man in New
England—where slaves were not permitted—was

never easy, but Randolph seemed to be capable of sur-
mounting any obstacle.

"Everything appears to be in fine order," he said.

"I have had considerable assistance from Mr. Wolf.
He spent the better part of three days here last week,
helping me repair fences. I am obligated to return the
favor next week, with some barn repairs."

"I must thank him personally," Beede said. "I have
to speak with him in any event, concerning another
matter. Have you heard about the unfortunate girl
whose body was found on the Concord road this morning?"

"Mr. Wolf mentioned it in passing. He stopped by
the farm to return your horse and to say you had arrived from Concord but would be delayed in returning
to us."

"Mr. Huff has asked me to assist him with his investigation," Beede said. "I'm on my way to the place
where the girl's body was found to see what else I may
learn from the scene. I thought it might be helpful if
you were to come with me. I think I can benefit from
a fresh pair of eyes. Are you free?"

"I'll be happy to help. I can finish spreading the
manure later."

"I suppose I should greet Mrs. Shelton before I go,"
Beede said.

"She has gone to the Tomkins house," Randolph
said. "Her assistance was needed in preparing the
body for burial."

"If we can identify her quickly," Beede said, "we
may be able to bury her before the ground freezes."

They made short work of the distance to the edge of
the fallow field where the girl had lain. Soon they
stood at the edge of the road and looked at the bed of

grass, still depressed from the weight of the girl's body.

"This is where she lay," Beede said. "An itinerant peddler found her."

"Are we looking for something in particular?" Randolph asked.

"Something that might help us to identify her. I confess, however, I have no idea what that might be. None who have seen her so far can put a name to her."

"A broken locket, perhaps."

"Or a Bible. What sort of possessions might a young woman have, do you think?"

Instead of answering, Randolph looked across the field toward the farmhouse. The house could not be seen from here; a stand of oaks and chestnut trees, interspersed with birches, blocked it from sight. In between the trees and the place where the two men now stood, the field of tall grass stood yellowing in the autumn sunshine.

"She came from there," Randolph said, pointing toward the field. "You can see where the grass has been bent aside by the passage."

"Do you think she was killed on this spot?"

"Perhaps, but I doubt it. There are no signs of a struggle here, and the passage through the grass is not wide enough for two people. I suppose she could have been followed by another, but it seems more likely that she was killed elsewhere and carried to this place."

"Across my land," Beede said. "Strange that no one saw a man carrying a girl in his arms. I would think such a sight would attract attention."

"The field cannot be seen from the house," Randolph reminded him. "And aside from an occasional peddler, this road is not much used during the autumn after the harvest is in."

"That is true enough," Beede admitted. "On the

other hand, it raises the question of why they were here, and how they came to be here."

"The bent-grass trail ends at the fence line separating your property from Mr. Wolf's woodlot," Randolph said. "On his side of the fence, the land has not been cultivated for many years. I doubt very much that we will be able to follow the trail through the trees and brush, and it's unlikely that Mr. Wolf would have seen anything untoward from his window."

Beede left Randolph by the roadside and carefully retraced the path by which the girl had most likely been carried. As Randolph had predicted, the trail ended at the fence line. Beede stood on his side of the property line and peered through the underbrush. In one direction, he could see the corner of one of Wolf's outbuildings, but he could not tell whether it was a smokehouse or a privy. It was too small to be the main house or a barn, but it had the same ramshackle thrown-together look of all of Wolf s structures.

Beyond the woodlot lay the Hanover road. Possibilities and scenarios ran through Beede's mind as he tried to piece together what had happened. If an unknown man had carried his lifeless burden from there, he might have come from anywhere in New England. However, he would have required a conveyance of some sort—a wagon, most likely—which someone might have seen. An abandoned wagon or carriage might arouse someone's curiosity. It would be worth investigation.

And was it really a man who had carried the girl all this distance? A stout woman might also have done so, though she might have had to put down her burden once or twice. But why would she then carry the body as far as she had? Would it not have been quite as effective to deposit the girl among the trees?

And a woman would not have caused the bruises

and bleeding on the girl's thighs. Bruises such as these were consistent with sexual activity forced upon an unwilling participant. A strong woman might be capable of such things, Beede thought, but a man seemed more likely.

Unless there were two people involved? But there was only one trail, and the existence of two assailants implied a conspiracy of the most depraved and distasteful kind.

"Mr. Beede!"

Randolph's voice jolted Josiah out of his thoughts, thoughts he was only too happy to leave behind for the time. He turned to see that Randolph was kneeling at the spot where the body had been found.

"I have found something that might interest you," Randolph said as Beede approached. He straightened up and handed Beede a small white object. Beede saw that the object was round, with a hole drilled through the center.

"Perhaps I can find another," Randolph said. He pawed the grass a moment and turned up yet another object like the first.

"I thought there might be more," he said.

"I have seen something like this before," Beede said.

"Yes, you have, sir. Don't you recognize it?"

"I feel that I should, but . . ."

"I knew it immediately," Randolph said. "It is a bead, meant to be threaded with others on a strand. Mrs. Beede used such a string every day."

"A rosary," Beede said, suddenly understanding.

"Yes, a rosary," Randolph said. "The girl who lay here was Catholic."

A diligent search failed to uncover any more beads, although they searched for almost an hour, both at the spot where the girl had lain and along the pathway through the field.

"Surely we are mistaken," Beede said, finally. "A rosary consists of more than two beads."

"It consists of many more than two beads," Randolph said. "I am as surprised as you that we have not found more of them, but I believe they are rosary beads."

"A young Catholic maiden lying by the side of the road in a small New Hampshire village," Beede said. "It is difficult to believe."

"There are quite some number of Catholics in America," Randolph said.

"Yes, in Boston, or New Orleans, or even Canada, but not here. I doubt there is a Catholic family between here and Boston. A hired man, perhaps. Young Irishmen are always passing through seeking employment. But a girl, and alone!"

"Perhaps she was not alone," Randolph said. "Perhaps she was killed by the person who accompanied her."

Chapter 5

There were two men standing in the dooryard as Beede and Randolph returned from their investigation. Beede remembered belatedly that he had agreed to put up the young peddler in his house.

"Yonder stand Constable Huff and the young peddler who found the girl's body," he said to Randolph, indicating the men who waited several yards away. "We dare not allow the peddler to leave the village until he is absolved of guilt in the murder, but Mr. Skinner could not continue to confine the boy in his storeroom."

"Certainly not without binding and gagging him," Randolph agreed. "Every customer who entered the store would hear his shouts. Is it your intention to house the boy with us?"

"We might put him to work for his keep," Beede said. "Surely we could use some assistance."

"The heavy work is nearly done," Randolph said.

"But I daresay I could find ways to keep him occupied."

"He's no stranger to farm work, I think. He may have been peddling most recently, but his hands still bear traces of the calluses of a farmer."

Huff had seen them coming before they reached the farmhouse. He grabbed the peddler by the ear and began pulling him in Beede's direction.

"Here's your young peddler," Huff said, the kindly manner he had displayed toward the boy earlier now gone. "I thought I might have to drag him out here. He tried to escape when we let him out of the storeroom."

"There's no point in running away," Beede said to the boy. "You'd only be brought back."

"I'm a peddler," the boy said bitterly. "I'm losing money sitting here."

"We have your merchandise under lock and key," said Huff. "You'll not have it returned until this business is over."

"You might as well hang me now, if you take away my livelihood."

"We'll see to it that you are kept alive and well," said Beede with a wry smile. He felt some sympathy for the boy, but it would not do to show it. "And you can pick up your trade again when you are released from our custody."

"But time is of the essence, and I cannot afford delay," the peddler said. "Winter is approaching, which will make travel difficult, if not impossible. I must sell my wares soon, while I can."

"I'll put you to work myself for the time being," Beede said. "There's always work to do on a farm, even with winter coming on. I'll pay you a fair wage and provide for your board and lodging. I'll hold your goods for security and return them to you if you are shown to be free of guilt for this crime."

"If I had wanted to be a farmer, I would have stayed in Massachusetts," the boy said grumpily.

"If you had stayed in Massachusetts, you would not be in your present circumstances," Beede said. "Until your circumstances improve, you had best make what you can of the opportunities available to you."

"To be trussed like a chicken and sacrificed to the hangman," said Sanborn. "Now, that is truly a golden opportunity."

"Have faith, boy," Huff said. "We're not all demons here."

"So you say." The young man stalked away and disappeared around the corner of the farmhouse.

"Perhaps I should follow him," Randolph said.

"No," Beede said. "He needs time for self-pity. He'll not stray far while we hold his goods."

The three men stood in uncomfortable silence, awaiting the peddler's reappearance. After a while, Randolph took his leave of the others and followed in the peddler's direction. When he had gone, Beede told Huff about the beads he and Randolph had found near the body.

"Rosary beads!" said Huff. "I have heard of them, but I have never seen them."

Beede fished one from the pocket of his frock coat and handed it to the constable.

"This!" said Huff, in exclamation. "You're sure this is not simply an Indian bead? I'd expected something more sinister in appearance."

"It's from a rosary," Beede assured him. "There should have been many more of them, yet we found but a few. Randolph is of the opinion, and I tend to agree, that the girl was killed elsewhere and carried to the spot where we found her. Otherwise, we would have found many more beads than we did."

"I wonder why we didn't find beads like these when we first discovered the girl," Huff sand.

"I don't know. Perhaps they were under the girl's body and were therefore hidden until the girl was moved."

"Curious," said Huff. He looked up at Beede. "And your man Randolph found them?"

"That's correct."

"I don't suppose you suspect Randolph of placing them under the body, as well."

"No," said Beede, a trace of annoyance creeping into his voice despite his intentions. "I can't conceive of that."

"I can appreciate your trust in your hired man, and I'm sure your judgment is sound," Huff said in a doubtful tone. "Nevertheless, it is my understanding that the charms of such a fair young woman might be more than a dark-skinned man could bear."

"Randolph is a married man," Beede said, his words tight. "He has a wife in Virginia, for whose freedom he has been putting aside most of his wages."

"Yes," Huff said. "You're right, of course. However, it is not my impression that the marriage contract is always as sanctified as it might be. And in fact, slaves are not permitted to enter into contracts, are they?"

"Randolph is a man of principle," Beede protested.

"I see," said Huff after a moment. "So I suppose we must look elsewhere for our murderer. I beg your pardon, Mr. Beede, for my untoward suggestion. I mean no harm."

Mrs. Shelton returned from the Tomkins house soon after sunset, wheezing from the exertion of the walk and murmuring sadly about the tragedy of it all.

"It were more than I could bear, Mr. Beede," she said as she settled her cumbersome frame into the Boston rocker near the fire. "I've seen young people die, of course. My own Benjamin was just sixteen when he fell from a ladder while patching our roof. I think that's what killed my poor husband, seeing his only boy lying there breathing his last. But this . . ."

"It is truly an unhappy event," Beede said.

"It is more than tragic, Mr. Beede," she said. "It's evil. To take a young girl just entering the prime of her life and to use her so . . . it's downright evil. I pray that the man who done this is captured and hanged. He deserves no less."

"I will do my best to see to it," Beede said. "Mr. Huff has asked me to assist him in the investigation. I share your sentiments."

"We must send word to Dr. Hutchinson over from Concord to conduct an autopsy," she said. "It's pretty clear how she died, I suppose, but we ought to do it anyway, just in case we missed something."

Supper that night was a glum affair, even by the relatively taciturn standards of Yankee households. Mrs. Shelton usually attempted to maintain conversation at mealtimes—one of her most attractive characteristics, in Beede's view—but she sat silently at her place, often avoiding even meeting Beede's eyes. Randolph, of course, received such treatment from Mrs. Shelton every day, but for Beede it was a new and uncomfortable experience. Albert Sanborn, the young peddler had retired sulkily to his sleeping place in the barn, claiming not to be hungry.

"The girl's body was discovered by the peddler," Beede said finally, in an attempt to initiate conversation. "He stopped at Jacob Wolf's house and told him what he had found. I suppose Jacob's house was more visible than ours, even though the body lay closer to us than to him."

"Poor man," Mrs. Shelton said. "Must have been a shock to him. Jacob's been alone so long in that rickety old house of his, I doubt he's seen a woman close up in four or five years."

"We ought to have him over for a meal sometime, if it's all right with you," Beede said. "Might do him some good, if you don't mind the extra work."

"Cookin' for four's easy as cookin' for three," she said. "Go ahead and invite him. I don't think he'll accept, though. He's been alone so long I think he's come to like it."

That night, the sky turned the color of milk, hiding the stars from view. Shortly after midnight, the first soft snowflakes of the season began softly falling. They lay gently on the barren village green in the center of Warrensboro and dusted the rooftops of the houses that clustered around it.

Three miles away, in his room at his farmhouse, Beede was awakened in the early morning hours by a snuffling sound somewhere beneath his window. Throwing open the window, he leaned out and saw an enormous spotted sow—not his own—rooting in his kitchen garden.

He pulled on a shirt and trousers and rushed downstairs, snatching a hoe that stood by the side door as he left. The sow heard him coming and scuttled quickly away through the fence. It turned then, with a snort of defiance, and rooted itself on the spot in four-footed arrogance.

It did not resemble any of his neighbors' animals, as nearly as he could determine in the darkness. Perhaps it had wandered many miles away from a farm in another town, living on whatever it could forage from the woodlands and from gardens such as his own. Beede could almost feel its desperation.

The sow remained on the road, glaring at him. Beede waved the hoe threateningly, and she backed away, but when he made no further moves toward her, she slowly came closer.

They remained thus, an uneasy truce prevailing. Beede stared at the sow. The sow stared at Beede. It was becoming a battle of wills, Beede thought, and he was by no means certain that he would win it, for it was cold, and he was not dressed for the weather. Fat, wet snowflakes assaulted his eyes and nose and burned through his linen shirt.

But the sow gave in first. Turning resolutely away, she trotted a few yards down the road, turned, looked back wistfully at the garden and its guardian. Beede could sense her thoughts; she was weighing her chances and concluding that they were slim.

When he was certain that she would not return, he entered the house and trudged upstairs to bed. But he did not sleep for some time.

Chapter 6

The snowfall amounted to little more than a light dusting, which looked in the morning like white chalk on the fields and fence posts. Beede awoke reluctantly and moved slowly to the window overlooking the kitchen garden. The sow had not returned.

He walked to the meetinghouse for the Sabbath service alone. Mrs. Shelton, who normally accompanied him, had complained of ill health that morning and had remained abed. Randolph avoided Sunday worship entirely, having received a cold reception from the congregation on his first visits.

It was religion, as much as agriculture, that had drawn Beede back to New England: sober, straightforward Congregational worship with its rigorous gospel and its levelheaded preaching. This was Christianity shorn of the wispy pieties and high-church folderol of the Southern Episcopalians and the French Catholics

of Louisiana. It embraced him like an old friend and
never failed to invigorate.

To be sure, it had its faults. It sought after perfec-
tion and was disinclined to tolerate those who fell
short of the goal. Beede himself was too aware of his
own shortcomings to be entirely comfortable pointing
fingers at his neighbors, particularly when the sins of
which they were accused seemed to have harmed no
one.

In that respect—that sole respect—he admired the
laissez-faire attitude that prevailed in Louisiana, with
all its hypocrisy and avarice. Was gluttony truly a sin
when Louisiana cooks could produce dishes that filled
the body and warmed the soul? For Pastor Gray, now
launching into what promised to be a lengthy sermon,
the answer would be yes. But Josiah suspected that
Pastor Gray had never experienced a New Orleans
bouillabaisse or a Creole gumbo.

And yet, he thought, the consciousness of guilt that
was so much a part of the New England version of
Christianity was also an ever-present spur to improvement. It distinguished man from the beasts of the field
and gave him a goal toward which to strive. He did
not, unlike the Unitarians, believe that man could perfect himself through his own efforts, but neither did he
believe that sins could be expiated through ritual acts
of penance as did the Catholics of Louisiana. Guilt, as
much as life itself, was a gift from Almighty God.

Normally, Beede forced himself to pay strict attention to the sermon, but he found it difficult to concentrate this Sunday morning. His thoughts kept turning
to the girl who had been so brutally murdered at the
edge of his property and to the sow he had discovered
rooting in his picked over kitchen garden the previous
night. For some reason, his mind had made some un-
explained connections between the two, and he found

himself puzzling over what those connections might be.

In the first place, he thought, both were out of their normal element. The sow belonged to someone, on a farm probably not very far away. The girl, too, belonged somewhere—or had—and would be missed. Like the sow, she might have run away from wherever she belonged, but she would have left a trail.

The sow, no doubt, had survived by foraging where it could. Beede doubted that the girl could have done as well. She would not know where to look for food in the woods, and she would need to find shelter. For those necessities of life, she would have had to turn to people. And in that event, someone must have seen her.

As Pastor Gray droned on in the pulpit about sin and salvation by grace, Beede considered the problem of the murdered girl. Who might have seen *her*? A storekeeper? An innkeeper?

Perhaps—if she had money. Otherwise, it would have been futile for her to attempt a transaction with either.

Of course, many people still preferred to conduct their business with goods rather than money. Barter had been an accepted form of commercial transaction in rural New England for more than a century; indeed, it had been the only form of transaction for many years. The girl might have acquired the necessities of life through some form of barter. But what would she have with which to trade?

The answer was obvious and distasteful, and he turned his mind to other matters. He tried to concentrate on the sermon, which was now developing into a description of the tortures that awaited unrepentant sinners in hell, but his mind refused, drifting instead toward his own personal experience of hell.

• • •

*A flash of blinding light and a noise that could
shake buildings. Another British mortar shell had exploded overhead. He attempted to sink into the spongy
earth beneath his feet and waited for the hot iron rain
to fall.*

*Beside him, Seth began to moan again, perhaps in
fear as much as pain. Josiah glanced at his brother,
who lay propped against a cotton bale. To his right,
one of the Kentuckians, a blond-bearded youth not
much older than he, bit off the end of a powder cartridge, cursed, and spat out the end of his cartridge
before ramming the powder home down the barrel of
his long rifle.*

*Behind them, the hot metal fell from the sky. Josiah
made himself as small as he could, attempting to meld
with the cotton bale, as he prayed for the salvation of
his soul and for the shelling to end.*

*And Seth moaned again, his lifeblood oozing to the
ground through the crude bandages. Josiah ran.*

There was another noise now, he realized. Not gun-
fire or mortar shells, but music of a sort. The organ—
third-hand but new to the congregation—wheezed and
brought him back to the present. The congregation
joined it in a chorus of "Old One Hundred," and he put
aside his thoughts for the moment.

After the service, Beede made his way to the meetinghouse door, greeting his fellow parishioners, ex-
changing information about crops, discussing the
weather, and engaging in the usual banter. He had been
pleasantly surprised at the way the town had taken him
in and accepted him as part of the community. New
Englanders had a nationwide reputation for standoff-
ishness, and he had feared that they would consider
him an outsider after all his years away. Instead, he

had been greeted enthusiastically by nearly everyone and made to feel welcome at once.

Well, except for Israel Tomkins, the squire of Warrensboro, who occupied the grandiose manor house at the far end of the green. He could see the little man bustling out the other door, shepherding his flock of daughters ahead of him, speaking to the few parishioners he considered his near equals but studiously avoiding Beede.

Tomkins was an enigma. From the day Beede had arrived in Warrensboro two years earlier, he had sensed the enmity in the older man. Later he had learned that Tomkins had made an offer for the farm but that Asa Rice had chosen to sell to Beede instead—and at a lower price than Tomkins had offered.

Clearly, the affront had angered and embarrassed Tomkins, but it had nothing to do with Beede himself. He had not known about Tomkins's offer when he had agreed to purchase the land, not that it would have made a difference in his decision. It was his money and Asa Rice's land, for each to do with as he wished. If Rice had chosen not to do business with the most prominent landholder in town, it was within his prerogative not to do so.

And in any event, it was done now. Beede watched Tomkins and his flock move out of the meetinghouse and across the green toward home. He turned and began the long walk toward his own house and farm. The afternoon worship service would begin soon enough.

A voice called after him. Beede turned to see the somber figure of Pastor Gray hurrying toward him. He ran, clutching his robe to keep the hem from rubbing the ground, like a woman lifting her skirt and petticoats.

Beede waited in astonishment. In his two years in

Warrensboro, Gray had rarely spoken to him aside from a perfunctory greeting at the meetinghouse door, much less actually run after him. Surely he must be bringing a message fraught with importance.

But he was not. As he drew closer and saw that Beede was waiting for him, he abruptly ceased running, dropped his skirts, and ambled slowly for the remaining distance.

"Thank you for waiting, Mr. Beede," he said at last, favoring Beede with one of his mechanical smiles. "I fear I am not the man I was in my youth."

Beede said nothing, and waited.

"I have been meaning to thank you," Gray went on, "for the delivery of firewood you left for us on Saturday last."

"No thanks are necessary. It was my turn." Everyone in the congregation provided firewood for the pastor and, during the growing season, with produce from their fields.

"Nevertheless," said Gray, "I am often forced to harass my flock to give up its due. I have never found it necessary to do so with you. I am grateful."

"I am happy to do my part, sir," Beede said. Gray was leading up to something; of that he was certain, but he had no idea what the clergyman's objective might be.

"I would be obliged if you could see fit to join my family and me for dinner today," the pastor said. "It would be our pleasure to enjoy your company, and I daresay you would be relieved not to have to return to your farm and then hurry back to arrive for the afternoon service."

"Thank you for the invitation, sir," Beede said, "but I have chores that must be done and may not be finished in time to return for the afternoon worship. Mrs.

Shelton is feeling ill, so Randolph and I must do her work as well as our own."

Gray seemed crestfallen, so Beede hastened to make amends.

"Perhaps some other time."

Gray brightened considerably. "Oh, of course," he said. "Why not join us for tea tomorrow if your duties permit it? My daughter Mercy has made some delightful cream cakes."

Beede hated tea but could hardly say so.

"I'd be delighted," he said.

Chapter 7

Josiah Beede had wanted, indeed expected, to be a farmer, but his dream had ended on an afternoon in July, a few days before his thirteenth birthday. He was present when the end came, but he did not recognize it as such until days later.

He had been in the fields mowing hay with his father and his brothers. It had been hard, tedious work, as nearly all farm work was in the summer, and no one had worked harder or longer than his father. In later years he could still see his father on the day of his death, far ahead of his three sons, wielding the scythe as if it had been grafted to his body.

Josiah had been resting and catching his breath when his father suddenly disappeared from sight. A moment or two passed before the meaning of what he had seen sank in. Then he was running as fast as he could, calling to Thomas and Seth to hurry and follow.

Their father was gone before they could reach him.

Thomas bent down and searched for signs of life, but even Josiah could see that there was no hope.

"It must have been his heart," Thomas said finally. "Josiah, you're the fastest runner among us. You must run to the house and tell mother, Sadie, and Louise."

His life changed profoundly on that day. Although his father's will bequeathed a portion of the farm to each of his children, the property was too small to support two separate households, let alone the five that would be required if all of his children were to receive their full inheritance. This fact led to considerable squabbling among the brothers and sisters. Eventually, Thomas, the eldest, solved the problem by buying out his brothers and sisters for pennies on the dollar. The two girls were happy with their meager sums; they had not wanted land that could not support a family. Seth, Josiah's middle brother, complained bitterly but took his portion of cash, nevertheless. Josiah, the youngest, had no say in the matter, and no opinion, either.

A few months later, Josiah succumbed to his middle brother's pleading and contributed his portion of the inheritance to further Seth's plan to set themselves up as peddlers in the new lands to the west.

For more than a year, they traveled through Illinois Territory, then south along the great Mississippi. War was abroad in the land, and Seth reasoned that wartime armies would be good customers. In Kentucky, they joined with a band of irregulars bound for New Orleans, where the Kentuckians intended to fight the British alongside Andrew Jackson.

By the time the battle had ended, Seth was dead, and Josiah had found, in Jackson, a mentor and patron. Jackson took him in and raised him almost as if he were a son. When the time came, he helped Josiah gain admission to read for the law. Then, with his new skill, Josiah returned to Tennessee to work with his mentor.

He returned to New Orleans to practice for a while, and married there.

When Jackson was elected president, Josiah was called by the great man to Washington. There, in the rowdy new seat of government, he became successful and moderately wealthy as a practicing lawyer and ex-officio advisor to Jackson.

But life in Washington City was not the bliss he had imagined. His wife, a New Orleans Creole, was unhappy there and yearned bitterly to return to New Orleans. He hoped for a while that the birth of a child would improve her outlook. Instead, he lost both Adrienne and their stillborn son to childbirth fever.

Without the ties of family—either his new one or the one into which he had been born—he found the trappings of wealth and public visibility less than appealing. The pace of life in the capital and the issues that engaged the administration hid his dissatisfaction for a while, but the time came when he could no longer deny it to himself. He was meant to be a New England farmer, dying breed though it might be.

Once the realization came upon him, Beede wasted no time. He booked passage on a ship to Boston. There he took a room, acquired a horse, and began riding the roads around the city in search of available land. It was, he soon discovered, a futile exercise. He had forgotten how close and congested New England was, particularly to a man who had spent his early adulthood in the West.

He found Boston particularly unsettling with its cowpath streets and cramped, narrow houses, and the outlying villages were little better. After a week he could stand it no longer. He packed his traps and caught a coach to New Hampshire, and as he jounced through the rocky countryside, he again breathed a sigh of hope, for the land here was much less densely settled.

He stopped for the night in Nashua, where the sight of a score or so of water-powered manufacturing mills threatened to plunge him into deeper depression. A companion in the taproom raised his hopes again.

"Go north," he said. "If you would have open land, you must go north—beyond Concord, even. It may seem that you're approaching the ends of the earth, so far will you travel, but the journey will be worth the effort."

"Then there is land, still? And it can be had?"

"For a song," the man said. He spat prodigiously, narrowly missing a spittoon nearly six feet away from their table. The brown liquid spattered at the base of the taproom bar.

"Here, now," said the innkeeper indignantly. "Aim better next time."

"Mind you," his companion said as if the innkeeper had not spoken, "it won't be an easy life. Farming in New England ain't like farming in the South. We have few Negroes here, and no slaves, and our growing season is much shorter. And we have two hardships no Southern planter ever had: boulders the size of horses and long, cold winters."

"I remember," Beede said. "Winter was always my favorite season."

"Well, we'll see how you like it when the snow lies all around, drifting as high as your second-story windowsill, and you must shovel your way to the barn at milking time," the man said. "As a boy, I cleared pathways to the barn and the privy until I could stand it no longer. That's when I made up my mind to pursue the itinerant mechanic's trade, honing knives and scythes. I left home at fourteen, and I've never returned."

"I was a peddler once," Beede said. "But it was a

decision of necessity, not preference. No, New England winters hold no terror for me. I look forward to them. And as for weather, for hardship there's nothing in New England to compare with summer in Washington City."

He continued northward, as the peddler suggested, until he reached New Hampshire. There he made inquiries, acquired another horse and saddle, and packed a few belongings in the saddlebags. Following the advice of a local lawyer, he set out in a westerly direction, asking at each village along the way about farmland that might be available for sale.

It was early on the morning of the fourth day that he topped the rise and saw below him the village of Center Warrensboro. It lay before him, pristine and white like fine china, and his breath caught in his throat. At one end of the green, which was beginning to blossom in wildflowers, was a meetinghouse like the one in which he had spent his childhood. At the opposite end was an imposing green clapboard house, enclosed by an equally imposing white picket fence.

Nearby, and only slightly smaller than the great farmhouse, was a house that swung a tavern sign from over the door. Adjacent to the tavern was a building that could only be a store. A single ox stood patiently before it, harnessed to a cart into which two men were loading burlap bags. Other, smaller houses dotted the perimeter of the green.

As he watched, the front door of one of them opened. A stubby woman stepped out and began shaking dust from an oval rug. A breeze blew up suddenly, causing the dust to blow back in her face, and she stumbled, coughing and sneezing into the front yard so that the dust would not reenter the house.

From his vantage point, he could see it all without being noticed, except by someone looking specifically

at the horizon. For several minutes he took in the scene
that sprawled before him. His eyes, his ears, even his
nose made note of the details of the tiny scene and
filed them away in his mind: the profusion of red, yellow, and fuchsia in the window boxes of the houses,
the soft plunk of tools now being loaded into the oxcart, the sharp scent of fresh manure closer at hand, in
the fields on either side of the road.

Everything about the scene said home as he remembered it twenty years earlier, before he had stolen
away in the night to pursue the life of a peddler. Before the towns of the western frontier had passed by:
Cairo, and Vincennes, and Ste. Genevieve and New
Orleans. Before Chalmette, and Andy Jackson, and
Washington City.

Why had it taken him twenty years to return to New
England, where he was meant to be? What had he been
waiting for? He knew it no longer mattered. He was
here. He was home. Now it was merely a matter of
finding a farmer who wished to sell his land and move
west.

He found several, but one stood out from the others.
The owner was a young man, who inherited the land
from his father, and his father before him, but who had
no interest in continuing the tradition and who, in any
event, had had only daughters. Beede walked the land
alongside young Asa Rice and noted with approval
that the house and the outbuildings were tightly fitted
even after nearly 120 years.

"My father did not do things by halves," Rice said
in agreement. "Nor did his father. It's a trait they
passed along to me."

"Why do you want to sell?"

"I shouldn't tell you this," said Rice, "but it's the
land itself that's the weakness here. Dig six inches
below the surface at any random spot, and you'll turn

up more rocks than soil. Dig twenty feet down, and you'll hit bedrock. You'll want to have two plows if you buy my land, because one plow will always be at the smith's for repairs. And it's all uphill and downhill here, hard plowing even without the boulders that are strewn in your path."

He paused at the edge of a fallow field, leaned against the split-rail fence, and looked Beede directly in the eye.

"I want to sell this land," he said. "But I want to make a friend and not an enemy. You must know what you're getting into here."

"You think I don't know what it's like?"

"You grew up on a farm in New England, so you've had a taste of the way we live here," Rice said. "But time dulls the memory and rounds off the sharp edges. Even now I remember mostly good things, and my experience is much more recent than yours. I remember husking parties and barn raisings, and I forget how long it required for me to plow a single acre of this rock quarry I call a cornfield. But this is a hard land. It wears out plows and oxen and people. I've had twenty-five years of it, and I'm ready to admit defeat. It's the western territories for me. I hear the land is flat there."

After leaving the farm, Beede stopped at the village center and purchased some writing paper at the store. He stood in a corner and, using the store counter as a writing surface, composed a letter to his bank, requesting sufficient funds from his account to purchase the Rice property. After finishing the letter and borrowing some sealing wax from the storekeeper, he waited to see the storekeeper dispatch the letter on the afternoon stagecoach. Two months later, as autumn began to color the ready hills, he took possession.

Randolph closed the house in Washington and came north to join him.

He had expected that he would have to practice law in order to supplement his meager harvest, but he doubted that the taciturn Yankees among whom he now lived would provide much income. He was mistaken.

One October afternoon barely a month after settling in as he sat in his parlor stoking a fire, he heard footsteps on the flagstone doorstep, followed by a series of sharp knocks on the door. Rising to meet his visitor, he found himself face-to-face with a heavyset man in a broad-brimmed straw hat.

"You're a lawyer," the man said without preamble.

"I am," said Beede.

"Good." The man heaved himself into a chair near the fireplace. "I want to sue someone."

"Who?"

"The squire."

"Who?"

"Tomkins," the man said, shouting as if he suspected Beede were deaf. "Old man Tomkins, in his big house on the green and his gentleman farmer airs."

"Has Mr. Tomkins wronged you in some way?"

"Well, I wouldn't be coming to see you if he hadn't, would I? Stole my sheep is what he done, and he won't make it right without I take him to court. If I let him get away with this, he'll be after my ox, next."

"I don't understand," Beede said. "Where are these sheep now?"

"In the pound. It'll cost me two dollars to get them out. I ain't got two dollars, and he knows it."

"What are your sheep doing in the pound?"

"Eating me out of house and barn," said the man. "They're getting better feed than they ever get from me."

It was not a difficult case. The farmer's sheep had been found grazing on another man's land, and Tomkins, as justice of the peace, had consigned them to the animal pound until the costs were paid. By demonstrating that his client could not pay the amount charged, Beede convinced the "squire" (as nearly everyone called him) to allow the farmer to work off the debt over time. But word of this minor victory made the rounds of the community, and Beede soon found himself with enough work to subsidize his farm to a considerable degree.

And if his legal work sometimes took him out of town for weeks at a time, it was a small price to pay. Many clients paid their debt to him from the produce of their own farms or the sweat of their brows. It helped as well that courts generally met after harvest and before planting time, for judges were farmers, too. And he had Randolph, who was learning the arts of agriculture quickly and promised to be of great assistance.

All in all, he had felt that his new life held much promise. It was a quiet life compared to his previous existence, but he was ready for quiet.

Except now he had a corpse on his hands, and the quiet he had worked so hard to find seemed very distant indeed.

Chapter 8

Someone came seeking the dead girl the very next morning. Mrs. Shelton answered the knock on the door shortly before noon and found a girl standing there—a girl who appeared to be in her middle teens with a round, placid face and dark hair parted in the middle and gathered in long braids on each side of her face. Mrs. Shelton stared dumbly at the girl in her woolen cloak and plain cap, and waited.

"Excuse me, ma'am," said the girl, looking up to the housekeeper. "I'm seeking a friend who I believe has come this way. Have you seen her, perhaps?"

"Come in, girl," Mrs. Shelton said, preoccupied, as always, with the practical. "Don't stand out there letting the heat escape. It's cold enough in this house as it stands. Where did you come from? Have you eaten?"

Beede was sent for. He left Randolph and Albert in the field, where they had taken up the manure-spreading

work that had been left off the previous day. He found
the girl seated in his favorite rocker by the fireplace,
sipping a cup of coffee in his parlor.

"Her name is Sharon," the girl told him once the
preliminaries had been established. "Sharon Cudahy.
Perhaps you've seen her? I'm certain you would have
noticed her and remembered. She's very pretty, with
bright red hair and the deepest blue eyes I have ever
seen."

"Is she perhaps seventeen years of age?"

"She turned eighteen last month," the girl replied.
"Then you have seen her? Is she still nearby? If not, do
you know where she might have gone from here?"

"What is your name, young lady?"

The girl colored. "Oh, I *do* apologize," she said.
"What must you think of me? I am Alice Patterson.
My father is Ephraim Patterson of East Sandwich. I
am employed at the Kerrigan cotton mills downstream
from here in Amoskeag Village. Sharon and I worked
side by side there until the day she left."

"And when was that?" Beede asked.

The girl seemed to sense something in his voice, for
she asked, "Is she no longer here? Have I missed her
again? I've been searching for her for more than a
week, and I had hoped that I was near."

"Miss Patterson, I fear that my information shall
distress you," said Beede, and he told her about the
young girl whose body had been discovered by the
road.

The girl began to weep, but she regained control
after a moment and looked steadily at Beede. "But are
you sure?" she said. "You have never seen Sharon, so
can you be certain it is she?"

"From what you have told me, I feel all too certain," Beede replied. "But if you think it will not be

too upsetting, I would be grateful if you could confirm it for me."

"You could not dissuade me," she said. "I must know what has happened to my friend. If it is the worst, then so it must be, but I must know."

Stepping outside into the cold, gray day, she became silent. Beede was made aware once more of the discomfort that every woman felt—except Mrs. Shelton, for some reason—when they were alone in his presence. Clearly, he harbored some malady, some character flaw, which would forever sour his relations with women. Of course, Adrienne had felt no such discomfort, but he was so much younger then.

He considered briefly whether to ask Mrs. Shelton to come with them to the Tomkins barn, where the body of the murdered girl lay. But it was not feasible; he had only one horse, and it would not be hospitable to ask them to ride together.

In the end he saddled the horse, and he led the girl, riding, through the village to the Tomkins house.

"Isn't it difficult for a young woman such as you to travel alone in these rural parts?" Beede asked. "And will you not be missed by your employers?"

"They closed the mill for two weeks," said the girl. "The looms are powered by belts made of leather, and one of the belts broke. It made no sense to go home to East Sandwich, which is much farther away, and I hadn't the money to stay on at the boardinghouse. I decided to go in search of Sharon."

"How long did your friend work at the mill?"

"Perhaps a year, perhaps more. We're all supposed to stay for at least a year. If you leave sooner, they add your name to the blacklist, and you can never get mill work again, at least in a nearby mill."

"And how long has she been gone?"

The girl thought a moment. "She left in late summer. August it must have been. This is the first opportunity I've had to look for her."

The Tomkins house stood at the upper end of the common on the location that Israel's maternal grandfather, Thomas Warren, had chosen for himself as one of the original settlers in 1750. It had been shrewdly chosen, with an eye not only for the lush meadowland that lay behind it but for the commanding facade it presented to its fellows, interspersed in less imposing positions along either side of the green.

At the far end stood the Congregational meetinghouse, and the two dwellings—one for Tomkins, one for the Lord—seemed to vie with each other for pride of place. If the meetinghouse won the competition, it was only by the slightest of margins and only because its whitewashed frame gleamed in the sunlight as the green Tomkins house could not. And on a gray day such as this, with the sun a silver sliver glimpsed occasionally through the clouds, the battle for preeminence was very nearly even.

"What a beautiful house!" Alice said.

Beede thought of the grandiose plantation houses he had seen in Louisiana, framed by their archways of live oaks. He thought of the magnificent mansions being erected even now in the American sector of New Orleans—houses that dwarfed this pompous edifice, with its mock-classical pretensions, looking grotesquely out of place in this country of boulders and scrub. He thought of his own house in Washington City, the city of pigs and mud and government, which nevertheless overshadowed this puny pomposity as the president's mansion overshadowed a toolshed.

Beede thought of all these things, but he said nothing. He understood the girl's reaction better than she knew. In fact, he realized that he, too, preferred the worn and weary honesty of these New England dwellings to the more elegant houses of the South and the cities. Better a farmhouse in New Hampshire, with a pasture and a cornfield and a woodlot, than a row house in New York or Philadelphia, cheek by jowl upon its neighbor.

They did not stop at the doorway. Instead, Beede led his horse and rider to the north side of the structure and paused before a barn nearly as imposing as the house it complemented.

"Sharon is in here?" the girl said, wrinkling her nose.

"I'm afraid it won't be a pretty sight," Beede said. "But it is necessary for someone to identify her, and you are the only one who can do that."

She seemed to catch her breath for a moment. Then she nodded and said, "Of course."

He helped her to dismount. She paused a moment before the door but entered without hesitation when he opened it.

Mrs. Tomkins sat in a chair beside the body, which had been covered with a sheet. She stood as the girl approached and looked questioningly at Beede, who nodded. Slowly, she drew back the sheet.

The girl looked at the reclining form, and Beede could see tears forming in the corners of her eyes. Finally she nodded and turned away. She strode quickly away through the still-open door.

When Beede caught up with her, the tears were gone. She stood beside an oxcart, staring out at the field behind the barn.

"I did not recognize her at first," she said. "Her face is so . . . twisted and ugly. She was so beautiful before, that for a moment I thought it wasn't Sharon at all."

"But you are certain now?"

"Yes. I recognize the dress, and the hair is unmistakable. But the face is so distorted. It is as if Satan had taken possession of her body in her last moment of life. She was a papist, you know."

"This thing was not the work of the devil," Beede said. "Strangulation causes the eyes to bulge in such a manner."

"But she was so fair, and now she is black."

"Her body has lain outside for several days. What you see is the work of sun and wind and rain. I'm sorry you had to see her in this condition."

"It is hardly the Sharon I knew," she said. "Please, Mr. Beede, find the person who did this awful thing." She turned from him and began sobbing once more while Beede stood by in embarrassed silence.

Chapter 9

"**O**ur young girl has been much in my thoughts," said Stephen Huff. He tilted his head and drained the ale from his tankard.

"And in mine," Beede said. "Although I fear I have no idea who killed her."

They had met at the Tomkins barn when Beede had brought Alice to view the body and had agreed to meet again at the tavern at the end of the day. Beede welcomed the opportunity to escape the tension of the farm, where Mrs. Shelton maintained a chilly silence in Randolph's presence and an austere formidability when he was out of her sight. Huff, Beede knew, had married for land, rather than companionship, and he was now thinking better of his bargain. The tavern meeting suited them both.

"The squire is willing to place the blame on an outsider," Huff said. "I suspect he favors the peddler for the crime."

"And what do you think?"

The constable shook his head. "I'm every which way," he said. "At first, we had a murder, and the peddler was at hand. But either he's a better liar than I could ever imagine, or he's not the cold-blooded killer he would have to be in order to have performed this deed."

"I agree," Beede said. "And you are the constable. Is it necessary that Mr. Tomkins be persuaded, as well?"

Huff stared morosely into his tankard as if in search of a wayward drop of liquid. "You should know, of all people, how the squire dominates the community," he said finally. "If he remains in doubt, he will worry us to distraction. And he has the ear of Pastor Gray, who will harry the entire village. Whatever the explanation for this crime, we must persuade Mr. Tomkins of its plausibility."

"Is that possible?"

Huff glared at him. "You are still new to the village, Mr. Beede, or you would not ask such a question. Mr. Tomkins is often irritable and sometimes arrogant, but he is a fair and decent man. It will not be a simple matter to persuade him, but he will listen to evidence."

Beede took a swallow of his rum flip and considered what Huff had said.

"We know a little more than we knew yesterday," he said finally. "We know her name. We know she worked at one of the cotton mills in Manchester. Miss Patterson tells me that she was from Ireland and was not long in this country. She was a Catholic."

"And you say she was violated not long before her death," Huff added. "That may point us to a motive."

"I think she was killed somewhere else and then carried to the spot where we found her body," Beede said, after a moment's thought. "There were no signs where we found her of the struggle that must have ensued. And someone—presumably her murderer—then straightened her clothing and folded her hands in her lap. That argues against a simple crime of opportunity. She was acquainted with the man who took advantage of her and killed her."

"None of this information puts us nearer to her murderer," Huff said.

"But perhaps it can show us where we must go for answers," Beede said. "To whom did our peddler go after he found her body? Jacob Wolf, wasn't it? Perhaps Jacob will remember something that will help us. I'll call on him tomorrow."

Beede slept late the following morning. He awakened after sunrise with the guilty realization that the business of the household had begun without him. He dressed hurriedly and descended the narrow stairs to find Mrs. Shelton working on the midday meal.

"Good day, sir," she said pleasantly enough as he entered. She did not, he noticed, say "Good morning," even though the sun had not been an hour in the sky. Mrs. Shelton would not venture to criticize her employer directly, but she had her standards.

Beede poured some coffee and savored the thick, hot liquid. It brought back memories of New Orleans, the smells of the market and the warm sunlight filtering through live oaks.

"Where is Randolph?" he asked.

"Your *darkie* went to Mr. Wolf's farm," Mrs. Shelton said. "Said something about owing him some work on a rock wall."

"I had forgotten," Beede said. "How long ago did he leave?"

"Soon after sunup. Took the peddler with him. Said he couldn't be trusted alone."

"I had better join him," Beede said. "I've been meaning to talk to Jacob, anyway."

On his way to Wolf's farm, Beede took the path that led past the place where the peddler had found the body of Sharon Cudahy. Strange that the unidentified girl now had a name like everyone else. With a name, he thought, she had suddenly become more real to him. The name reminded him that she had once been a living person, not some inanimate object originally made in the form of a girl now distorted almost beyond recognition.

He looked at the place where she had been found, but he did not stop. It was difficult to see where she had lain, in fact, because the grass was no longer pressed flat by the weight of her body. The earth was healing its wounds. It remained to be seen whether its inhabitants could do the same.

Wolf's house stood open as a barn. It was typical of the man, Beede thought. Wolf stood in little danger of theft, both because few strangers came this way and because Wolf owned little of value. "If there is no danger," Wolf would reason, "why close the door at all?" He had been a widower for twenty-five years, and men who lived alone did not do things strictly for the sake of appearances.

Beede stepped inside and called his neighbor's name, but there was no response. He passed through the front room to the small chamber Wolf used as a bedroom. There was an upstairs portion of the house, but Wolf had told him that he had sealed it off, being unable to climb the stairs as easily as he had in the past.

The room was not quite as bare as Beede had anticipated. In addition to the wooden bed there was a small table containing a pitcher and basin. Beside it sat a lead comb—unusual since Wolf had almost no hair except in fringes around his ears—and a razor. The bed was rumpled from sleep. An oval rug lay in tatters on the floor, and Beede suspected it had lain there since before the death of Wolf's wife. Perhaps the comb had been hers, as well.

But he was not here to inspect his neighbor's house, Beede reminded himself, but to assure himself that his neighbor was not at home. He had already been inside longer than was, perhaps, seemly. Beede looked out the window toward the rock wall, which led upward over the top of the hill behind the house. He could see no men working along the wall, but perhaps they were working on the other side of the hill.

The three men were, indeed, working over the hill as Beede discovered when he came upon them in a few minutes. Randolph saw him first. He grinned at Beede and gestured to Wolf, who was working beside him. The older man stood slowly and waited for Beede to approach. The peddler, Beede noticed, labored on in unhappy silence.

"I'm embarrassed that I was not here earlier," Beede said when he came within earshot. "Randolph mentioned to me yesterday that he would be coming to help you today. I should have come with him."

"We're nearly finished," Wolf said. "It would have been a difficult job for a tired old man such as me, but your two strapping young lads made short work of it. But I daresay I can find some work for you, if you're determined to help."

It was less age than melancholy that afflicted Wolf, Beede thought, but he let the comment pass.

"Perhaps I can be of *some* assistance," Beede said.

"But I would like to talk with you somewhere in private, first."

They walked together some distance from the others. As it happened, it was Wolf who spoke first.

"Josiah," said Wolf, as they walked together back to his house, "I believe I have something that belongs to you." He motioned toward the rear of his house, where his chickens were pecking and scratching. He pointed to a hen standing off by herself in a corner of the chicken yard, studiously ignoring—and being ignored by—the others.

"She's not one of mine," Wolf said. "I noticed her a couple of days ago. The others won't have anything to do with her, of course, but my rooster is enamored of her and won't let them harm her."

"I recognize her," Beede said. "She has wandered off before. I'm fortunate to have such an honest neighbor. Many a man would have eaten her by now."

"That isn't my way," Wolf said. "I'll fight for my own, but I want no more than what's mine. I'll find a sack so you can take her home with you when you go."

Wolf walked on toward the house. He walked slowly, Beede noticed, as if each step pained him.

Wolf seemed to sense what Beede was thinking. "I am an old man," he said. "And what is worse, I am an old man without issue. I have no one of my blood to help me, and I cannot afford a hired man, except only on occasion. And no wife, and no heirs."

"Randolph and I are more than willing to assist you," Beede said. "And Mrs. Shelton would not mind an extra place at the table."

Wolf shook his head. "I am already too much a burden to my neighbors. I'll not increase that burden as long as I can hold out. Still, I've half a mind to sell, as Asa Rice sold to you. I have a nephew in Illinois Territory who might have me, if I make myself subservient enough. Wouldn't you like to buy my farm from me?"

"I have more land than Randolph and I can handle, at present. Remember that I have no family, either. The peddler is some small help, but I do not expect him to stay with us forever."

"Perhaps you would permit Randolph to buy my farm," Wolf said. "I would be pleased to sell to him. He's an industrious fellow, and he has learned quickly."

"It isn't up to me to permit Randolph to do anything," Beede said. "I doubt that he has saved enough to make such a purchase, but I'll mention it to him."

They were at the doorstep now. Wolf motioned for Beede to precede him, and he closed the door behind them. He strode quickly to the banked fire and began to stir it to life.

"Since you didn't care to have our discussion in the presence of the others, I assume it has to do with the murdered girl," he said over his shoulder. "I don't know that I can tell you much."

"I didn't want to discuss the murder in the peddler's presence," Beede admitted. "Mr. Huff and I do not think him a likely suspect, but until he is ruled out, we must be discreet."

"And Randolph? He was around when the girl was killed. Do you suspect him, too?"

"I can't believe it was Randolph," Beede said. "Perhaps I do not wish to believe it. He's been faithful in my service for many years, and in my wife's service for many years before that. I have always found him to be upright and of the highest moral character."

"For all that, a man can break," Wolf said, still stirring the embers. "The most upright man can be faced with a temptation that he cannot resist."

"That is so."

"But I confess I don't fancy Randolph for such a crime, either. And I would be greatly disappointed if he were to be accused of it." He hung the poker on its stand again and stood. He walked to one of the two chairs in the room—a rocker—and settled into it. Beede took the other and turned it so that it faced Wolf.

"It would help me," Beede said, "if you could recall the incidents of the morning when we found the girl's body. Could you do that?"

"It wasn't so long ago, and there's little enough to report. I had finished the morning milking and was carrying the pails back to the kitchen when I encountered the young peddler in the barnyard. He told me what he had found, and I followed him to the site."

"Immediately?"

"Almost. I put the milk pails down in the house. Then I followed him straightway."

"And what did you find?"

"Exactly what you found," Wolf said. "We touched nothing."

"What was the peddler's demeanor at the sight of the girl's body?"

"Rather calm, I would say. Of course, he had seen her before and so, I suppose, had had time to compose himself."

"Did he say anything?"

"Not much, and what he said was of little consequence. 'It's terrible.' He said it over and over."

"What happened then?"

"I went for the constable," Wolf said. "I left the boy there to guard the scene. I found the constable at the tavern, where he is usually found, and he returned with me as rapidly as we could go."

"So the peddler was alone with the body for a period of time."

"Yes, of course," Wolf said. "But, then, he was alone with the body before he reported to me, as well."

"And the girl was dead already," Beede said.

"Yes. So what could he have done in my absence that would have made any difference? I can't think of a thing."

Neither could Beede. He continued his interview for a few more minutes but learned nothing that seemed relevant or substantive. He thanked Wolf for his cooperation and made ready to leave.

"I hope you know," he said, "that you are welcome at my house at any time. In fact, I would be honored if you would join us for our thanksgiving dinner next week."

Wolf shook his head. "Thank you, Josiah, but I cannot. I require little food these days, and less meat. My needs are simple, and my appetite is meager. And I fear I'm not much in the mood for giving thanks anymore."

"If you change your mind . . ."

"I will not. But thank you for the gesture."

Wolf shut the door behind Beede as he left the house. As he did so, Beede thought for a moment that the old man sobbed.

Taking tea with Pastor Gray and his family was every bit as tiresome as Beede had feared. Afternoon tea socials sometimes became community affairs, particularly during the autumn and winter when neighbors often had time on their hands and used their leisure in rounds of amiable gatherings. In this instance, however, there were no other guests. Faced with the prospect of relying on their own resources for the afternoon's amusement, both the host and hostess and their sole guest found themselves lacking for conversation. After the predictable topics had been exhausted—the weather, the harvest (for Gray was a farmer, too, in a small way), and the state of the meetinghouse roof—they lapsed into an uncomfortable silence that stretched for long minutes while the clock in the corner of the parlor ticked off the inexorable seconds.

But the cream cakes were quite good, as the pastor had promised, and Mrs. Gray had coffee available, as well as tea. Beede decided he should be content with small blessings.

During one of the interminable silences, he found himself studying the pastor and his small family at close range. They were a loving family, responding to each other with unfeigned affection, laughing easily and often. Louisa Gray, the pastor's wife, was as round and soft as the pastor was cadaverous. Timothy, the son, had his father's blue gray eyes and narrow shoulders, and he moved with a poise and grace that belied his years.

But it was Mercy, Gray's daughter, who clearly was the favored child in this household. Beede could see why. She was, he estimated, sixteen or seventeen years old, with golden blonde hair set in spit curl ringlets. Her delicate figure was clad in a shimmering material—satin, perhaps—that made it a simple matter for an observer to follow her gentle curves. She was dressed, Beede thought, in a fashion more suitable for a Beacon Hill soiree than for an afternoon tea with one of her father's parishioners.

He was embarrassed to find himself becoming unsettled as she flitted gaily about the room, engaging him with her eyes and her lilting voice. It occurred to him that, despite the differences in their ages, she was deliberately seeking to attract his attention. He had to remind himself that she was merely trying out her charms in an experimental way, to perfect her powers for the courting games that she would engage in during the coming years.

"Do you also play, sir?" It was Louisa Gray. Beede was suddenly aware that she had been speaking to him for some minutes.

"I beg your forgiveness," he said. "I seem to have been woolgathering. I didn't hear your question."

"It's quite all right, sir. I asked if you played a musical instrument. Our Mercy is becoming quite accomplished on the fiddle. Mercy, dear, please find your fiddle and play for Mr. Beede."

"Oh, no, really," Beede began, but he realized with dismay that the girl had already left the room. With a sinking feeling, he resigned himself to his fate. In the adjoining room, he could hear the girl already tuning her instrument.

It was a painful two hours. Mercy Gray was diligent but without discernible talent. She had learned a smattering of traditional fiddle tunes and attempted to make restitution for her poor skills with seemingly boundless enthusiasm. What was worse, once having played through her entire repertoire—a performance of about thirty minutes' duration—she was prevailed upon by her doting parents to reprise her most successful efforts once more, and then once again, on the pretense of "practicing." Beede smiled faintly and suffered in silence.

As he made his manners, Gray led him a little away from his wife and family, wrapping his arm familiarly around Beede's shoulder. It was a gesture that seemed entirely out of character for the circumspect minister, and it caught Beede by surprise.

"I have been meaning to talk to you, Mr. Beede, about Mr. Wolf," he said in an intimate tone. "I worry about him very much."

"As do I," Beede said. "I would guess that he is in his sixties, but he seems much older. He grows more despondent with each passing day."

"What might the congregation do to help?"

Beede thought. "Feed him," he said at last. "I cannot believe his crops have yielded sufficient food to see him through the winter. Indeed, I'm certain they are *not* sufficient, and yet he will take nothing that he perceives as charity."

"Your observations coincide with mine," Gray said. "If you could suggest a way to overcome his resistance, I would appreciate hearing it. You may call upon me at any time." He clapped Beede on the shoulder and released him to go his way.

It was a curious incident, Beede thought as he walked home. Nothing of importance had transpired during this allegedly social occasion—nothing, in fact, that could not have transpired during a brief moment's conversation following the Sabbath meeting.

Except, of course, for the fiddle concert. Clearly, Pastor and Mrs. Gray were inordinately fond of their beautiful young daughter and doted on her every move. But the child's atrocious, unmusical efforts had averted conversation and misdirected the entire afternoon. Beede could not make sense of it.

Unless the concert had been the point of the affair. Could it be that the Grays were hoping that Beede might be sufficiently attracted to their daughter to pay suit? She was certainly lovely to look at, in a simpering sort of way, Beede thought. She caused a stir inside him that he had almost forgotten. But he could not imagine marrying anyone as long as his guilt about Adrienne lay heavy on his heart. And he could not imagine a time when it would not do so.

• • •

"**S**he *walked*, do you say?" Jacob Wolf said. He braced himself and slowly lowered the stone from his shoulder to the top of the rock wall. "Thirty miles?"

"Thirty miles," Beede agreed, lending a hand to steady the rock. "Perhaps a little more. I've not measured it, and I daresay she hasn't, either."

Wolf let go of the stone and leaned against the wall, breathing so heavily that Beede began to fear for his health. "Long way to walk, for a young girl," he said.

"I quite agree," Beede said. "Why do you not sit in the shade for a bit? Randolph and I can finish up here." He gestured in the direction of Randolph, who was working alongside Albert Sanborn perhaps twenty feet away.

Wolf shook his head. "You and Randolph have a farm of your own to work. Mind you, I'm grateful for your assistance, but I fancy I must do for myself as much as I can for as long as I am able."

"A bit of a rest will not hurt you," Beede said. "Nor will a bit more labor hurt us. Rest a bit. This is what neighbors do for each other."

"I am already in your debt," Wolf said, but nevertheless, he sat wearily on the nearby stump of a white oak tree. Beede and Randolph carried on hauling boulders from a nearby pile and setting them in place on the wall.

"So what do you make of this young lady?" Wolf asked. "What is her interest in the dead girl?"

"She says the girl was a friend, and I have no reason to think otherwise," Beede said. "She has come a long way for someone she considered an enemy."

"Or for a friend, either, seems to me," Wolf said. "A long, long day's walk in the best of times, for a strong, fit man. At least two days for a girl. She has put herself out considerable for someone she could not have known well."

"I have the impression that young ladies form fast friendships quickly," Beede said. "I confess I have little personal experience to rely on in these matters, however."

Wolf sighed. "Nor I," he said. "It has been so long since my Livvy died that I can hardly remember her. There is a hole in my soul where she used to live, but I can hardly picture her face anymore. Sometimes, in my dreams at night, I can almost touch her, but the image dances away when I awaken, no matter how I try to hold on to it."

It was as near to self-pity as Beede had ever heard from Wolf. "Did you ever think that you might marry again?" he asked.

Wolf was silent for a moment. "There was a time when I thought . . ." he said. He was silent for a moment more, "But it could not be. I do not think of it anymore. And what of you?"

"Me?"

"You, also, have lost someone you loved. Do you ever think of marrying again?"

Beede shook his head. "No, never," he lied. "I have everything I need." And he lifted another stone.

Chapter 10

"**M**r. Beede, do you feel that Vice President Van Buren will be a good president?"

"I do, Miss Tomkins."

"As good as General Jackson?"

This impromptu meeting had been called by the squire for the purpose of planning the funeral of Sharon Cudahy. But New England funerals were simple affairs—no point in making an elaborate occasion out of what was, unfortunately, an everyday occurrence—and the details had been settled in a matter of minutes.

Strangely, no one seemed in a hurry to leave, and Tomkins was not attempting to break up the gathering, either. Beede had the sense that the squire was pursuing an agenda of his own, the purpose of which was not yet clear. Indeed, Tomkins had not attempted to introduce a new topic of conversation, seemingly content to follow the discussion wherever it might lead.

From the corner of his eye, Beede was dimly aware that Tomkins was watching him closely, with a slight smile threatening to break out at the corner of his mouth. The old squire was enjoying Beede's discomfiture. As the community's leading Whig, no doubt, Tomkins felt that Beede, the son of a struggling Yankee farmer, had been elevated to a high place in the town without the proper antecedents. No matter that he had trained for the bar, had served as an advisor to the president, and had amassed a fortune of some size. It was this sort of attitude among the gentry that had persuaded Beede that he was a Democrat.

"That I can't say, Miss Tomkins," he said, after a deep breath. "And of course he isn't president yet. The electors have not met."

"But he *will* be president, don't you think? Could anyone in this era run on General Jackson's coattails and lose an election? I should think no one else would stand a chance."

"Deborah, watch your tongue," said Tomkins quickly.

"I believe in the discernment of American voters, Miss Tomkins," Beede said. "I believe they chose correctly when they selected General Jackson in three separate elections. I believe they will choose correctly again this year."

"They will choose Mr. Van Buren?"

"I believe so, yes."

"And is Governor Van Buren also a slavery man like General Jackson?"

"I do not believe so."

"You don't know?"

"I have never asked him."

"But he is General Jackson's man, is he not? And General Jackson is a slaveholder, is he not?"

Beede sighed.

"Miss Tomkins," he said with as much patience as he could muster, "no one in this country has more respect for General Jackson than I. He was a father to me when I had none, He was my mentor and benefactor and confidant. I have seen him on the battlefield and in the president's mansion, and I admire his honesty and his upright nature. But I do not agree with him on all things, and slavery is one point on which we disagree."

"And Governor Van Buren?"

"Governor Van Buren has never owned slaves, I believe. I daresay his views on the subject are closer to my own than to General Jackson's."

"But you do not know for a certainty?"

"I know *one* thing for a certainty," said Beede. "I know he believes in the continuity of the Union. He is not a nullifier. And in this respect, he and General Jackson—and I—are in complete agreement."

"Deborah, don't you think we've talked enough of politics?" The speaker was Sarah, the second oldest of the squire's daughters, whom everyone called Sally. "You know that you and Mr. Beede will never agree on anything."

Beede had forgotten how forward Yankee girls could be, and he waited, inwardly cringing, for Tomkins to explode in wrath at her effrontery. The explosion never came, however. To Beede's amazement and grudging admiration, Tomkins accepted the girl's interruption as he would the remarks of a tavern companion who had inquired about his crops.

"On the contrary, my dear, I suspect that Mr. Beede and Deborah—and I—agree on many things. After all, he has retired from the life of a Southern gentleman and returned to his childhood home. He is a New Englander somewhere, though his true nature may be buried deep beneath the trappings of a Democrat."

"I am truly a New Englander," Beede agreed. "And I am truly a Democrat, if by that term you mean I am an admirer of General Jackson. And so, I would venture to add, are many New Englanders, particularly in New Hampshire."

"That is so," admitted Tomkins. "Many of our neighbors have been afflicted with that dread disease, which makes them envy their betters' possessions without coveting the diligence by which they were acquired. Yes, General Jackson's unprincipled appeal to the basest of human emotions has found fertile ground in New Hampshire. I only hope, sir," he said with an eye toward Beede, "that this fervor for democracy stops short of the bloodbath that engulfed France. Few events in history have been so devastating in their effects."

"We are all children of revolution, sir," Beede pointed out.

"Children of it, yes. But not creatures of it. There must be some stability in the world."

The meeting went on for an hour more, with the conversation meandering from subject to inconsequential subject. As Beede prepared to leave with the others, Tomkins took him aside.

"What are your future plans concerning Alice Patterson, the mill girl?" Tomkins inquired.

"She must be returned to her proper place soon, I think," Beede said. "But I fear I don't know how to do that."

"By coach to Concord, and by canal boat to Manchester, I should think. Surely that isn't difficult."

"The route isn't difficult," Beede said. "But it's hardly proper for her to travel alone, and it would be equally improper for me to accompany her. There would be talk that could do serious damage to her reputation."

"And to yours?" Tomkins said.

"Mine is of no particular consequence. But the trip will take most of the day. If the weather is bad, we may have to put up somewhere for the night. Mill girls are employed on the condition that their reputations are not tarnished. I don't care to be the instrument of her termination."

Tomkins smiled. "Your thoughts are much like mine, I see," he said. "It speaks well of you that you have considered these things. Many men would not."

"Thank you, sir."

"However, I believe I may have a solution to your dilemma."

"And what is that?"

"Deborah."

"I beg your pardon?"

"Deborah. My eldest daughter," Tomkins said. "She informed me recently that she believes she might enjoy a year or two in the mills. If she were to accompany you, it would serve two purposes. She could see for herself what the life is like, and she could serve as chaperone and companion to Miss Patterson."

"Surely you wouldn't allow her to take employment in the mills."

"I might very well. In fact, it might be good for her. She would see more of the world than she could see from Warrensboro, and she would earn cash money that would be helpful to her in the future."

"But her reputation would suffer."

"That only goes to show that you don't know her reputation, sir. No one in Warrensboro would think ill of her. Deborah is a strong-willed young woman. No one will take advantage of her weakness, and everyone is aware of this. Her reputation is above reproach."

"But she is a girl. A strong man could overpower her and force himself on her against her will."

"But she will have you to protect her, sir. Unless you mean that you would perform the deed yourself?"

Beede racked his brain for a reply but found none. He could only stand dumbly. He had the sense that his mouth was opening as if to respond but no sound emerged.

"I thought not," Tomkins said, with a smile. "Then it's settled. We'll work out the details tomorrow, after the funeral. I bid you good evening."

A lbert Sanborn was tired.
    Three hours of hacking and hoeing, even in the weak November sun, had taken its toll. Two years of peddling, hawking his cheap wares up and down the New Hampshire back roads, had hardened his calf and thigh muscles, and hauling his heavy peddler's chests had broadened and strengthened his shoulders. He had been pleased to think of himself as a strong man for his size, and his size was not inconsiderable.

But this was backbreaking work in ways that he had forgotten, and it was almost more than he could bear. He could feel his back stiffening, his legs cramping.

What was worse, to his mind, was that he knew he had been given the easy work. The Negro man, Randolph, had sized him up accurately and had accounted him unfit for other tasks. Randolph had left Sanborn to dig up the few remaining potatoes, while Randolph forked manure into the dog cart and led the oxen to the fields to spread it. Then he had spent an hour stacking the ubiquitous New Hampshire boulders into a rock wall that divided Beede's land from that of his neighbor, Jacob Wolf. Then he climbed a precarious makeshift ladder up the side of the barn to patch and replace portions of the roof.

Meanwhile, Sanborn dug up potatoes. There seemed an uncommon lot of them for so late in the year. If it had been his own farm—heaven forbid—he would long since have declared himself finished and retired to the house.

And yet, if the potatoes were left to rot in the fields, it would not bode well for next year's crop. And if, as now seemed likely, he continued to be confined here for several months, he would be grateful to be eating these same potatoes during the winter to come.

So he worked on, mindful of Randolph's casual but systematic scrutiny, aware that he had not been forgotten, no matter how preoccupied the black man seemed to be with shingles and boulders. Sanborn knew Randolph had been aware of his every action. He had said nothing to the peddler, but Sanborn could feel the man's eyes upon him when his back was turned. The knowledge filled the peddler with anger bordering on rage. He wanted to strike out at the dark man who was both his overseer in these hated tasks (a Negro!) and the representative of the supercilious lawyer who had confiscated Sanborn's meager fortune of tin and trinkets.

He was startled out of his thoughts by the shadow of a man that fell upon him. Looking up, he saw Randolph towering over him.

"Midday," he said. "We'll rest now before dinner."

Sanborn left his hoe in the potato patch and followed.

At the well, Randolph drew water, dipped the ladle, and offered Sanborn the first sip. After Sanborn had drunk, Randolph dipped a drink for himself after first carefully wiping the lip of the ladle with his shirttail. Sanborn realized with a start that he was offended by that gesture, although he knew he would have done the same thing if Randolph had taken the first drink. Somehow, it seemed right to wipe the ladle after a black man had drunk from it. But he said nothing about the incident and joined Randolph on the bench that stood along the front wall of the house.

They sat together in silence for a while, soaking up the precious sunshine. Sanborn wondered what Randolph was thinking. While Sanborn struggled to wrest a few potatoes out of the earth, Randolph had single-handedly done the work of two men without complaint or comment. How could he work so hard, Sanborn wondered, for another man, on land that was not—and would never be—his own?

"Hard work," Randolph said, breaking into the peddler's thoughts.

"What?"

"Farm work, I mean," Randolph said. "Hard work. Takes a while getting used to it, even if you've done it before."

"Are you some sort of witch?" Sanborn said, crossly. "Are you reading my thoughts?"

"No need," Randolph replied. "They're all over your face. And I know what it's like. It was hard for me at first. Still is hard, if I think about it."

"How do you live with it, then?"

"Like I said, it's hard if I think about it. So I don't think about it."

Sanborn sighed and stretched his legs.

"It ain't the work I mind so much," he said. "It's knowin' that I'm doing all this work for somebody else. I worked on a farm, growin' up, down in Massachusetts. It was hard work, but the worst of it was that I was not workin' hard for me; I was workin' for my father. That's why I became a peddler."

Randolph nodded. "Yes, I can see that might be

hard for someone unaccustomed to working for another."

"Have you never wanted to work for your own benefit?" Sanborn said.

"Oh, yes. Many times. And someday perhaps I shall."

"Why have you not done so before now? Do you lack the courage?"

"You might say so. But it was difficult. I was a slave, you see."

"A slave! In New England?"

"Oh, no. In the South. You may have heard that Mr. Beede acquired this farm rather recently, when he moved here from Washington City. I came with him."

"Did he buy you from your master, then?"

"Mr. Beede *was* my master," Randolph said. "Now he's my employer, and I believe we both prefer this relationship."

Sanborn pondered this new information. "I find it difficult to think of you as a slave," he said. You're well-spoken, almost like a . . . like a . . ."

"Like a white man," Randolph said with a smile. "Is that not the term you were struggling to find?"

"As a matter of fact, yes."

Randolph nodded. "You are not the first to notice and comment upon it. It is unusual, I admit, though not so uncommon in New Orleans, where I was living. I received the rudiments of an education from a former mistress and a from a free colored man who took an interest in me. I suppose he saw something in me that I did not see, myself, at the time.

"And later, when I accompanied Mr. and Mrs. Beede to Washington City, Mr. Beede worked with me on my reading until I became quite proficient. This happened more since Mrs. Beede died than before."

"She did not approve?"

"It was a point of contention between them. One of many."

The dark man rose from the bench and entered the house. Sanborn followed quietly, lost in thought.

So Randolph was a former slave—Beede's slave. Perhaps Beede was a fair man after all, and Sanborn need not fear the consequences of this murder investigation.

The rise in his spirits was short-lived. *What investigation?* he asked himself. To date, the investigation of Sharon Cudahy's murder seemed to consist of a few desultory conversations with a handful of people—that discussion with Jacob Wolf the previous day had clearly been about the murder—and no new suspects had arisen to shift the pressure from Sanborn.

No, he decided, the so-called investigation was going nowhere. In fact, it was not an investigation at all. And why should there be an investigation, when a perfectly suitable suspect was already in custody and laboring here in the fields? He wondered whether he would be executed immediately after the harvest or kept around to help with the spring planting.

As he sat down to Mrs. Shelton's dreary meal, Sanborn made a silent promise to himself. He would get away from this death trap at the earliest opportunity. And if it meant that he must abandon his beloved goods, then so be it.

Chapter 11

Late the following afternoon, her identity having been established to everyone's satisfaction, Sharon Cudahy was buried on a corner of Beede's property. The funeral had had to wait until an autopsy could be performed, with Mrs. Shelton in attendance to a physician called from a nearby town, Warrensboro having no physician of its own.

Mr. Gray had refused to permit the girl to be interred in the churchyard, and most of his parishioners were unwilling to brook his determined opposition. Beede had no such concerns. He had no fears for his soul—no new fears, at least—since he had been married to a Catholic woman for several years. Moreover, he told himself, the girl had been abandoned on his property and had, in a sense, become his responsibility.

But if Sharon's body was denied the protection of the churchyard, her little band of mourners was also

spared the presence of Mr. Gray, whose eulogies often
left survivors feeling more bereft than they had previously. The pastor had found it inconvenient even to attend.

In Gray's absence, Beede was forced to improvise.
Since no hearse existed in all of Warrensboro, and he
deemed it unreasonable for the hastily recruited pall-
bearers to carry the coffin on their shoulders the four
miles from the Tomkins place to his, he borrowed a
dog cart from the squire and loaned his horse to Alice
Patterson. Everyone else was required to walk, but this
was the customary mode of transportation, and no one
minded.

So the girl was sent from this world to the next accompanied by plain singing and plain speaking from a
handful of villagers, none of whom were Catholic. The
group of mourners was small, in part because few villagers who had not been personally involved in the funeral had even known of the grisly discovery of
Sharon Cudahy's body. The customary practice of
ringing the meetinghouse bell had been omitted out
of respect for Mr. Gray's convictions.

Those who attended, except for Alice Patterson,
were those who had known the girl only in death.
Beede recognized all the members of the little party
that had gathered around the body that Saturday morning. Huff was there, as was Jacob Wolf, who stood
apart from the others. Tomkins brought his entire family and stood quietly with his three daughters arranged
before him in stair-step order. Randolph was there, and
Mrs. Shelton, and Beede's temporary employee-guest,
Albert Sanborn. A few families from the village also
gathered near the gravesite as much from curiosity,
Beede thought, as from sympathy or grief. They had
not known the girl, or even known of her existence
until it was no more.

After the funeral, Beede conveyed Alice Patterson back to his house, where Mrs. Shelton took her in tow. Almost immediately, the girl brightened perceptibly and became more animated. Within an hour, she was chattering incessantly to the housekeeper. Beede, who by now was accustomed to his dampening effect on the female gender, was not surprised or offended. He was, in fact, pleased to find that the grueling routine of the mill—which he knew only by reputation—and the sadness of the occasion had not ruined her spirit, and he made it a matter of principle to remain at a distance from her, in order that her newfound spirits might not again desert her.

The chatter continued almost without respite, through the supper and into the evening, Beede marveled at Mrs. Shelton's forbearance. Long after he could take it no more—he excused himself from the small parlor and found chores to do alongside Albert and Randolph in the barn—the old woman continued to rock by the fire mending one of Randolph's two shirts and seemingly listening to Alice Patterson's childish prattle.

In the course of the evening, Beede learned more about Alice Patterson than he had ever been interested in knowing. She had two brothers, both older than she, and a sister who was approaching five years of age. She came from a farm farther north near the White Mountains, which meant that she now worked and lived far from home. Like many mill girls, she contributed to the maintenance of the family homestead by sending most of her pay back to support the family.

"When I can save enough money, I'll go back home. Then Peter Taylor will have to look at me different because I'll have a dowry."

"You're quite right, child," said Mrs. Shelton, who

clearly had no more notion than Beede as to who Peter Taylor might be. "He'll pay attention to you then, without doubt."

After the girl had crept up to bed in the extra room, Beede apologized privately to Mrs. Shelton, assuring her he had had no idea how talkative young girls could be.

"Why bless you, sir, it's a tonic to me to hear her," Mrs. Shelton replied. "Reminds me of my own young Sally, who's now married and removed to the Ohio country. She used to prattle just like this. It's music to my ears; don't you worry about that. I'll be sorry to see her leave us."

The chatter began again in the morning and continued until it was time to leave.

The trip to Manchester the following morning was uneventful. They were, indeed, a party of three. Beede was secretly pleased, for he reasoned that Deborah's presence would relieve the painful silences that would otherwise prevail. He knew of nothing to say to young women that would interest them.

For the first couple of hours, the two girls amused themselves, chattering happily about matters that Beede did not understand. The girls' preoccupation with their own concerns left Beede free to turn his mind to other things. Tomkins had loaned his carriage to Beede, who had none of his own, and the trip was as comfortable as it was possible to be on the roads they were obliged to travel. Only once was it necessary for the party to alight from the vehicle and help to extract it from a hole, and it was only a small hole, at that.

Eventually, the girls seemed to tire of each other, and silence reigned once more. Alice Patterson reached into a bag at her feet and drew out a bit of knitting. It caught Deborah Tomkins's attention, and she expressed delighted approval of the workmanship.

"I'm knitting a pair of stockings for my brother," Alice said. "He is in need of a second pair, and I promised him that I would send these to him when I finished. I have not had much time to work on them recently, however."

"I can knit, of course," said Deborah. "But I confess that I do not enjoy it overmuch."

"I find it a great pleasure," Alice said. "I think that the agreeable clicking of the needles is like music. It eases my cares and brings me contentment. I'm never without my knitting."

For a time, the only sounds that could be heard were the clopping of the horse's hooves, the squeaking of carriage wheels, the distant sound of wind in the nearly leafless birches, and the metallic clicking of Alice Patterson's steel knitting needles.

"Mr. Beede," said Alice Patterson, at last. "May I ask you a question?"

"Of course."

"Are you an important man?"

Beede hesitated. "I'm not sure that I understand your question," he said, at last.

"Come, sir. It can't be that difficult. Are you an important man? Do other people look up to you? Are you a leader of men?"

"We are all leaders of men, Miss Patterson. Every man depends on every other man for his survival. We learn from each other. Every man teaches another by his example. I hope that my example will be useful, and I work with that end in mind."

"You are equivocal, sir," she said. She turned from him on the seat, as if she had lost interest in him, and stared off into the pastureland beside the road. Two young working steers grazed placidly there, and she seemed to study them with the intensity of a gentle-man farmer at an agricultural fair.

Beede glanced at Deborah Tomkins, who sat be-tween them on the rigid bench. She, too, was looking away from him, apparently equally fascinated by the grazing animals. He could not see her face.

"Why do you ask such a question?" he said, at last.

"Because it is an important question," Alice said. She turned back to face him, and he was alarmed at the fierceness in her expression. "Do you not feel some re-sponsibility, sir, to those who look up to you?"

"Of course. It is a great burden at times."

"Then why do you not live as the important man you are?"

"I beg your pardon?"

"You live in a house that does you no justice. I be-lieve, from what I have seen, that you are as wealthy as Mr. Tomkins, and you are rapidly gaining in influ-ence among your townsmen. And yet you live in . . . in a hovel, sir. A hovel! My father is not a man of wealth, but he lives much more comfortably than you. Do you have no pride?"

It was a direct question, and it deserved an answer. He fumbled for something to say but came up with nothing. He had not thought of his farm in those terms before—many New England farmers were too busy eking a living from the recalcitrant earth to care over-much about tidiness—but compared to the Tomkins house, Beede's property did, indeed, seem unkempt. Appearances, apparently, were quite important to Alice Patterson.

The silence stretched on, and he grew more frantic with each passing moment.

Pride is sinful. No. As a response, it was altogether too pharisaical.

I need no showy palaces. No. It would be an insult

to Deborah and her father, who lived, comparatively, in a palace. In addition, he wasn't sure it was true.

He searched his mind for a response, but none came to him. The silence stretched on uncomfortably. It was broken, finally, by Deborah Tomkins, who pointed out the rooftops of Concord in the distance.

Chapter 12

At Concord they stabled Beede's horse, stored the carriage, and took passage on a canal boat. The novelty of the experience distracted the girls, sparing Beede the necessity of making further conversation or of answering unwelcome questions. He took the opportunity to look around him and take in the sights on the river.

As a farmer, he lived daily with nature, and it held few surprises for him. The river, however, was different. Sounds carried farther here. The heat reflected off the water's surface, even in autumn, and scalded his face. And then there were the birds—not the birds who visited him in the fields but water birds such as ducks and geese, who dove and paddled around him as if the canal boat did not exist. He became engrossed in their activities and so lost track of time.

They heard the falls long before they arrived—the rushing of water and, high-pitched above the sound of the water, the clacking of wooden machinery. As the boat drew closer, the boatman poled it toward the shoreline. There the bow of the boat was attached to a line extending to a gray draft horse, waiting patiently with his handler on the towpath.

"We're almost home," said Alice Patterson. There was an eagerness on her smiling face that surprised Beede nearly as much as her use of the word *home*.

The great gates opened, and the boat glided into the lock with the onrushing river current. The gates shut behind them, and Beede heard the water rushing out of the lock, lowering them to the level of the next segment of the canal. And there was another sound, a deep-voiced basso continuo of cogwheels and tumblers that issued from somewhere below them like the seamless rumble of a hundred field artillery pieces.

"What is making that low rumbling sound?" he asked Alice.

"Waterwheels, Mr. Beede," she said. Her eyes were shining. "Huge, great waterwheels like none you've ever seen. They turn the shafts that operate the looms and spinning wheels."

The gates opened ahead of them, and the boat moved into the next locking pool. At each step in their descent, the noise from the mill seemed to grow louder.

After disembarking from the canal boat, Beede and his companions crossed over the canal on a footbridge. The mill building towered above them, and the clacking of the looms was louder than before. Beede noticed that all the windows in the building were shut tight against the November chill. He tried to imagine how noisy it must be inside and how much louder it would be outside in the summer when the windows were open.

They walked along the canal, with Alice Patterson

eagerly leading the way, until they came to a break in the line of buildings. Alice turned abruptly and disappeared into a doorway. Beede and Deborah Tomkins followed.

The interior of the building resembled nothing so much as a shop on Beacon Hill. A small room with a small table in the corner. A journal, outspread on the table, into which Alice Patterson entered her name. A door to the rear of the room, and another door to the right, both resolutely shut to the outside world. A shop without clerks, or merchandise, or custom, and with no apparent reason to exist.

Alice Patterson turned to the door on the right and raised her fist as if to knock. But she did not.

"I'm late," she said, looking wildly at Beede. "I should have been here two days ago. Perhaps my position has been filled by someone else."

Beede stepped forward to knock for her, but the door swung open before he could set his fist upon it. In the doorway stood a red-faced man whom Beede realized was familiar to him from Democratic Party meetings.

"Mr. Beede," he said, beaming. "This is certainly an unexpected pleasure. Come in! Come in, please!"

"John Kerrigan," Beede replied as his mind seized upon the correct name. "The Kerrigan Cotton Mills. I confess I had not made the connection."

"I'm happy to see you, sir," Kerrigan said. "What brings you to my establishment? Not that it matters; you're welcome. You will stay for dinner, I trust? I flatter myself that my domestic staff is the finest in New England."

"That's very kind of you, Mr. Kerrigan," Beede said. "But as you see, I am not alone. Permit me to introduce my traveling companions."

Upon meeting Deborah Tomkins, Kerrigan bowed

low, took the girl's hand, and looked into her eyes, murmuring pleasantries all the while. Beede noticed the consternation on her face as she submitted to his attentions, but there was pleasure in her eyes as well, and she blushed.

Turning from her, Kerrigan looked at Alice Patterson. "I do believe that we have met before," he said.

"Yes, sir, we have," Alice said before Beede could make an introduction. "I am Alice Patterson, and I work here."

"In the weaving room," Kerrigan said. "I remember."

"Loom forty-six," she replied. "Although I am late returning. I pray that my position is still open."

"I'm sure we can find work for you, my dear," Kerrigan said. "There are always opportunities for the diligent." He turned his attention back to Deborah. "And are you also in my employ, Miss Tomkins? I confess I believe I would have remembered you."

"Miss Tomkins is merely visiting," Beede said hastily. "I came to Manchester to return Miss Patterson to her place of employment. Miss Tomkins accompanied us as Miss Patterson's companion."

Kerrigan arched an eyebrow. "A chaperone? Well done, sir. But if she returns with you to your home, will she not require a chaperone, as well?"

"I will return her to her father," Beede said, "not to my farm. And I must answer to him if anything should befall her. Her father's house is in my village only a few miles from mine."

"I see," Kerrigan said. "So Miss Tomkins is safe in your hands. You have been very thoughtful. In any event, you are both welcome to stay with me for as long as you remain in town. Perhaps you would like to see a bit of my mill while you are here."

"I'd like that very much," Beede said.

"Excellent," said Kerrigan. "Then perhaps we can begin at once. Miss Patterson, why don't you take Miss Tomkins with you and introduce her to Mr. Coolidge?"

Leaving the little office with Alice and Deborah in tow, they strode along a wide pathway fringed with dry grass to a long brick building. Three rows of windows marched the length of the building. Each window was shut tight, but a muffled roar could be heard before they were closer than forty feet away.

Kerrigan seemed to read his thoughts. "I should warn you that cotton mills are not peaceful places. But the sound you will hear is the sound of industry."

He opened the door and stepped through into the interior of the building. Beede followed and was nearly floored by a massive wall of sound unlike any he had heard before. If the noise on the battlefield at New Orleans had been louder—and he was not certain that that was the case—it was at least intermittent, where this was constant and unremitting.

They ascended the narrow steps and emerged into a long room filled with young women and cacophonous machinery. The late afternoon sunlight cast grotesque shadows on the planked floor and glittered on the lint, which floated in the air so thickly that the air was almost opaque. Beede was reminded of fog, floating like a living thing off the Mississippi River on a long-ago morning in New Orleans.

"Here, sir," said Kerrigan, "is the face of the future."

The noise from outside the building had been loud; from inside it was painful. The clatter of shuttles shooting like bullets across the looms, the clacking of wooden machinery, the rumble of the thick leather belts as they transferred energy from the waterwheels below—Beede tried to imagine spending day after tedious day in this maelstrom of noise and furious movement, but he could not.

Nor was the noise the only irritant. The heavy fog of cotton lint was causing several of the girls to cough like consumptives.

Kerrigan led his party quickly down the narrow aisle between the rows of hulking looms. The sounds of the spindly wooden arms clumped and clacked in his ears. They passed face after face, with their haunted eyes fixed firmly on the shuttles as they passed inexorably from left to right.

"Think of it, sir," Kerrigan shouted over the noise, with an expansive sweep of his hand. "In this room alone, I can produce more cotton cloth in a month than thousands of household weavers can make in a year. Think of the benefits to mankind."

"And what are these benefits?"

"Clothing, sir. Well-made clothing at a fraction of its former price. Better than homespun and far less dear."

Beede surveyed the room with newfound curiosity. After a bit, he recognized some similarities between the tasks these girls were performing and the steps his mother had followed on the old loom she had worked on during his childhood. In fact, the girls did not actually perform most tasks but merely stood and watched as the machines clattered on deafeningly. Occasionally, a girl would pull a lever at her side, and the machine would come to a quivering halt. While the machine waited obediently, she would perform some minor adjustment, after which she would again pull the lever, and the loom would roar into life once more.

Kerrigan pointed to one such girl, whose shuttle had leaped from its path and landed on the floor.

"We teach the girls never to stand beside their loom while it is in operation," he said. "We employ a flying shuttle, which is spring-loaded. It flies across the shuttle race with great force and cannot always be counted upon to come to rest safely in its compartment. If it were to fly out of the box that is there to receive it, it might cause a serious injury to someone standing beside the loom."

Beede wondered how the girls could work amid the brown haze of cotton lint.

"I realize the day is cold," Beede said to Kerrigan, shouting to be heard above the noise of the machinery. "But could you not open the windows a bit, to disperse the cotton dust? These girls are suffering terribly."

Kerrigan shook his head. "No, sir. The windows are nailed shut and are never to be opened. Outside breezes might disperse the lint, but they would also destroy the humid conditions we require to prevent the thread from breaking. That is something we cannot afford."

"But look at them, coughing and sneezing," Beede replied. "Surely this cannot be healthful."

"They're paid to do a job," Kerrigan said. "They must accept the conditions imposed on them."

"And if they cannot?"

Kerrigan shrugged. "They're free to move on. They're not slaves, you know." Beede glanced quickly at Alice Patterson who was nodding vigorously.

They ascended the stairs to the uppermost floor, where Kerrigan showed them how the machinery drew in the cotton fibers and spun them into tight, even threads in preparation for the looms below. From there they passed downstairs through the weaving room again and on to the floor below it.

"Here is my pride," Kerrigan said.

He pointed to where water poured downward through an overhead pipe into a waterwheel that had been laid on its side. But unlike all the waterwheels

Beede had seen before, the water seemed to pour into the central hub, from which it was flung violently outward as the wheel whirled.

"What is it?" Beede asked.

"It's my waterwheel," Kerrigan said proudly.

"It's like no waterwheel I've seen before," Beede said. "It looks like a tub wheel, but a tub wheel with no sides. I've heard that overshot wheels are most powerful, but this is obviously not an overshot wheel."

"Quite true," Kerrigan said with a smug smile. "Nor is it a tub wheel. Tub wheels are primitive creations, perhaps suitable to operate a few carding machines, but totally inadequate to our needs. No, sir, this is a turbine wheel, and it is a distinct improvement over even an overshot wheel."

"In what way is it superior?" Beede asked. "Open at the sides as it is, I would think it would quickly dissipate its power."

"Far from it, sir." Kerrigan said. "For while your overshot wheel generates power from the weight of the water as it fills its buckets, my wheel makes double use of the same amount of water. Not only does it use the weight of the water, it also uses the force of its fall."

"I must take you at your word on that," Beede said.

"Moreover," Kerrigan said, continuing on as if Beede had not spoken, "my wheel receives water from below the surface of the canal. Even when the river and the canal freeze over, my wheel can continue to operate."

"So you can continue running the mills in December?"

"December, January, February. All through the winter."

"Is there any time when you cannot operate?"

"Sometimes in high summer, when the level of the

river is too low, I must shut down for a little while. And when a belt breaks, as it did recently, it becomes necessary to lock my doors. And on the Sabbath, of course."

There were, Beede now realized, two of these strange turbines operating side by side in the subterranean half light. These, clearly, were the waterwheels of which Alice Patterson had spoken so proudly and which he had heard during their journey down the canal.

"They cost me a pretty penny, I must tell you," Kerrigan confided. "To my belief, mine are the first such wheels in New Hampshire, although I believe one or two of the Lowell mills may have installed them."

He turned away from the turbines and led Beede up the iron staircase to the exit.

"Have you seen the falls?" Kerrigan asked as they left the mill.

"We passed it on the canal as we arrived," Beede said.

"Then you haven't really seen it," Kerrigan said. "You cannot grasp its full nature from the canal. Come with me, sir, and I'll show you the real falls."

He led Beede to a place where they could look out over the river, and Beede concluded that Kerrigan was right. What had appeared to be merely a roar and a layer of mist from the canal was, from this vantage point, a sight of awesome power. The waters of the Merrimack had been falling continuously since leaving its headwaters in the mountainous north. Now they plunged over the precipice in a torrent, bringing with them the debris of upriver forests and towns. Tree limbs, many with brown leaves still attached, plummeted over the edge and disappeared into the churning froth below, often to reappear suddenly on the surface again, many yards downstream. There were wood planks, as well, and the detritus of upcountry households: bottles, shards of pottery, a wicker basket or two, even clothing.

"Can you imagine the power available to us here?" Kerrigan shouted over the roar. "This is the *real* treasure of New England. I doubt not that England has nothing to compare with the industrial potential that awaits us here. Even Lowell, with its congregation of manufactories, has nothing on us."

"I have heard that the falls downstream at Lowell are also impressive," Beede said.

"Indeed they are, Mr. Beede," Kerrigan said. "But they do not compare with these. The drop is greater here, and the power produced is greater in consequence."

"You must look forward to a profitable future, indeed," Beede said.

"Alas, no," Kerrigan said. "I fear my days here are numbered. In another year or two at most, I must be gone from this spot. The investors who own and operate the mills at Lowell have purchased the land and water rights here and far upstream. I continue only at their sufferance until their own mills are in operation across the river, and I pay a pretty price for the privilege."

He pointed across the river. Beede could see workmen laying brick and rockwork.

"There's the new Manchester. This side of the river has always been known as Amoskeag Village," Kerrigan said with a touch of bitterness. "They're building a new canal over there to power new mills. They're building boardinghouses and company stores. They'll soon be laying out streets and offering lots for sale. An entire city will soon rise there, and my enterprise will not benefit from it in the slightest."

"Are the Boston investors as wealthy as that?"

"Indeed, sir. As wealthy as kings. My Southern backers cannot hope to compete with them."

"What will you do when you must close your doors?"

"In truth, I don't know. Perhaps I can hire on as an overseer at their mills. More likely, I'll take my capital and return to the South in hope of buying plantation land of my own. I believe land might still be had in the Mississippi valley at a price I could afford. At least, I should be able to sell my turbines to the Boston investors for a good price. Buying from me will be a good deal less expensive than shipping two turbines upriver from Lowell."

Kerrigan lived in a large, brick Greek Revival house about three blocks from the mill. It was the sort of house that would have been called a town house, had it stood in Boston or New York. Here, in this dusty little village, it appeared out of place, like a white birch draped with Spanish moss. Beede surveyed the structure in astonishment. Kerrigan had come from the low country of South Carolina to the rock-strewn land of New England, and he still, apparently, carried a piece of the South in his soul.

Inside the house, a sweeping staircase spiraled upward from the foyer, which was graced by an ornate crystal chandelier. In the parlor to his right, Beede saw a fire blazing in a marble fireplace. Deborah rejoined them here, having been directed to the house by Alice.

He and Deborah were shown to their rooms. Beede's room was comfortably furnished, and a fire was already blazing in the fireplace here, as in the parlor. He supposed that Kerrigan had sent word ahead to his domestic staff that they should be expecting overnight visitors, and the rooms had been made ready before the party had arrived. If the appointments were any clue, Beede was apparently considered an important visitor.

They descended again a short while later to a dining room set with imported china and silver plate, which sparkled from the light of yet another chandelier. The meal about to ensue, he surmised, was to be dinner in the Southern fashion. He thought briefly of Randolph, and Mrs. Shelton, and his unwilling employee, the peddler Albert Sanborn. They would also be sitting down for the evening meal, but it would be nothing as elaborate as this.

Here, the meal was presented in courses. First came oysters: big, succulent Belon oysters from French Canada. It had been several years since Beede had been presented with such a meal. Mrs. Shelton could not have even conceived of not bringing everything to the table at one time or of having portions ladled out onto each diner's plate individually. He had eaten in many taverns and ordinaries, following the court circuit from town to town, and there, too, the food was brought all at once and plopped hastily upon the table lest the deliverer be stabbed by the knife of an overeager trencherman. He wondered what Deborah would make of this. He glanced at her, sitting across the table from him in the chair closest to Kerrigan, but he could make nothing of her expression.

"So, Mr. Beede, to what do I owe the honor of this visit? What brings you out of the hills to this place? Surely you had more on your mind than serving as an escort to a young factory girl and her charming companion." Kerrigan smiled at Deborah, who responded with a very becoming blush.

"That would have been sufficient reason," Beede said. "But I do have another."

"And it is . . . ?"

"I have been asked by the citizens of my village to assist in a murder investigation," Beede said. "A young girl, about Miss Patterson's age, who I believe was employed in your mill."

"And am I to know her name?" Kerrigan asked. "Or am I considered suspect?"

"I have no reason to think so. Her name was Sharon Cudahy, and she was found foully murdered and left by the side of the road."

"Irish," Kerrigan said, musing. "We have employed a few, I believe, but I'm not familiar with their names. Why do you believe she worked for me?"

"Miss Patterson says she worked side by side with her for nearly a year," Beede replied. "After the girl disappeared, Miss Patterson went in search of her and arrived eventually in our village."

"Where she was apprised of her friend's unfortunate demise, I assume," Kerrigan said. "Well, I'm afraid I can add nothing to what you already know." He hesitated a moment, as if in thought. "Was the girl possessed of a fair complexion and reddish hair?" he said.

"Yes, she was."

"Then I believe I do remember her, but she left my employ some months ago. I have no idea where she might have gone from here."

"I thought perhaps you might be able to suggest someplace to begin my search."

At that moment, servants appeared with the next course, effectively ending their conversation for the moment. Turkey, chicken pies, scalloped oysters, duck, and rabbit came steaming on magnificent platters accompanied by white potatoes, sweet potatoes, and several loaves of bread made of both corn and wheat. But it was the rice that caught Beede's attention, for it had been several years since he had eaten any. He had grown to love it during his years in New

Orleans but had seen it only rarely since then. He loaded his plate shamelessly.

The meal was followed by a bewildering variety of pies and puddings. Beede found it nearly overwhelming after two years subsisting on Mrs. Shelton's begrudging meals. Kerrigan, however, was apologetic. Iced cream would have been appropriate for the occasion, he said, but his supply of ice had run out, and it would be a month or more before the lakes and ponds would freeze over again.

"**I**t is possible," Kerrigan said, after dinner as they sat by the fire, "that my overseer may be able to help you trace the unfortunate girl. Mr. Coolidge is closer to the girls than I can be. At the very least, he may be able to direct you to the girl's residence when she lived here." Deborah Tomkins had retired to a room upstairs, and Beede and Kerrigan shared pipes and brandy below.

"Did she not live with the other girls?"

"Oh, no," Kerrigan said. "That would never have done. She was Irish. A Catholic. It would have been a gross disservice to my other girls to have put them together. I should lose the confidence of their families if I were to do so. They did not put their daughters into my keeping so that they might be catechized by a papist."

"Was Miss Cudahy a proselytizer?"

"As I told you, I didn't know the girl, except by sight. But prudence would dictate that she be separated from the other workers. You should ask Mr. Coolidge in any event. He will know where she lived."

After their brandy was finished, Beede was shown upstairs to his room for the night. As he passed her open door, Deborah Tomkins called his name. She was sitting in a straight-backed chair in the middle of the room, as if waiting for him to appear in the corridor.

"You called me, Miss Tomkins?"

"Yes," she said. "Please come in and shut the door behind you."

He did so reluctantly, not wanting to cause talk among the servants. Deborah, however, seemed unconcerned.

"I have received a message from Alice Patterson," she said when he had done her bidding. "She asks me to visit her at her boardinghouse this evening and to stay the night. I have decided to accept her invitation."

"Are you certain that is wise?" he asked.

"Quite certain," she said. "Staying with other girls in the boardinghouse will offer me a much more intimate exposure to their way of life. Alice says she believes I would be permitted to observe her life in the weaving room, if I would care to do so, and I think I would. If I choose to come back for employment, I'll be grateful for that experience. And perhaps Alice will be more forthcoming in my presence than she has been in yours."

"Has she been lying to me?"

"I don't believe so, but neither do I believe that she has told all that she might. You intimidate her, I believe."

Beede could think of no one less intimidating than himself, but he did not say so.

"It would be useful to learn anything she can tell us," he replied instead.

"I think so, too," she said. "There is another reason to accept her invitation, however, and that is to put some distance between Mr. Kerrigan and myself. I do not like the way he looks at me, or the things he says, or for that matter, the way he says them."

"Has he been forward?"

"No," she said. "Perhaps that is not his intention, or perhaps I have simply not given him the opportunity. But in any event, I prefer to remove myself from his presence. In fact, I would rather not tell him myself that I am leaving. I would be grateful if you would do that for me."

"Of course."

She looked into his eyes with an expression of great concern.

"Please be careful of him, Mr. Beede," she said. "I fear him greatly, and I would wish you to do the same."

"Why do you fear him? Is it something he said?"

"In a sense. I find it odd, for example, that he would remember Alice Patterson was an employee but could not recall Sharon Cudahy, who was not only far more striking in appearance than either Alice or myself but was also Irish."

"You believe he is dissembling?"

"I am certain of it, Mr. Beede. My only question is why he would do so."

Chapter 13

Escape, Albert Sanborn concluded, was easier to imagine than to effect.

True, there were no barred windows or high stone walls at Josiah Beede's farm, as there would be in a town jail, and there was no one standing over him with a musket aimed at his chest. Nevertheless, the obstacles to flight were greater than he had anticipated.

There was, for one thing, the workload. As a peddler, he could work or not as he wished. His load might be heavy, and his feet might grow weary, but he could always declare his work at an end for the day and stop to rest. There were periods of rest on the farm of course, but it was rest under supervision. The colored man—the *nigger*—was always about.

The workday extended from sunup to sunset, with barely a break for meals. Even the Sabbath offered little relief. As a peddler, Sanborn had enjoyed leisurely Sundays. Many farm households in New England still

treated Sunday as a day of worship and were unlikely
to be receptive to a peddler's call, even if they were
home to receive him. So Sundays had become a day of
rest for Sanborn, as well.

No longer. Mrs. Shelton, the austere housekeeper
whom Mr. Beede had employed, had not attended
worship the previous Sunday, and Randolph, from all
that Sanborn could gather from his conversation,
never went at all. Perhaps he wasn't even Christian.
Perhaps he observed some strange pagan religion inherited from his African ancestors. Or perhaps he had
not been welcomed by the meetinghouse congregation; Sanborn could well imagine the reactions of
these taciturn Yankees to the appearance of a dark-
skinned man in their midst.

In any event, whatever the explanation, it left Sanborn in dire circumstances and greatly complicated his
plans for escape.

He had done what he could. He had squirreled away
food from the table, stuffing his pockets with bread
and cheese, in anticipation of the opportunity that he
hoped would come. He would take only the clothes on
his back, and he would forgo (oh, how reluctantly!)
the merchandise that remained under lock and key in
Samuel Skinner's storeroom in the village. Fortunately, he had some cash money that had been concealed in his boot and overlooked when he was placed
in custody.

Now, as he struggled to help Randolph lift a heavy
crossbeam into place at the cider press, he began to
doubt that an opportunity for escape would ever arise.
This would be the perfect time, with Mr. Beede away
in Manchester, if only he could shake off the hired
man.

"Easy with your end, Albert," Randolph said. "This
beam's too heavy to take chances with."

Sanborn seethed with barely concealed fury. To be called by his Christian name by this savage was almost more than he could bear. But he put his back into the effort, all the same, and cursed himself for his cowardice in doing so.

The beam slipped into place with a satisfying clunk, completing the A-frame structure that would serve to support the milling shaft.

"A good job of work, if I do say so myself," said Randolph.

Sanborn grudgingly agreed. There *was* a form of satisfaction in building a structure such as this that could not be equaled in the peddler's trade, no matter how much money he made doing it.

"Now," Randolph said, "we must put the tub in place. I've had that made for us by Thomas Brown, over in the center village. I'm afraid I don't trust my skills at coopering."

"I didn't think there was anything you couldn't do," Sanborn said.

"Well, now you know," Randolph said in good humor. "I flatter myself that I've acquired most of the skills needed to run a farm. I hope to have land of my own, someday. But barrels—barrels and wheels—are beyond my ken just yet."

"Did you learn your farming skills working for Mr. Beede?"

"I had acquired some knowledge of planting as a slave, but farm work was largely new to me. Fortunately, Mr. Beede was a skilled and patient teacher."

"I thought Mr. Beede was a city lawyer."

"Ah, but he was a New England farmer first, and I believe it's where his heart has ever been."

"I don't understand how anyone can leave this place, become successful somewhere else, and then return here," Sanborn said. "And to be a farmer! I'll stick to my peddling; it's more to my liking."

"Mr. Beede was a peddler at one time, too," Randolph said. "He left home at thirteen and took up a peddler's trade with his brother. I don't think he enjoyed it."

"But he enjoys farming?"

"He certainly seems to. He often complains that his legal duties take too much time away from the farm chores."

"I wonder," said Sanborn, "if he would still enjoy farming if he couldn't get away to the court circuit now and again."

Randolph, however, had been inspecting the A-frame while Sanborn had been talking and had clearly found something not to his liking.

"I don't think this crossbeam is as secure as it ought to be," he said. "Come give me a hand in settling it into a firmer position."

Sanborn complied reluctantly, having had his fill of construction work for the time being. He clutched the beam firmly with its weight upon his shoulders as Randolph began slowly rotating the beam to a better position.

A sudden shift in his feet caused the great beam to slip from Sanborn's shoulder. He grappled frantically in an effort to regain control, but it was too late. The beam rolled into the A-frame structure, and the structure collapsed in a heap on the ground. The crossbeam hit the ground behind it, bounced prodigiously, and caught Randolph in the ribs.

It was over in a second. Randolph lay on the ground with the crossbeam resting on his right foreleg. He was still and silent. Sanborn rushed to his side, fearing the worst, and was relieved to see that the man, though unconscious, was breathing regularly.

He would need assistance in moving the crossbeam from Randolph's leg. No doubt he would also need a physician, but there was none in Warrensboro. The nearest physician was sixteen miles away.

Sanborn set out down the road at a run, stopping briefly at Jacob Wolf's place to summon his assistance.

A mile or so down the road, he realized that he was free.

Chapter 14

"Josiah, wake up!"

The voice was soft but insistent. Josiah turned over away from the voice calling in his ear, but it did no good, for the voice followed.

"Josiah, it's Seth! We need to go before the sun comes up."

He felt his brother's rough hands shaking him by the shoulder.

"Come on, 'siah. I can't shout at you. I'll wake Mother."

Sitting up slowly, Josiah stared groggily at his brother, who was already dressed in his one linen shirt and one pair of trousers. Seth stood, hands on hips, glaring down at him.

"Is it time already?"

"Come on," Seth said. "We must leave quickly. I have everything we need, but we must go now."

Josiah dressed hastily. He rolled his nightshirt and

began to place it in Seth's open carpet bag, which sat at the foot of the bed.

"Leave it here," Seth said. "We'll be sleeping on the ground for a while."

"On the ground?"

"For a while. Until we can establish ourselves. You can buy a new nightshirt then. We'll have cash money."

"Seth, are you sure we're doing the right thing? Mother will miss us. So will Thomas."

"Thomas will miss our arms and legs and backs. No matter, he can hire someone. There's nothing for us here, now that Thomas stands to inherit the land. We've got to make our way for ourselves."

Beede opened his eyes. Seth was gone. The old farmhouse was gone. Both had been left behind many years ago, and he was alone . . . where? It came to him after a moment: the home of John Kerrigan, the mill owner.

It could be said that Seth had left *him* behind, Beede thought as he lay in the bed. On that cold January day at Chalmette, Seth had taken his soul and departed, leaving behind only a pool of his lifeblood as a legacy for his younger brother. Their merchandise, what remained of it, was sold to cover Seth's gambling debts. The wagon had been destroyed during the battle of the cotton bales.

Two years on the road with Seth had left him without money, family, or land. Not that there would have been land, or money, in any event, but there would at least have been family. But he could not go back. He doubted that his mother had outlived his father by more than a year or two, and his eldest brother, though he might have taken him in, would not have been happy to see him.

It had been up to him to make his own way, and he had done so, with Jackson's help and encouragement. He thought of the years studying the law, the years practicing in Washington, serving Jackson behind the scenes. He thought of Adrienne, whom he had married while she was still in her teens and he was barely in his twenties.

A lifetime had passed since he had run away with Seth. It had been only twenty years or so, but it felt like an eternity.

Lying in a strange bed in a strange house, Beede realized once again that he had lost virtually all connection to the world in which he had lived as a child. The ties had been irrevocably broken, and there was nothing left for him but the present.

He wondered again if he had been hasty in leaving Washington City and Jackson. They were the closest things to home and family that he had known in many years.

But Jackson would soon be leaving, also. The voting had already taken place, and in December the electoral college would formally elect his successor, almost certainly the little Dutchman from New York, Martin Van Buren. Beede liked and admired Van Buren, but he could never have the same relationship with Van Buren that he had shared with Jackson. Beede and Van Buren had politics in common, but Beede and Jackson had New Orleans.

But there was no time left for what might have been. It was time to be up and doing. Beede rolled over, sat up, and began to dress.

Noah Coolidge, Kerrigan's overseer, was a barrel-chested man whose neck threatened to burst out of his shirt collar. When Kerrigan introduced him,

Beede felt his hand being enveloped by a gigantic paw and squeezed with considerable force. Coolidge was clearly a man who was proud of his physical strength. He had shed his frock coat and hat in the mill, which was at least as warm as it had been the previous evening. Although it was still early in the morning, Beede could see that the overseer's shirtfront was already soaked with perspiration, and beads dotted his forehead below his widow's peak.

"Oh, yes, I remember her right enough," Coolidge said. "Sharon Cudahy, aye. She weren't easy to forget."

"Do you recall when she left your employ?"

"Not offhand, but it'll be in my journal." He turned to the high desk behind him and began riffling through the pages.

"It would have been a while back," he said. "Summertime, I think. She didn't even give notice. One day she was here, next day she was gone."

"Is that common?"

"Well, not as uncommon as I might wish it. When these girls get an itch to go, they just up and go without so much as a by your leave."

"Why do they leave you?"

"Many reasons," Coolidge said, still leafing through his records. "Some girls come with the intention of earning money for a dowry. Once they have enough put away, they go back home. Some are saving for education. Some go home to help with the chores. And of course, some can't handle the work."

He straightened up and called to a younger man in the office next door.

"Richard, I'm looking for the daybook for August. Do you have it?"

The young man appeared in the doorway, holding a book like the one Coolidge had been looking through.

"I was counting up work hours," he said in a thick Scottish burr.

"Well, give it to me, man," Coolidge said irritably. "This gentleman wants to know when one of our girls ended her employment." He took the book from his assistant's hand and began quickly thumbing through it.

"Here it is," he said. "Sharon Cudahy left us on August seventh."

"And she offered no explanation?"

"Nor farewells, either. We learned she was gone when she didn't show up at the morning bell. We sent someone to her boardinghouse, and she wasn't there."

Beede turned to the assistant. Unlike Coolidge, the assistant was thin and bookish in appearance, with fragile-appearing eyeglasses that threatened to slide from his hooked nose in the sweltering heat.

"Are you familiar with the girl we're inquiring about, Mr. . . ."

"My apologies," Coolidge said, quickly. "Josiah Beede, Richard Hamilton. Richard Hamilton, Josiah Beede. Mr. Hamilton is new to us, only recently arrived from Scotland barely six months past. I daresay he never met the girl."

"Is that true, sir? Did you ever meet Sharon Cudahy?"

"Nae, sir," Hamilton said. "Saw her, though. Irish lass. I remember her, for she was one of a kind. No other Irish here, none other in the whole town, I believe."

"And what," said Beede, "was your opinion of her?"

"No opinion, sir. Never met the young lady personally. We have so many girls here, and I was only beginning to learn their names when she left us."

"I'd like to talk to her landlady," Beede said, turning to Coolidge. "Can you tell me where to find her?"

"I'll do better than that," Coolidge said. "I'll take you there."

"Free."

Sanborn said the word aloud, liking the sound of it. It had been only days since he had been placed in involuntary servitude, but it seemed already like ages. Now, with no one to watch over him, and no one seeking him, he was free again. They would be seeking him soon enough, he did not doubt, but he was, for the moment, at liberty.

But could he leave Randolph lying unconscious on the ground, with his leg pinned beneath the log? The log might well have broken a bone in Randolph's leg, rendering him unable to work on the farm for many months. Could he leave him not only helpless but likely to remain so?

Sanborn considered this question and concluded that he could, indeed. Jacob Wolf would see to Randolph's immediate needs. Furthermore, Beede would be back soon, and Sanborn's assistance would no longer be required. Indeed, when Beede returned, it would be advisable for Sanborn to be far away from this place. No good news for Albert Sanborn could emanate from the place to which Beede had gone.

But where should he go?

If Beede were south, the obvious direction for Sanborn would be north, to reduce the risk of crossing the man's path during his flight. But north was also the direction of the White Mountains, and the Whites were notoriously inhospitable, particularly with winter on the way. They were sparsely settled and inhabited by hard-bitten men and women whose hostility to strangers was infamous. As a peddler, he would have had a means of bargaining, something to trade for life's necessities. As a fugitive, without his merchandise, he would be on his own. Already there would be snow on the mountains, and soon it would fill the passes and make transportation on foot nearly impossible.

So north was a poor choice. Nor would east or west be better. And south was out of the question.

Or was it? Far from being a poor choice, it might actually be the best. A lone man in the north would be conspicuous. In the crowded south, he might very well escape notice.

And there was, when he thought about it, another reason to go south rather than north. If he were ever to be relieved of suspicion for Sharon Cudahy's murder—and recover his precious stores—another, more suitable suspect must be found. The best opportunity to find another suspect was likely to be in the vicinity of the mill where the girl had once been employed. And no one was better situated to find that suspect—more motivated—than he.

He would have to be careful, of course. It would not do to stumble upon Beede on his way. But a different hat, a bit of a beard and, perhaps, something to darken his yellow hair . . .

And he would approach the village from across the river, on the eastern side. Beede would have no reason to cross the river—none, at least, that Sanborn could think of.

In the meantime, he thought, he should travel as far and as fast as he could, ever watchful for traffic on this back-country road, prepared to slip off the road into the woods at their approach. His mind set at last, Sanborn lengthened his stride and moved purposefully toward the east, away from the village that had been the cause of all his troubles.

A quick image of Randolph, lying unconscious in

the farmyard, passed through his mind, but he pushed it away. Randolph was established in the community. He had neighbors who would take care of him; Sanborn had only himself. It was time, Sanborn concluded, to look out for Albert and let those who cared about him look out for Randolph.

The road diverged not far ahead. Sanborn squared his shoulders and set out on the southern fork.

Chapter 15

The boardinghouse was across the river. Beede followed the big man across the narrow bridge to the eastern bank and down dusty streets that were little more than cattle trails. The journey took nearly an hour, and Beede wondered how long it had taken Sharon Cudahy to walk to and from the mill each day. Even if one accepted the need to separate an Irish Catholic girl from her Congregationalist coworkers, this seemed less like segregation than quarantine.

They arrived not at the town house Beede expected but at a farmhouse surrounded by wood lots and orchards. Coolidge strode to the front door and hammered it with his massive fist.

"Mrs. Webb, it's Noah Coolidge. I know you're at home. Open up."

He had to hammer the door twice more before Beede heard a stirring inside. The door opened to reveal a wizened little woman, who glared at Coolidge in what Beede took to be trembling defiance.

"What do you want from me, sir? The girl still ain't come back, and I still don't know more'n that."

"No," said Coolidge. "She ain't coming back, neither. This gentleman with me found her dead some miles up north of here."

Beede winced with embarrassment at the acrimony that passed between Coolidge and the woman, who was perhaps twice his age. He had apparently come into the middle of a long-standing feud.

"Dead?"

"Ask for yourself if you don't believe me," Coolidge said. "Violated and strangled, I heard. Isn't that right, sir?"

Beede confirmed the report, and the woman grew pale.

"The poor child," she said. "I must sit down." She toddled away into the house as Beede and Coolidge followed.

It was a poor enough house. It more resembled those of his neighbors in Warrensboro than that of the one resident of this village—Kerrigan—he had met. The front door had no lock, merely a string latch like his own. Furnishings were sparse, as well: two cheap Hitchcock-style chairs—one of them a rocker—and a low bench by the fire. The embers in the fireplace grate were damped, despite the cold. Mrs. Webb took the rocker, and Coolidge moved quickly to the remaining chair. Beede leaned against the mantel.

"Dead, you say?" The words were barely a whisper. She looked to Beede, and he nodded in confirmation.

"She must have suffered terribly," she said. She glanced at Beede as if seeking contradiction. When none was forthcoming, she sighed.

"Poor lost child," she said. "She had a harder life than most."

"She had work," Coolidge said shortly. "She earned good money, in cash. There's many who'd like to have that. She had friends, and a roof over her head, and enough to eat."

The old woman laughed bitterly. "Friends!"

"Many of the girls in the mill were fond of her," Coolidge said.

"There was others who was fond of her, too," Mrs. Webb said with a snort. She looked at Coolidge. "Too fond, if you catch my meaning."

"Now hold on, Mrs. Webb. Don't you go making accusations. That's dangerous business."

"Is it so? And who was it who came to call on Sunday afternoons? And who was it brought her back long after dark, with her garment stained from the grass?"

"I visited her once or twice," Coolidge admitted. "I was one of those who tried to ease her way in this strange new world. I plead guilty to being a friend in need."

"It were your need you was helping," she said. "Not hers."

"Now, see here—"

"And you wasn't the only one, either," she said, triumphantly. "Now I surprised you, didn't I? There was another, and you know who it was, I don't doubt."

"I won't sit here and listen to this," Coolidge said. "This gentleman has come to ask you about the girl. You answer his questions and don't be going off on your flights of fancy."

"Flights of fancy, indeed," Mrs. Webb said.

She turned her attention to Beede, who had been standing there quietly transfixed by the exchange. "What is it you want to know?"

"Anything you can tell me," he replied, as he tried to gather this thoughts. "I never knew the girl at all."

"Nobody knew her, sir. I suppose I knew her better than most, but she kept her own counsel."

"How did she get along with the other girls?"

"Well enough, I think. Didn't see the other girls much. We're a bit of a long walk from the mill, and the other boardinghouses are farther still."

"How did she spend her free time?"

"She had little enough of that," Mrs. Webb said. "They work 'em long at the mill."

"Even on the Sabbath?"

"No, Sundays she had to herself, aside from church, of course."

"Is there a Catholic church in the village?"

"She went to Episcopal, like the other girls. Mr. Kerrigan's church. They all go there."

"Not a Congregational church? Surely most of the girls here are accustomed to attending Congregational meeting."

"I'm sure," she said. "And there *is* a Congregational church in the village. But Mr. Kerrigan insisted on Episcopal."

"I see. And on Sundays she had callers?"

"Indeed she did."

"Mr. Coolidge among them?"

Mrs. Webb shot a scalding glance at Coolidge, who colored visibly.

"That he was."

"Were there others?"

"There was many others, from the village, and from the farms around about," she said, still glaring at Coolidge. "He was the main one, though. Him and that peddler."

"What peddler, Mrs. Webb?"

"Don't know his name," she said. "Yeller-haired

fellow. Young one. Younger than him," she said, indicating Coolidge. She shot a triumphant glare at the overseer. "Didn't know you had competition, did you?" Coolidge reddened and turned away.

"How do you know he was a peddler?" Beede asked. "Did he bring his merchandise with him?"

"Brought two big chests with him, most times," she said. "He'd leave 'em in the parlor, here, and they'd go walking. They'd be gone for hours."

Beede considered this information carefully. The woman's description would easily have fit Albert Sanborn. It was something he would have to ask the peddler about when he returned to Warrensboro. It was curious that Sanborn had not admitted being acquainted with the girl when he had been questioned. Sanborn might have been afraid that such an admission would simply add to the burden of suspicion he already carried.

"Do you know where they went on their walks?" he asked.

The landlady shook her head. "Don't know. Didn't ask. I weren't paid to be the girl's chaperone. Other girls go out on their own, and they have families. Sharon didn't have nobody here who'd care where she went or when, long as she showed up for work on time."

Beede wasn't sure why the information bothered him so. Sharon Cudahy was, by all accounts, an attractive young woman, and it was only natural that she would have suitors—if that was what they were. Listening to Mrs. Webb's assertions, he wondered if the men who came to call were interested in a relationship that outlasted the evening or the afternoon.

Another thought also occurred to him. The girl whose body he had seen could not have been carrying a child. Had she been with child when she left the mill? It might explain her sudden departure.

Of course, the disgrace that once accompanied unwed motherhood had largely dissipated; Beede guessed that a considerable number of New England brides were pregnant on their wedding days. But those pregnancies were followed quickly by marriage; it was unthinkable that a community would allow a child to grow up without someone to care for and support it. If Sharon Cudahy were to give birth out of wedlock, there would not likely be a prospective husband in the picture. The prejudices against Catholics—and Irish Catholics, in particular—would weigh against it. An unscrupulous man out for a quick bit of fun would know that he could take his pleasure in Sharon Cudahy without being saddled with a tiresome obligation.

The turn of the conversation clearly made Coolidge uncomfortable, and Beede felt the need to move it to safer ground.

"Mrs. Webb, you had the girl under your roof for a year. You must have formed some opinion of her in that time. What can you tell me about her?"

The old woman beamed. "Oh, sir, she was a joy. Such a cheerful countenance and such a lovely voice. Always singing, she was. She knew the old songs, and she sang them so sweet. I can almost hear her now, when I close my eyes."

"Was she always cheerful?"

"At first, yes, sir. Even coming home in the evening from the mills, often in the darkness, I knew when she was approaching. I could hear her, you see. I know she was tired from a day at the loom, but there was always a song. In the beginning, at least."

"Did a time come when she no longer sang?"

She sighed. "Just a month or two before she left me. I can't remember just when it was, but she grew melancholy. I didn't hear her singing but very seldom after that."

"Did this happen suddenly or was it gradual?"

"I don't know, sir, and that's the truth. I just know that one day I realized she hadn't sung one song in, oh, I don't know how long. Many days had passed. She gave up weaving. Just sat up in her room reading by candlelight. Finally had to take 'em away from her, the price of candles being what they is."

It was Coolidge's turn to be astonished. "You mean to tell me that she spent the day in the weaving room and then came here and wove some more?"

"Yes, sir, I do," Mrs. Webb said. "And right good at it she was, too. She used to say she was from County Mayo, and that County Mayo was known far and wide for its weavers."

"Maybe we didn't work her hard enough," Coolidge said with a laugh that fell on impassive ears.

"I think that's why she stayed here so long," Mrs. Webb said. "I had this loom that came down from my grandmarm. I'm not much good with it, but Sharon was a wonder."

"**M**aybe you could have made better use of Miss Cudahy when she was in your employ," Beede said as he and Coolidge made their way back across the river. "If she was such a skilled weaver, perhaps she could have been of great assistance to your endeavors."

"If I'd known she was skilled, I would have fired her," Coolidge said. "Last thing I need is some experienced hand weaver trying to tell my girls what to do."

"But if she were able and willing—"

"We don't do hand weaving at Kerrigan Mills, Mr.

Beede. We're not craftsmen here; we're manufactors. Skill has nothing to do with producing our products."

"Skill is always helpful, I should think."

"No, sir. The machines have all the skill we need. What we need are bodies. If a girl can learn enough to keep her hair pinned up and out of the way of the machinery, and to stand away from the shuttles so she don't get hit by one, that's all the skill she needs. Any more than that, she's a liability."

"But surely—"

"Come, sir. Let's move along smartly. I want to be back at the mill in time for dinner."

Chapter 16

Over the next two days, Beede made the rounds of local businesses and outlying farms. The lack of a horse limited his range somewhat, but he made a thorough canvass of the dwellings and business establishments within walking distance.

The effort was fruitless. Many people remembered the girl, for she was striking in appearance. None, however, had seen her since the end of summer. At harvest time, of course, everyone was occupied with the backbreaking work of bringing in the crops, and neighbor helped neighbor single-mindedly until the job was done. Still, Beede doubted that a girl like Sharon Cudahy would have been overlooked if she had happened to appear on a rural road during harvest. It was almost as if she had vanished from the face of the earth.

But if Sharon Cudahy had not lingered in the area after giving up her employment in the mill, perhaps some trace of her might be found on the road to Concord. On his return to Warrensboro, therefore, it might be prudent to take the stagecoach rather than the canal boat.

From time to time, mindful of his duty to Tomkins, he returned to the mill. There he saw Deborah Tomkins working at a loom as if she had been doing it for years.

"Oh, yes, she's working out nicely," Coolidge said. "If she wants, and can sign on for a year like the others, I can use her. She's picked up the tricks right well."

But when he stopped by her boardinghouse on the second evening, he found her eager to return to her home.

"I'm used to hard work," she said. "But this is not merely hard, but mindless drudgery. I admire the girls who can adjust to the work and the rules, but I've lost any desire to become one of them."

"In that event," he said, "I propose that we leave in the morning, if that is satisfactory."

"I'll be ready," she said. "I've had a chance to talk with Alice at greater length, and I'll pass on what I've learned about Miss Cudahy. This is not the place to discuss it, but we'll have time to talk on our way back home."

"I trust your efforts have produced useful information," Kerrigan said to Beede that night at dinner. Deborah had remained in the boardinghouse. "Do you have an idea concerning the murder of the Irish girl?"

"I fear I'm no nearer a solution than when I arrived," Beede admitted. "I have learned interesting things about the girl, however, and I'm grateful for the assistance you have provided."

"Mr. Coolidge tells me you visited Mrs. Webb, Sharon's landlady. Was she helpful at all?"

"She certainly gave me a better sense of the girl herself," Beede said. "I'm not sure that it will help me discover the identity of her murderer, however."

Kerrigan poured a glass of Madeira and offered it to Beede before pouring another for himself.

"In any event, I'm pleased to have had the opportunity to show you my mill," he said.

They moved to the withdrawing room, where a fire was blazing, providing far more warmth than was strictly necessary. Beede supposed that, as a native of a warmer climate, Kerrigan was uncomfortable during the gray days and long nights of winter. Even in Washington City, residents who came from farther to the south were known to complain frequently about the cold winters. New Englanders, by contrast, complained about the sweltering heat of Washington summers and were known to state that the winters were not cold enough—indeed were not really winters at all.

"I have the impression," Kerrigan said, when they were seated, "that you suspected me of some involvement with the girl's death."

"The thought had crossed my mind."

"I must say that I'm disappointed in you," said Kerrigan. "I had assumed you were a man of the world. I assumed you would discern the nature of my business better than you have. With your experience, I thought you would realize that I couldn't be a murderer. Not, at least, in this instance."

"The girl worked for you."

"The girl worked for me," agreed Kerrigan. "And that is why I would not murder her. I did not need to murder her."

"She left your employ," Beede pointed out.

"Precisely!" Kerrigan thumped the table with his

fist. "Precisely! She had ceased to trouble me. She was no longer any concern of mine."

"She knew what goes on here," Beede pointed out. "It occurred to me that her witness might be an embarrassment to you, if she were to report what she knew."

Kerrigan waved his hand as if dismissing the issue. "What goes on here, goes on in every mill. I have nothing to hide. I offer work, for cash, to people who need cash in order to augment their living. It is hard work, but farm work is also hard, and less remunerative."

Beede studied the round, pink face carefully but saw neither remorse nor shame there.

"The work you offer is little better than slavery," he said.

"Precisely," Kerrigan said triumphantly. "It is only a *little* better than slavery, but it *is* better. And I am never short of applicants. Whenever an opening becomes available, someone inevitably appears at my doorstep. From my standpoint, it is better than slavery, of the southern form. It is slavery with a waiting list."

"I am astonished."

"It is better than the Southern form of slavery in many ways," Kerrigan went on. "For example, if I buy a slave, and the slave later becomes of no value to me, our relationship does not change. Perhaps he has grown old and can no longer carry his burden. As a slaveholder, I remain bound both morally and legally to continue providing for him until he dies or is sold, and a slave who cannot carry his weight will be difficult to sell. If, on the other hand, that man is an employee, I am under no such obligation. He has worked for me, and I have paid him. I may dismiss him at will, with no further commitment of any kind. The contract is fulfilled. He—and I—are both free men."

"Someday you are likely to push these young girls to the snapping point," Beede said. "They may decide to work for you no longer."

"Quite true," Kerrigan replied. "Some have done so already. I would have no one work for me unwillingly, particularly when there are others who will be happy to take their places. It's but a short distance to French Canada, where workers can be had for a song. And the Irish, wallowing in poverty across the ocean. It would take little to encourage them to take passage to America. They believe America is the new El Dorado."

"You speak like a zealot," Beede said. "As if this were a holy crusade."

Kerrigan laughed. "In a way, I suppose that's exactly what it is. I believe that slavery is a great boon to mankind, and that attempts to divert us from that cause are wrongheaded. I have had the opportunity in this place to demonstrate that slavery is a natural form of social organization. It is only natural that I would be proud of my accomplishment."

"But you have said that your future here is limited," Beede said in protest. "The Boston investors have bought you out, and they are good Yankees. They have said, in fact, that they believe their system will offer an alternative to slavery."

Kerrigan waved his hand in dismissal. "That's what they say."

"You don't believe it?" Beede said, astonished.

"I believe they'll try, though I doubt their fervor will endure very long. However they may wish it were not so, their fortunes depend on the success of slavery."

"In what way?"

"In two ways, sir. First, there is the small matter of cotton. The mills must have cotton in order to function, and cotton is planted, tilled, and harvested by slaves. Second, there is the question of market. There are not enough people in all of New England to purchase the cotton cloth produced by the mills of New England. No, sir. The mills of New England are dependent on the slaveholders of the South, who buy their manufactures in order to clothe their Negroes."

"Then the slaveholders must also be beholden to the mills of New England."

"Oh, they are, sir," Kerrigan said, beaming. "As long as New England can produce cotton cloth that sells at a lower price than Southern homespun or factory-milled cloth from England, slaveholders will be pleased to buy in the North. But we in the mills must always keep our prices as low as possible in order to discourage Southerners from establishing mills of their own."

Beede's mind struggled to encompass the vision that Kerrigan presented him: men, women, and children gathered in the mill yard, their fearful faces waiting expectantly for the word that they had been chosen for the right to join the harried little group on the inside, which worked from sunrise until well into the evening, in wretched conditions, for a man who treated them with less dignity than most people would give to barnyard animals.

Beede shook his head sadly. "I've never before seen greed displayed in so pure a form," he said.

"You may think of it as greed, if you wish," Kerrigan said smugly. "I prefer to think of it as frugality. And while greed is a vice, frugality is a virtue."

"And you see no distinction between the two?"

"Certainly I do, sir. But the distinction is in the viewpoint, not in the acts themselves. Greed is frugality seen from below, from the underside, if you will. If I have wealth, yet choose to spend as little of it as possible, then I am frugal. If you have wealth, and I am envious of you, then you are greedy."

Beede felt suddenly fatigued and depressed. He paid his respects to his host and retreated to his comfortable guest room. Kerrigan bade him farewell with his usual cheer.

Chapter 17

"She left Ireland two years ago," Deborah Tomkins said. "Alice said Sharon did not speak of her previous life but once or twice. Alice believes she had an unfortunate experience on shipboard."

They were sitting on the rude bench in front of a tavern, waiting for the arrival of the stage coach to Concord. Deborah had been brimming with information to impart and could not wait for the coach to be under way before imparting it. In reality, Beede thought, it was unlikely that they would have the privacy they needed once the coach arrived. Coach lines were known for squeezing every penny of profit by overcrowding their vehicles with paying passengers.

"Did she explain the nature of that unfortunate experience?" Beede asked.

"Alice believes she was violated during the passage from England. Sharon told her that she was the only girl on board the ship, and that she could find no safe place to hide. Perhaps she was violated more than once; Alice was under that impression."

It seemed, when he thought about it, all too likely. Six weeks on the open sea with a ship full of men and one pretty girl would be a temptation to which many men might fall prey. Many captains would have refused to take her on board at all for fear of precisely such a development. The captain who accepted her would have to be ever vigilant to maintain discipline among passengers and crew alike—or else recklessly unconcerned with the possible consequences. Both types of captains were known to exist.

"I have gained some new information myself," he said. He told Deborah about his conversation with the girl's landlady across the river. He refrained from speculating about the nature of the Sunday afternoon visitors Sharon Cudahy received, but Deborah understood the ramifications without prompting.

"Truly she suffered grievously at the hands of many men," she said. "Are all men as callous and unfeeling as that?"

"Not all," he assured her, wondering if he had answered truthfully.

If he were presented with an opportunity to gratify his desires without concern for the consequences, would he also succumb to temptation? The question lay at the heart of his feelings about Adrienne. They had both been young when they married, and consumed with passion for each other, but in five short years the strain had worn them down. What would have happened if they had remained together long enough for the fires to die? Would he have remained faithful when the passion had cooled, or would he have sought another? In New Orleans, where men routinely took mistresses, often spending more time with

their paramours than with their wives, the temptation
would have been strong.

"What else did you learn from Alice?" he asked.

"Alice didn't mention Mr. Coolidge," Deborah
said. "But there was another, and I'm certain you
know him. Albert Sanborn, the peddler."

"Mrs. Webb also mentioned a peddler with yellow
hair, who came to call on Sundays."

"Not merely on Sunday," Deborah said. "When the
workday was done, Sharon would often go with Alice
to Alice's boardinghouse, rather than walk all the way
back to her own lodgings. Mr. Sanborn would meet
her at Alice's boardinghouse and escort Sharon
home."

"And did Alice believe that theirs was an intimate
relationship?"

"I don't believe she knew with certainty," Deborah
said. "But the idea clearly had occurred to her, and she
was pleased, I think. She thought Sanborn would be a
fine 'catch,' as she put it: industrious, clever, and
rather comely. I think Alice rather fancied him, herself."

"Anything else?"

Deborah thought for a moment.

"I don't know what it means," she said, after a moment. "Perhaps it means nothing. But Alice has the impression that Kerrigan Mills will not continue long in
operation."

"So Mr. Kerrigan told me," Beede said. "I gather
from him that the Boston owners of the mills in Lowell have acquired both the land and water rights in
Manchester. He continues to operate his enterprise at
their sufferance until their own mills begin to operate
across the river."

The stagecoach clattered around the bend in the
road and pulled up before the tavern in a cloud of dust.

Two passengers alighted and entered the tavern, and Beede helped Deborah to enter the vehicle. He placed their baggage on the rack above the coach and then climbed aboard himself.

The sole passenger already aboard the coach was a fellow lawyer, whom Beede had often met on the circuit, a corpulent but good-natured fellow with thinning sandy hair and watery blue eyes. Beede and Deborah took the forward-facing seat opposite him.

"Mr. Beede, isn't it?" the man said. "I was under the impression you lived farther north!"

"That is so," Beede said. "I'm here on business."

"And is this your lovely wife? Will you not introduce me to her?"

"My apologies, sir. I forget my manners. Miss Tomkins, may I introduce Mr. Thomas Meeks. Mr. Meeks, Deborah Tomkins of Warrensboro. She is the daughter of Mr. Israel Tomkins of that town."

"So you are not husband and wife? This is, indeed, encouraging information, sir. I must make it a point to call upon you in the very near future, in order to further my acquaintance with your charming companion. That is, unless I would be encroaching upon your territory."

Meeks was having some fun at Beede's expense, and Beede knew it. But he knew, also, that rumors often took flight on the flimsiest of breezes, and a rumor concerning an unwed man and a young, single woman could have devastating consequences for the woman. He searched his mind for the proper response.

Deborah's wits were sharper than his own.

"I've been to Manchester to visit an acquaintance in the mills," she said with a smile. "Mr. Beede has graciously agreed to accompany me on my return. We are neighbors, in a manner of speaking."

Meeks was about to respond, but at that instant the stagecoach jerked into motion. Beede, who was leaning forward, found himself thrown backward against the hard wooden bench. The force of the movement momentarily robbed him of his breath.

"Are you all right, man?" Meeks asked. Beede could only nod in response. The concern in Meeks's eyes seemed genuine, and Beede saw a worried expression on Deborah's face, as well.

"I'm not hurt," he said. "Do not concern yourself with me."

They relaxed visibly and turned their faces to allow him a moment to compose himself. He took advantage of the opportunity to study his companions.

Meeks was clearly taken by Deborah Tomkins. Strange, Beede thought, that he had never noticed her before, despite having seen her every week at Sabbath meeting, at Skinner's store, and around the village. He had, in fact, spent several days and evenings in her company without paying her any particular attention.

But now that a casual acquaintance was showing interest, Beede began to see her in a new way, and he realized that she was, indeed, pretty. Too young for him, of course, even if he were inclined to remarry (and he was not), but Meeks was yet several years younger than he. Further, he was established in his profession, quite wealthy for a New England lawyer, and might be accounted handsome by women. Beede did not understand why women were attracted to some men and not to others, but he thought that Meeks might be considered a prize.

Watching now as they chatted animatedly, Beede felt the confusion he always felt in the presence of young women. He admired Meeks's easy gift of sociability, his ability to make a woman whom he had never met before comfortable in his presence. It was a gift Beede had never possessed, although he had tried mightily to acquire it for Adrienne's sake.

"Are you feeling better now, Mr. Beede?" Deborah was smiling expectantly, her conversation with Meeks temporarily interrupted.

"Oh, yes. Much better, Miss Tomkins. Thank you for inquiring." She smiled again and turned away, and he knew she had put him out of her mind once more.

So it had been with Adrienne. After those early days, when they burned with passion for each other and seemed to feel each other's touch even from a distance, they had drifted apart. She had fallen in love with the boy hero of New Orleans, but she had soon realized that he was no hero. She objected to his phlegmatic manner and contemplative nature. She desired a young Jackson—hot-blooded and mercurial—rather than an impassive young Yankee, and she resented what she considered his deception in failing to meet her expectations.

For his part, there were few men he would rather have emulated than Jackson. But it was not in him. Duels were fought in New Orleans with frightening frequency, but Beede had never settled a difference on the field of honor. Indeed, he had never felt the need to do so, and he knew that his reluctance stemmed in large measure from fear for his life. Adrienne knew this, also, and held him in contempt for it. It was one of the many ways in which he failed to live up to his mentor's standard. Jackson was never reluctant to issue or accept a challenge, and he carried in his body at least one relic of those encounters.

So the marriage had endured for five long years, and then the childbirth fever had overtaken her, and she had died. Beede still carried with him the memories of lost hopes and missed opportunities. He suspected that they would remain with him forever.

Chapter 18

The coach stopped twice on the road to Concord. At both stops, Beede and Deborah Tomkins inquired about Sharon Cudahy, to no avail.

At Concord they said their farewells to Meeks, who was traveling on by coach to the northern mountains, and walked to the stable to reclaim Tomkins's carriage and Beede's horse. From there, they began the final leg of their journey home to Warrensboro.

They rode the first few miles in silence, but Beede found it to be a much more comfortable silence than had prevailed on the trip south. They sat wordlessly on the carriage bench, gazing at the bare gray trees and yellowing pastures. When he glanced in her direction, Deborah turned to him and smiled—an open smile containing neither flirtation nor derision—before turning her gaze to the countryside again.

It was difficult to think of this as land carved out of the wilderness. There was so little wilderness left.

Acre upon acre of cropland and fallow field stretched over the hillocks in every direction, sometimes with a fringe of trees to provide a spot of shade for grazing cattle, but more often not.

Not every field was cultivated. Many were returning to the wild as weeds and bushes began reclaiming their territory. These were fields that had been cultivated but were now abandoned by farmers who had died without living heirs, or who had finally thrown up their hands and moved west with their families and all their possessions. Beede was ambiguous about these abandoned fields; he had come to New Hampshire in search of isolation, but these abandoned farms were promising to bring him far more isolation than he had desired.

"I have been thinking about Sharon Cudahy," Deborah said as they approached another village. "Her life in America began in Manchester and ended in Warrensboro. If we were to inquire along the way, should we not be able to trace her movements? And would that not provide us with a clue to her last days?"

"You're quite correct," said Beede, and he reined his horse to a stop.

The village was little more than a crossroads, dominated by a ramshackle tavern. The wooden sign, hanging by a single hasp from a yardarm, proclaimed it to be the Hart and Crow. The inn's namesakes had been crudely rendered by an itinerant painter in a manner that made the hart look more like an ox.

Adjacent to the tavern was a two-story house accompanied by a lean-to shed, from which came the clanging sound of metal on metal. Beede hesitated a moment, considering first the tavern with its unpromising appearance and then the blacksmith's shop with its sounds of activity, and decided to begin with the smithy.

The smith was a bit of a surprise. Blacksmiths, in Beede's experience, tended to be large men with broad shoulders and well-developed upper arms, the product of a lifetime of pumping an overhead bellows and wielding heavy hammers. The man at the anvil, however, was thin and wiry. Beede judged him to be in his late teens or early twenties—old for an apprentice but not impossibly so.

The young man looked up briefly and returned to his work.

"With you in a minute," he said. The hammer rang out in a rhythmic tattoo as it struck first the iron bar and then the anvil in regular alternation. First-year apprentices often dissipated their energies by arresting their hammer after each stroke. Beede noticed that this young man had learned to let the hammer bounce on the anvil, so that the anvil became, in effect, his partner rather than his adversary.

At length, he put down his hammer and turned expectantly to his visitors. "How may I help you, sir?" he said to Beede, sparing an interested glance for Deborah.

"Perhaps some information," Beede said. "We're seeking to retrace the steps of a young woman who may have traveled through here about three months ago. Were you here during that period?"

"Every day for the past three years," the young man replied. "Except for Sabbaths, of course. I inherited the smithy from my father-in-law about that time when he passed on."

"She had bright red hair," said Deborah. "And blue eyes. Perhaps you recall seeing her."

"That I do," the young man said. "Saw her and talked to her. She was a striking young lady and hard not to notice. She came on foot, which was also unusual."

"Was she alone?" Beede asked.

"Now that would have been striking, indeed," the smith replied. "No, she was accompanied by a peddler. They sought directions. The young woman was seeking a physician."

"And were you able to assist her?"

"In a manner of speaking," the smith said. "We have one such creature in the village, though I'm not persuaded that I did her much service by directing her to him. He's not the man I would trust with any ailment that couldn't be cured with a good puking."

The young smith's directions led them through the village to a modest saltbox house set well back from the road. The physician had established a small office in a front room of the house. Beede knocked on the door and waited. In a moment, they could hear a chair scraping on the floor followed by the sound of a shambling gait approaching the door. It opened, and a wizened head appeared in the opening.

"Dr. Goodwin, I presume?"

The head withdrew from the doorway, and the door opened wider. Taking that to be an invitation, Beede ushered the girl ahead of him into the house.

The old doctor was already shuffling his way down the hall ahead of them. Reaching a door, he pushed it open and motioned for them to enter. He settled himself into the only chair in the room while his visitors stood awkwardly before him.

"So which of you is ailing?" he said in a sandpaper voice. He looked up at Beede. "You could use some bleeding, by the look of you," he said. "And perhaps some calomel, also."

"I feel fit enough," Beede said. "And so does the lady. It's someone else we've come about."

"A girl about my age," said Deborah. "With bright

red hair and deep blue eyes. We believe she may have visited you sometime last summer."

"I do recall such a girl," the doctor said. "She came to me in September, I believe. Do you know her?"

"She is dead," Beede said. "I am trying to trace her movements in these past few months."

"If she is dead, it is through no fault of mine," the doctor said defensively. "She was fine when she left me."

"I don't doubt it," said Beede. "We have no reason to suspect you of any involvement in her demise. I only wish to know the circumstances of her visit to you."

"And what business of yours is that? I do not discuss my patients' ailments with others."

"We are merely attempting to trace her movements," Beede said again as patiently as he could. "And since the girl is dead, she can have no objection to this discussion."

"Yes, I suppose you're right," the old doctor said. "In any event, her ailments were common enough. She asked for help in calming her stomach. She complained of nausea and said she had been uneasy for a week or more. I treated her in the usual fashion and sent her on her way."

"The usual fashion?" Deborah said.

"Yes," the doctor said, plainly irritated at being interrupted by a female. "I followed the time-honored practices. Clearly her humors were out of balance."

"You bled her?" Deborah said incredulously.

"Of course," said Goodwin. "It is a commonly accepted procedure for ailments of the body, particularly when the body is so obviously unsettled. When I was done with her, she felt much more at ease, I assure you."

"You *bled* her!"

"A procedure that is proven by time," Goodwin said. "I know that there are those who question its efficacy, but it has also been approved by no less than the great Dr. Benjamin Rush. It was the treatment afforded our first president. Why should I offer less to my patients?"

"General Washington died," Deborah said dryly. "It was widely held that he would have lived much longer if not for being bled."

Goodwin shook his head. "The general was gravely ill and would not have lived much longer—as indeed he did not. No, I stand with the great authorities of my science, who have almost unanimously endorsed the procedure."

Beede stepped in to redirect a conversation that was quickly deteriorating. "Was there a gentleman with the girl when she came to you?"

"I'm told there was," Goodwin said. "I did not see him, but my wife said he waited in the front yard until the girl departed."

"And where did they go after leaving you?"

"North, I believe. I did not follow them."

Beede thanked the doctor for his time and escorted Deborah, who would have stayed to pursue her argument with Goodwin, back to the carriage.

"So we know that she was here in September," he said, when they were on their way again. "But she was not murdered until nearly two months later. I wonder where she spent those two months, and with whom. Do you suppose the peddler was with her all that time?"

"I can't imagine."

"I shall have to question him closely about this," Beede said.

They rode together in silence for a while. Deborah was clearly perturbed.

"He bled her!" she said, finally, catching Beede by surprise. "I do not doubt that he purged her and puked her, as well."

"They are, as he said, common procedures," Beede reminded her, confused by the vehemence of her reaction. "Why does it upset you so?"

"They are not common treatments for a woman who carries a child," she replied. "I would have thought a physician would have recognized the symptoms and known what the girl was really requesting."

"Pregnancy?"

She turned to him fiercely. "Surely you discerned it, sir! Were you not a married man, and did your wife not conceive a child? Sharon Cudahy came to this backwoods charlatan seeking the means to abort the child that was growing within her."

"An abortion?"

"Yes, sir. An abortion, sir. I wonder sometimes that men are so blithe and unobservant. She came to him for the means to remove an unwanted child. He responded by opening her veins and dosing her with mercury!"

Chapter 19

Home.

They topped the hill and saw the familiar scene spread below. Below them, the road veered eastward, skirting the rock wall of Beede's own south pasture. The place where Sharon Cudahy had lain was hidden again by the merciful grass, and the wooden cross that marked her grave site was barely visible on the other side of the wall.

He hadn't intended to stop, had planned instead to continue on to the Tomkins property, thereby returning Deborah to her family as soon as possible. As they passed, however, Deborah begged him to rein in so that she might visit the grave site.

"I've been thinking of her," she told Beede simply. "She has been on my mind almost constantly since leaving the mill. I would have regretted not stopping to pay my respects."

"I have been intending to replace this meek little

cross with a headstone," Beede said in apology. "Now that I am home again, perhaps I can see to it."

"It is no less than she deserves," Deborah said. "You know, do you not, that Pastor Gray says Sharon's soul will not be accepted into God's presence because she was a papist?"

"My Adrienne would have said much the same about Pastor Gray," Beede said. "I confess I don't know who is right and who is wrong."

"What was your wife like?" asked Deborah, a curious expression on her face. "Was she very different from New England girls?"

"Very different," Beede said. "Though I believe the difference was less due to her religion than to the fact that she was French. They are a very dissimilar people, in my experience."

"In what way?"

Beede thought for a long moment before speaking.

"The French people of Louisiana live for pleasure," he said. "Their sense of moral duty seems far less advanced, in my impression. Perhaps it's the climate, or the soil, or the fact that they depend on slaves to perform so much of the unpleasant work. Even their religion is made into a source of pleasure. They celebrate Christmas—quite elaborately and expensively—and the period immediately before Lent, which they call carnival, is given over completely to music and dalliance."

"And your wife? What was she like?"

Again Josiah paused before speaking. "She was elegant," he said finally. "She was small, and dark, and beautiful, and very young, and she fit snugly in the crook of my arm. She wore long dresses that made it appear that she was floating as she walked. I felt quite large and clumsy when I was with her. She could dance like an angel."

"Are New England girls not elegant?" she said with a trace of a smile.

"No, of course they are," he said, hastily. "But Adrienne was elegant in a different way. I never saw her composure break. She never failed to find the right words to put another person at ease. I was always roiling the waters—unintentionally—and she invariably calmed them."

"Was she skilled at the domestic arts?"

"No. She had always had . . . servants. Even after we were wed, we had servants. Randolph had been in her family and came north with us to Washington City. He was, in a manner of speaking, part of her dowry."

"You were a slaveholder?"

"I regret to say I was, though not without discomfort. But it was the custom of the Southern states, and Adrienne would not have abided my freeing them. She had no qualms of conscience about owning another human being, and in fact the slaves belonged to her, not to me."

"But Randolph is now a free man, is he not? How did that happen?"

"My wife died in childbirth, and her property was bequeathed to me. Randolph was the most valuable part of that inheritance."

"What happened to the slaves you inherited?"

"I freed them, gradually, as I thought I could afford to do so. There were not so very many by that time. We had only a small household in Washington. When I decided to return to New England, it seemed only logical to offer Randolph his freedom and a job—if he wanted it—on my new farm. He agreed, with the understanding that he would leave when he had acquired the skill and the money to strike out on his own."

"A noble gesture," she said.

"Hardly that," he replied. "Randolph was the last to

be freed. Probably he should have been the first, but I enjoyed his company and was loath to let him go."

They had been walking back to the carriage. At the wall, he climbed over, lifted her easily, and set her on the opposite side, noting that she was nearly as light as Adrienne, though much taller.

"Tell me, Mr. Beede," she said in a little while as Beede's horse plodded on toward the village. "How did a New England man make the acquaintance of a young French girl from New Orleans, let alone marry her?"

"My brother and I left home after my father died," he said. "My eldest brother inherited the farm, and there was little left for Seth and me. We took up the peddler's trade and headed west to the new lands. Eventually, we found ourselves in New Orleans."

"Why New Orleans?"

"We thought it would be profitable to sell our wares to soldiers," he said. "Soldiers always need goods, and their supply trains are often far in the rear. We made it a point to stay as close to the advance columns as we could. When we reached Kentucky, the soldiers were all moving south toward New Orleans. We simply followed them."

"Your wife must have been very proud to be married to such a man as you," Deborah said.

"I do not believe so."

"Not proud? They called you the boy hero of New Orleans."

He bought a few seconds to think by clucking at his horse and slapping the reins lightly on the Morgan's rump.

"I was called that, it is true. But I was no hero. I was a spindly boy of fifteen who had never been fired upon by another man. I did not acquit myself well."

And then they were at the village common. Whatever response may have been on Deborah's mind seemed to die instantly as they caught sight of the Tomkins house on the far side of the common.

"We are home," she said simply. And she was out of the carriage and flying across the flagstones to her front door before Beede could bring the carriage to a full stop.

Chapter 20

"So the trail has grown cold," Huff said. "I had feared as much."

"I'm not certain," Beede said. "We know she was in the vicinity of Warrensboro—at least within a few miles—in September. And the peddler was with her."

"But not a trace since then," Huff pointed out. "Two months are unaccounted for. She could have gone much farther north on foot in that span of time."

"She might," Beede agreed. "But in November she was found on my property, recently murdered. It seems likely to me that she did not go so very far away from here."

They sat in the parlor of the Tomkins house. Israel Tomkins, Stephen Huff, and Josiah Beede warmed themselves at the hearth and discussed the information that Beede had acquired, with Deborah's help, on his trip south. Huff lived nearby—his house also faced the green, although in a far less imposing position—and

Tomkins had summoned him immediately upon Beede's arrival.

"What is our next move, Mr. Beede?" Tomkins said. "If we assume, as you say, that she remained in the vicinity of Warrensboro, how do we trace her movements?"

"Simple enough," said Huff. "We conduct inquiries throughout the village and the town."

"We should do that, certainly," said Beede, "but I doubt that it will yield us much. If someone had harbored her for two months, I don't believe they will tell us so. Not now, since we have found her and determined that she was murdered. Not even an innocent party is likely to admit it, for fear of having the crime fastened upon him."

"But surely someone must have seen her," Tomkins said. "Some disinterested party might have come upon her along the road."

Beede took a sip of the exceptionally fine Madeira that Tomkins had brought out and savored it before he replied. For the first time since his arrival two years earlier, he seemed to have been accepted by Tomkins as a neighbor, if not a friend. He supposed his agreement to escort Deborah to and from Manchester had been a factor in Tomkins's gradual warming.

"It's certainly possible," he agreed. "And we mustn't curtail our efforts, in any event."

"Then it's agreed," said Huff. "Shall we begin immediately? We can survey all those who live on the green as a start."

"I'll be happy to join you later," Beede said. "But I should return home as soon as possible. Several questions were raised in my mind during my trip south, and I'm eager to put these questions to Albert Sanborn as soon as possible."

Huff laughed. "Might be difficult to do, sir."

"Well, I can only try."

Huff looked at Tomkins. "Has no one told you? "

"Told me what?"

"Your man Randolph was injured two days ago while building a cider mill," Tomkins said. "He was unconscious for some little time. Sanborn used that opportunity to make his escape. No one knows where he is."

"I have put the word out among all the villages hereabouts," Huff said. "It'll take a day or two, but we'll find out which way he went soon enough."

Beede made his apologies and hurried back to the farm. He found Randolph sitting up uncomfortably in Beede's own bed, his right leg splinted and bandages on his head. Beede saw that he was in considerable pain but managed a rueful grin.

"I fear that I'll not be much value to you for a little while," he said.

"No matter, as long as you are out of danger," Beede said. "Your injuries look painful."

"They're not so much now," he said. "Though I admit that for a while I was seeing two of everything."

"What happened to cause this disaster?" Beede asked.

Randolph winced as if the mere memory was painful to him. "The beam slipped out of its seating," he said. "It fell upon us, and I must have taken the brunt of it. All I know is that when I awakened, Jacob Wolf was standing over me, and the peddler was gone. I suppose he took advantage of the opportunity to escape."

"Did he plan this, do you think?"

"I don't think so. He could not have known that we would be working on the cider mill that morning, and the beam was heavier than even I expected. I believe he simply benefited from a fortuitous chain of circumstance."

"We'll catch him," Beede promised. "Mr. Huff has sent notices to all our neighboring villages. Someone will surely see him."

"I don't know that the recapture will be worth the effort of fetching him back," Randolph said. "I'm persuaded that he could not have had a hand in this murder. It is not in his character. He might be capable of rape and murder, as might almost anyone, but I don't believe he would have had the foresight to carry her body from the scene of the crime."

"Perhaps not," Beede said. "But there are a number of questions I'm eager to put to him, based on my discoveries on my visit to Manchester. Our young peddler, it seems, knew Sharon Cudahy rather better than he let on."

If the invitation from Nathaniel Gray was not a command, Beede felt, nonetheless, that he must make the effort to appear. Therefore, prior to leaving the farm for the morning Sabbath service the following Sunday, he asked Mrs. Shelton to pack some bread and cheese for his portable dinner.

After the service had ground to a close, Beede waited for the congregation to file out of the meetinghouse so the pastor could join him in one of the pews. On summer Sundays, a number of the congregation might have chosen to remain behind and enjoy a picnic dinner on the grounds, but the late fall weather rendered such indulgences foolhardy. Even in the relative shelter of the meetinghouse, Beede and the pastor were obliged to wear their winter cloaks in order to maintain some degree of comfort.

"I fear I have had little time to think about Mr.

Wolf's difficulties," Beede began, when they were settled. "I'm aware that the problem is acute, particularly as winter is coming on rapidly, but Jacob is a proud man who will not submit to charity, no matter how useful or well-intentioned."

Gray dismissed the matter with a gesture. "I'm certain that you will think of something, sir," he said. "I have faith in your acumen. Frankly, it is of another matter that I hoped to speak today."

"And that is . . . ?"

Gray hesitated, and a moment of embarrassed silence followed.

"It is about Mercy, Mr. Beede. My daughter."

"I don't understand."

Gray regarded him steadily for a moment. "No, I see that you don't. Very well, sir. I shall be blunt. I must know your intentions."

"I beg your pardon?"

"Your intentions, sir. Toward my daughter. Surely you must be aware of her feelings toward you. They are quite plain to everyone else."

"My intentions? Toward your daughter?"

Gray emitted an exasperated sigh. "Oh, come, sir. She is enamored of you. She speaks of you at length in the most acclamatory manner. She seeks opportunities to call upon you. Surely you are not so blind that you have not noticed this."

Beede had, in fact, noticed her presence on a number of occasions. He would return from the fields, or the tavern, or from Samuel Skinner's store, to find Mercy Gray engaged in earnest conversation with Mrs. Shelton. But he had not made the connection that Gray had made. He wondered whether he had been stupid or whether Gray was reading more into these incidents than was actually there.

"I have noticed your daughter, of course," he began.

"I confess that I did not see in her what you profess to see. Are you certain of your conclusions?"

Gray shook his head condescendingly. "It is difficult for me to believe that you do not see what I see, sir. I'm inclined to believe you're being disingenuous."

"No, sir. I—"

Gray held up his hand. "It's of no significance. You may trust me in this matter. My daughter is infatuated with you, sir. If you have not been aware of it before, you have at least been made aware of it now. I expect you to consider your intentions carefully."

"I assure you, sir, I have no intentions regarding your daughter."

"You mean to say that your intentions are not dishonorable?"

"I mean to say that I have no intentions of any sort toward your daughter. I am not now seeking a wife. Therefore, I have no interest in paying suit to Miss Gray."

Far from reassuring the pastor, Beede's denial seemed to upset him further.

"Come, sir, this will not do," Gray said, sternly. "Not at all. Do you mean to say that you have *no* interest in my daughter whatsoever?"

"I thought I had said so quite plainly."

"Do you find her . . . unattractive?"

"Far from it. I find her exceedingly handsome."

"Then perhaps you are of the belief that she is insufficiently skillful in the domestic arts?"

"I'm quite certain that she is skillful."

"Or of a shrewish disposition? Because I can assure you that that is not the case. Her manner and countenance are of the sweetest sort."

"I had always assumed so," Beede said, unsure of where the pastor was headed.

Gray shook his head. "Then you will no doubt agree that she will make an excellent life companion."

"I'm certain."

"Do you believe that she will have no suitors?"

"I'm certain that she will have many."

"Then I fail to understand," Gray said, "how you can turn so blind an eye to her obvious virtues."

"I do not, sir. I am simply not seeking a wife at this time."

"You are thirty-five years old, are you not?"

"Yes, and married."

"Your wife is dead, sir."

"Not to me."

"This is foolish, sir!" Gray said. "You are still a young man. You have many years to live. Your wife was taken from you some years previously—"

"More than five," Beede said.

"And yet you continue to mourn her! This does you no credit, no credit at all. We must all know how and when to let go of the past. Life goes on, sir! Life goes on!"

"I know you are correct, Mr. Gray," Beede said. "It is my earnest hope that I shall be able to do so someday. But I cannot. At least not yet."

Gray stood and moved to the window, where he peered out at the gray November silence.

"Then you must promise me something," Gray said, after a moment.

"If I can."

"I would ask you to consider paying suit to my daughter for her sake, if not for yours."

"I don't believe I heard you correctly. I thought you said I should court your daughter for *her* sake."

"That is exactly what I said, Mr. Beede. It would be embarrassing if you were to resist her blandishments entirely. We are a small community, and it has got about already that she has set her cap for you. If you were now to reject her, it would be unbearable for her."

"As you pointed out yourself, she will not lack for suitors," Beede reminded him.

"None who are as well situated in life as you," Gray said quickly. "You are mature, a man of accomplishment, with property of your own and the means to acquire more. You are a serious man who has read widely. A man of some influence in the community, indeed in the nation. My daughter *deserves* such a man as you."

Not for the first time in his life, Beede could think of nothing to say.

"I see that this has been presented to you rather suddenly," Gray said. "But I hope you will give the matter some thought, and quickly. To be frank, I fear that too long a delay may cause her to despair and to seek someone younger and more passionate, who will lead her away from the paths of righteousness and into a life of debauchery and licentiousness. I call upon your sense of responsibility to save her from such a fate."

"I—"

"No response is required at this time, sir. Indeed, I see the first of our faithful members are returning from their nooning. I must go and prepare for the service. I bid you good day."

He swept away toward his study in the rear of the meetinghouse, leaving Beede sitting dumbfounded in his wake.

Albert Sanborn had spent the day trekking through the village of Manchester without success. He had knocked on doors, accosted strange people on the street, inquired of every merchant and merchant's customer, and had come up empty-handed.

Some of the people he met remembered the girl. As Sanborn knew firsthand, she was hard to forget. Their memories, however, were inconsequential. None had met her or talked to her at any length, and none, he was sure, had raped and murdered her and then transported her to the side of the road in a village nearly a day's ride distant. If he were to discover the murderer of Sharon Cudahy, it seemed clear, he would have to return to Warrensboro and make his inquiries there—the one thing Sanborn could not and would not do. The outlook for clearing his name of suspicion and regaining his merchandise seemed dimmer than ever.

He was heartened by one discovery. Nearly everywhere he went, Beede had been first. Perhaps there was a real investigation going on, after all. As far as he could tell, Beede was asking about the girl, not about the peddler, even though he seemed to know that Sanborn had accompanied her. Perhaps his sole purpose was not to lay the guilt upon Sanborn at all.

Not that it mattered. If another suspect could not be found, the temptation to blame the stranger would always be there. And in truth, he was beginning to think another suspect would not be found, no matter how hard he searched.

He stopped and sat upon a boulder at the side of the road, ever watchful for passersby who might recognize him and attempt to capture him. Was he to be a fugitive for the rest of his life? Would he be forced to leave New Hampshire—perhaps even leave New England—entirely? He toyed with the idea for a moment. Perhaps he could go west, as Beede himself had done, or even south to New Orleans. Warm winters, fragrant springs, dark-eyed Creole girls, and what was generally believed to be an easygoing life—bordering, some said, on the libertine.

It sounded promising on its face, but it would be a major decision. He would never see his family again, at least until the death of Sharon Cudahy was forgotten. Even in New Orleans, someone might recognize him; notices concerning fugitives appeared on walls and nailed to trees everywhere, although without a likeness, it was unlikely that he would be recognized on the basis of a sketchy description on a circular. The odds would favor him in a faraway city, but distance was by no means a guarantee of safety.

And, of course, he would have to survive long enough to gather what he would need. He would need shelter, however temporary, while he prepared for flight.

Where would he find it? He thought he knew at least one person here who was acquainted with him and would believe in him. He set out immediately for her door.

On his way, he reviewed the possible suspects in his mind. Beede, he knew, was out. He had been in Concord at the court.

Randolph? He had to admit to a certain grudging respect for the man but could not rule him out. Where had he been at the time of the murder? Did anyone know?

Could the murderer be someone else in the village? It was certainly possible, even probable, but Sanborn did not really know anyone else in the village, except for the old man he had called on after finding the girl's body. And this was a crime of passion; what could rouse such passions in a man clearly reaching the end of his life?

This was futile speculation, he decided. He did not know these people well enough even to form an opinion. Let the villagers of Warrensboro search among their own, if they would. He would concentrate his efforts here, where Sharon Cudahy lived and worked.

He picked up his pace. The house he sought was now in sight.

Chapter 21

Word of Albert Sanborn's whereabouts reached Warrensboro two days later. A postmaster in a village farther south had seen a young man resembling the peddler striding through the village center a few days previously. He had not been positively identified, but the description left no doubt in the minds of Stephen Huff or Josiah Beede. Clearly, it was the man they sought, and apparently he was bound for Manchester.

"I can't imagine why he might return there," said Beede. "But in any event, I have a duty to find him and bring him back. I'll start at once."

"It will keep until after Thanksgiving," Huff said. "No one should have to be away from home tomorrow. You can leave on Friday."

On the eve of the holiday, a dance was held at the tavern. Beede had not felt like dancing for many

years, but he attended the festivities as a matter of
courtesy. There were too many memories associated
with dancing, for it had been on the dance floor that he
had first met Adrienne.

"And this," said Jackson, "is the young man I was
tellin' you about. His name is Josiah."

"I'm pleased to meet you, Josiah," said the short,
round woman who happened to be the general's wife.
"I've heard about your bravery."

"Wasn't bravery, ma'am," Josiah said shame-
facedly. "I was mad, and I was scared. That's all it
was."

"Yes, I know," said Rachel Jackson. "General
Jackson's told me about your modesty, too. Must be
the Yankee in you that makes you want to hide your
light under a bushel like that. Men in our parts don't
see nothin' wrong with braggin', if you can follow
through on it like you done."

"Ma'am, I'm not being modest. It's just the way it
was," he said in protest.

"Oh, I'm sure," she said and patted his hand. "I
want to talk to you some more, but the general is after
me to dance with him, and he's gettin' awful impatient.
Now you wait right here, and I'll be back in just a few
minutes. Don't move, now."

The long soldier and his round consort moved out
on the dance floor. Seeing them together, the other
dancers gave way. Creole and Kaintuck alike moved
aside for the general and his wife. A ripple of applause began somewhere on the other side of the
floor and spread throughout the room. Seeing them
on the floor, the orchestra put aside their quadrilles
and struck up an "American" tune in their honor.
The ripple of applause became a torrent as Jackson

and his wife began bobbing to the rhythms of a mountain fiddle air.

Josiah marveled at the hypocrisy of it all. When he and Seth had arrived in New Orleans early in December, the city was in turmoil, and Jackson was vilified at every turn. He was, to the Creoles, the heathen, arrogant backwoodsman who treated Creole aristocracy as he had treated the Creeks whom he had subjugated. Now, with victory over the British in his grasp, the backwoods bully had become hero of the hour. How long could Jackson remain in the good graces of this fickle band of French-speaking snobs?

The music ended, and Rachel, Jackson sailed off the floor, the décolletage of her (probably) borrowed gown displaying her ample bosom.

"I swear I ain't danced so much since I was a girl," she said, laughing. A wine goblet was placed in her hand, and she took a long sip as she fanned herself with her free hand.

"You ain't been out there on the floor, Josiah. This is a ball, son. You should find yourself a likely young lady and dance with her."

"Ma'am, I cannot," he said.

"Of course you can, Josiah. You're a hero. Didn't the general explain that to you? There are dozens of young ladies here who are dying to dance with you."

"Can't dance, ma'am."

"Don't be silly, boy. Course you can. They ain't doin' nothin' fancy out there; it's just plain country dances like you done at home in New England. And look at that little girl right over there; she's been lookin' at you doe-eyed all night long."

If the truth were told, Josiah had been looking at her, also. She was small and dark, with a waist so narrow he felt he could fit his hands around it and feel his fingertips meet. She wore something dark red in color, off her delicate shoulders, exposing a vast expanse of creamy skin. He had been finding excuses to steal glances at her for more than an hour. She had not, as far as he could tell, noticed his existence or acknowledged it in any way.

He glanced once more in her direction. As he had thought, she was paying him no attention at all, chattering gaily with other young Creole girls and their formidable mothers. Now and then her eyes would wander the ballroom as if searching for a familiar face, but her eyes would slide past Josiah as if he were not there before coming to a halt at some point in the middle distance beyond him. After a moment of this, she would often wave gaily to someone across the room before returning to her friends nearby.

"She is not looking at me, Mrs. Jackson," he said. "She looks over this way some, but she does not notice me at all. She's got friends all over the city, I'll bet, and she won't want a tongue-tied Yankee to get in her way."

"And you don't think she's trying real hard not to notice you? She's depending on you to make the first move. That's how it's done."

"Ma'am, I'm certain she isn't interested in me. She's looked right through me many times without even seeing me. She don't see me at all."

Rachel Jackson shook her head. "I swear, boy. Have you been hiding under a rock your whole life? Don't you know how these things are done? Don't you know nothin'?"

"I think I know when a girl isn't interested," he said hotly. She might be the wife of the great general, he thought, but she was clearly unacquainted with the ways of young women in the sophisticated cities. Of

course, he admitted, he hardly knew more than she, but he had had the advantage of numerous prolonged discussions with the men and boys of the army during the preceding weeks. It was their all-but-unanimous opinion that New Orleans girls were haughty and coldhearted.

Rachel Jackson sniffed.

"Reckon I'm going to have to show you how you go about it," she said. She grasped his arm in a viselike grip and nearly dragged him across the room to stand in front of the girl.

"How do," she said to the startled girl. "I want to introduce myself to you. My name is Rachel Jackson, and I'm the wife of the general, over there."

"Oui, yes, madame," said the girl. "All New Orleans knows who you are. I am honored to meet you."

"And who might you be?"

"Oh, I apologize, madame. I am Adrienne Dumont. I am the daughter of Pierre and Margarethe Dumont, merchants of Rue Royale."

"Well, Miss Dumont, I'd like you to meet my young friend, Josiah, here. Josiah is a hero. "

"I have heard of him," said the girl. "How many British soldiers he killed. He is famous."

"Well, he's also real modest and real shy," Mrs. Jackson said, as Josiah squirmed in embarrassment. "He's been achin' to ask you to dance, but he ain't got the nerve. So would you dance with him?"

The girl blushed. "Certainement. Of course," she said. "I would be much pleased." She smiled at Josiah and extended her delicate hand to him.

"Well, don't just stand there, boy," said Rachel Jackson. "Take her hand. It ain't polite to leave a lady waiting."

As Rachel Jackson had predicted, the country

dances came back to him as if they had been burned into his memory. It was good that they did, for Josiah walked through the steps as if in a daze. The dance patterns took him away from the girl who called herself Adrienne (Ah-dray-ahn, she pronounced it, with an emphasis on the final syllable), and he would return momentarily to his senses, only to melt again like warm butter when the dance brought her back to him.

He lost count of the number of dances they did together, though he was vaguely aware that others in the ballroom were glancing furtively in his direction, then turning away to speak quietly to their companions.

And then, according to some signal that Josiah did not understand, the cotillion foursomes suddenly dissolved, and everyone moved to the fringes of the dance floor. The orchestra struck into music of quite a different sort, and the dancers returned to the floor in couples, holding each other in attitudes of great familiarity. The girl took his hand again and smiled expectantly.

"Ma'amselle, I'm afraid I do not know this dance," he said.

"It is merely the valse," she said. "I teach you."

During his remaining days in New Orleans, they had been together almost constantly. They could not get enough of each other. Whatever trepidation her parents must have felt—and it must have been considerable, for she was Catholic and French, and he was Congregationalist and American—it could not withstand the force of their attraction for each other. Her father, a prominent wine merchant whose shop was situated conspicuously on the Rue Royale, seemed to accept and even take pleasure from the company of the spindly teenager who had so won the favor of the great General Jackson. Adrienne's mother, while less enthused, eventually acquiesced to her daughter's clear affection and accepted him into her house, if not her heart.

Perhaps her mother and father had hoped that the infatuation would dim when Josiah left New Orleans, but Josiah was determined to prevent that from happening. When he finally left the city to accompany Mrs. Jackson back to the Hermitage, he exacted a promise from Adrienne that she would write to him regularly, a promise she agreed to eagerly, but did not, at the outset, keep.

Although he made a point of writing to her daily, more than a month went by before he received a reply. It came soiled and almost unreadable, due not entirely to the hardships of the road. Reading it— with considerable difficulty—Josiah became aware that writing was a painful process for his beloved. She formed her characters crudely, with almost as many words crossed out as not. Her grammar was a strange jumble of English and French, and she had a tendency to let her sentences dissolve into hazy nothingness, as if they had finally grown tired of the effort to make sense for her, That she had attempted to write to him at all was astonishing, and he considered it a testament to her love for him that she had done so.

And so he wrote more, and longer letters, which continued until he could stand the separation no longer. Borrowing a horse from the general's stable, he rode back to New Orleans with his heart in his throat. A year had passed since he had seen her. Would his absence have dimmed his image in her mind?

It had not. She threw herself into his arms the moment he had appeared at the door of her father's emporium, which, like most Creole establishments, occupied the ground floor below the family apartments.

Their reunion was fervent. For more than a month he remained in the city, living as a guest in her household, seeing her every day, taking long walks through the town and along the river, sharing secrets and endearments that they would have been embarrassed to disclose in the presence of others. He told her of his intention to read for the law with one of the prominent practitioners in New England. She told him of the balls and masques, of the operas and recitals, and of the everyday life of the city. He listened and absorbed it all, elated merely to be in her presence.

And in the end he asked her to wait for him. It would be hard, he told her, because reading for the law was a long and arduous course, but it would be worth the effort. He would emerge as a professional man, respected in whatever community he chose and able to provide a home for her that would satisfy her every wish. She smiled, with tears in her eyes, and promised him eagerly that she would be waiting when he returned. Neither had realized that some needs would necessarily go ungratified, and that small disappointments would loom ever larger in their lives. It had not been until later, after they were wed, that familiarity had begun to breed contempt.

"Mr. Beede, how delightful to see you here," said a musical voice that interrupted his reverie. "You have not attended one of our social gatherings before, I believe."

"I think you are as surprised to see me as I am to see you," Mercy Gray added, as if she could read his mind.

"I had not wished to thrust myself into company too soon," he said, finally. "I am a newcomer in your midst after all."

"Two years, Mr. Beede?" She was laughing merrily at him. "I hardly think you are too presumptuous, sir. I believe we have made it clear that you are considered an important member of our community."

"Oh, yes, of course. Nevertheless . . ."

"Would you consider me too forward if I were to request a dance with you?" she said, extending her hand to him.

"I would be delighted," he said, as flattered that she noticed him as when Adrienne had noticed him in that earlier life. He was not inclined to seek a wife, he told himself, but he had to admit that Mercy Gray was an uncommonly attractive young lady.

He let her lead him onto the dance floor—surely it was supposed to be the other way around—and they stood waiting for the music to begin. There was a small orchestra, recruited from where he could not imagine, with a fiddle, a pianoforte, and a clarinet. The tunes were familiar, however, as they were when he had heard them as a boy and again in New Orleans.

"You dance marvelously, sir," she said, gushing. He knew it to be a lie, but he accepted the flattery with embarrassed pleasure, nonetheless. And, indeed, he did seem to step on fewer toes than usual. She made it easy, as Adrienne had made it easy, and Beede felt his step—as well as his heart—grow lighter.

On several occasions he glanced across the room at Deborah Tomkins, who seemed to be enjoying her-

self thoroughly dancing with different young men. At
one point he happened to catch her eye. She smiled
briefly in his direction before she was whirled away
once more. He considered whether to ask her to
dance, but he concluded that it would be unfair to en-
croach upon her in that way. Mercy Gray, at least,
had come to him.

They danced long into the night and were among
the last to leave. Beede returned home with much on
his mind. Was it simply the power of her father's suggestion that had altered his view toward Mercy Gray,
or was he prey to deeper feelings that he had not even
been aware of until now? At the age of thirty-five, he
had thought himself to be beyond the reach of physical passion, but an evening in the company of an attractive young woman had shown him that he was
wrong. The realization was both bracing and curiously
frightening, and he lay awake for hours poring over its
implications.

The day of Thanksgiving dawned bright and cold.
A thin mist hung over the barnyard at sunrise, and
frost nipped the few brown stalks remaining in the
now-depleted kitchen garden. Beede was up early,
feeling at loose ends with no legal work pressing and
the heavy work of the farm largely completed. He contented himself with restacking rocks that had fallen
from a stone wall on his back acreage until it was
nearly time to go to meeting. He ate a sparse breakfast
and then elected to walk into the village rather than
saddle his horse.

During his years of exile in the southern states,
Beede had often dreamed of Thanksgiving. In the
sober and somber environment of New England,

Thanksgiving stood out as the bright spot of the year.
It was one of the few festive occasions on the Yankee
calendar, neither Christmas nor Easter being much observed, and nearly every man's childhood memories
revolved around the day.

Those memories had often sustained him through
the low points of his life. The reality, alas, was now far
gloomier than he recalled. Thanksgiving was a day for
families, and Beede was no longer a man with a family. There was an older brother, still tending the family
farm in Connecticut, but he and Thomas had never
been close because of the difference in their ages. His
two older sisters had long since married and moved
west with their families. And Seth, the brother to
whom he had always been closest, had died in
Louisiana twenty years before.

As he walked home from the meetinghouse after
worship, Beede thought glumly of the dinner to follow. His mother had been no great shakes as a cook,
and his sisters had inherited her indifference to the art.
Nevertheless, they were infinitely superior to Mrs.
Shelton, who feared flavorful food almost as much as
she feared an eternity in hell.

He could picture the meal that lay ahead, and he
shuddered at the thought. There would be no turkey
this year, for one skill Randolph had not yet mastered
was marksmanship, even if he had been physically
able to go hunting with his splinted leg. A turkey could
be purchased, but Mrs. Shelton would not hear of it.
Instead, there would be one of those dull little hens
that Mrs. Shelton insisted on keeping, and it would be
roasted until it was dry and tough. There would be
only one chicken, for she would not risk a significant
depletion in egg production for the sake of a single
meal, however festive.

The meal was as he had expected. In addition to the
hen, there were potatoes, and the last of the greens
from the kitchen garden—long past their prime and
boiled to mush in the New England tradition—and the
obligatory pies. Mrs. Shelton loved pies of all sorts
and lavished on them the loving care she applied so
meagerly to the rest of the meal. The meal was eaten
in the spirit with which it was prepared—silently and
joylessly.

When the meal was ended, Beede and Randolph sat
by the fire discussing farm chores. Even in the slow
season, which winter definitely was, there were fences
to be mended, equipment to be repaired, and livestock
to feed. Fortunately, the peddler had shown himself to
be a useful hand. He had helped to ease the workload
considerably before he had run away.

Randolph suddenly went quiet, however, and Beede
realized that Mrs. Shelton was hovering near him with
an anxious look.

"I wonder if I might have a word with you, Mr.
Beede," she said, indicating the kitchen with a nod of
her head.

"Certainly, Mrs. Shelton."

"I was hesitant to speak in Mr. Randolph's presence," she said when he had followed her out of
the room. "I know you set great store by him, but
I'm bound to show you something I found this morning."

She opened her hand to display a small bead like
the ones the two men had found on the day the murdered girl had been discovered by the roadside.

"Where did you find this?" he asked.

"In the chicken."

"I beg your pardon. *In* the chicken, you say?"

"The chicken I served for our Thanksgiving feast,"

she said. There was an unaccustomed glitter in her eyes.

"In the chicken? *In* it?"

"In the gizzard," she said. "Chickens often swallow small stones to help them digest their food. The hen I prepared today must have swallowed this."

Beede stared dumbly at the round, white object with the neatly drilled hole.

"Do you not recognize it, sir?" Mrs. Shelton said. "Does it not look exactly like those two small beads that you found by the side of the road?"

"Yes, indeed. But Mr. Randolph found them, not I."

"I know that, sir," she said. "That's why I felt duty-bound to show this one to you."

"I'm not sure I follow your meaning, Mrs. Shelton," Beede said, although he feared he followed her all too well.

"It's a prayer bead, ain't it? Just like the other ones. They belonged to the dead girl, and Mr. Randolph found them. And now this one turns up in one of my chickens."

"Are you saying that Mr. Randolph is responsible for its appearance?"

"Stands to reason, don't it? There's been nobody here but you and me—and Mr. Randolph. Well, that young peddler was around for a week or more, but he didn't turn up until after the dead girl had been found. And you were off at the court for two weeks before that."

"I'm afraid I still don't understand," Beede said, shaking his head. "What does that have to do with the bead?"

She leaned forward and fixed her eyes on his face. "Suppose it was Mr. Randolph that murdered the poor girl?" she said in a conspiratorial whisper. "It's been nobody but him and me here for two weeks, at the very time that the girl died. Don't he seem like a likely suspect?"

"I'm sure you're wrong, Mrs. Shelton," he said. "I've known the man for years, and I'd swear there isn't a violent bone in his body. It isn't in his nature."

"The girl was found on your land, Mr. Beede. Mr. Randolph and I were the only people here. I spend my days and nights here in the house, or in the kitchen garden, but Mr. Randolph's duties take him over the farm. Maybe he killed the girl right nearby and broke them beads off the string while he was doin' it. It could of happened right here in the barnyard. He had the opportunity to do the deed without anyone knowing it."

"I suppose that's true," Beede said. "But why would he do so?"

"I'd have thought that was obvious, sir," she said. "He's a black man, ain't he? And a former slave? And the girl was as white as they come, and very pretty, besides. If he was to come upon her when she was alone, and helpless, the anger and the lust might just take over his better nature."

"You do not like Randolph very much," Beede said suspiciously.

"I never have said a word against him," she replied. "I *will* say I'm uncomfortable around him. He's only a step or two out of the jungle, no matter how many airs he puts on. Civilization ain't natural to him, Mr. Beede, the way it is with you and me, Sooner or later he's going to snap, and I fear it may have happened already."

There was, Beede admitted reluctantly, a certain odd logic to Mrs. Shelton's allegation. Randolph certainly would have had the opportunity to commit the crime, a greater opportunity than anyone else who came to mind. And as for finding the beads, he might well have done so in order to divert suspicion from himself. Though it seemed alien to Randolph's nature, Beede knew that crimes of passion were not merely the province of outwardly violent men. Even those of phlegmatic disposition had been known to strike out when they were denied something they desired above all else.

Now that the accusation had been made, he felt an obligation to pursue it, however distasteful it might be. "I will look into the matter," he said, after a moment.

But not today, on the day of the feast. Tomorrow would be soon enough, and in the meantime, he would consult with Huff and Tomkins.

"I agree that the matter must be investigated," Huff said when they met the following morning. "Knowing how you feel about the man, however, I could understand if you don't want to do it yourself."

"I don't want to do it," Beede said. "But I believe I'm obliged to do it. Perhaps someone else should make the trip to Manchester in search of Albert Sanborn."

"No," said Huff. "You've been there and talked to the people. You'd know better where to look for him. If he's on his way to Manchester as it appears—and God knows why he'd go back there—he's undoubtedly looking up his old mates. Finding him will be easier for you than for us."

"Your darkie can't run away, with his bum leg," Tomkins said. "What I'll do is move him here to my house, where he'll be easier to keep an eye on. That way you can conduct your search without worrying. In fact, I'll send over a couple of hired men first thing in the morning."

Beede broached the subject to Randolph as gingerly as possible.

"I've been asked to return to Manchester to seek out the peddler," he said that evening. "He's been spotted in that vicinity. Squire Tomkins has graciously agreed to move you to his house where you can be cared for more effectively. He's sending over some hired men in the morning."

"It isn't necessary," Randolph said, smiling. "Mrs. Shelton may be reluctant, but she's been caring for me quite well these past few days. And I hardly need much caring for with this crutch that Jacob Wolf made for me."

"We worry, though," Beede said. "Mrs. Shelton is none too happy about the arrangements, as they stand."

"She will complain, but she will come through," Randolph said. "I'm content here; I do not need to move."

"Nevertheless," Beede said, "I think it would be best. They can take much better care of you at the Tomkins house. I believe I must insist."

"I think this is not about helping me recover from my injury," Randolph said. "Am I now a suspect in the murder of Sharon Cudahy? Has it come to this?"

Beede hesitated, and Randolph drew an inference from his hesitation.

"Surely, Mr. Beede, you don't think I would have had something to do with murder," he said. "I thought you knew me better than that."

"Mrs. Shelton believes you were involved," Beede said, his cheeks burning in shame. "For your sake, I believe it's best if you were somewhere else."

"Yes, for my sake," Randolph said bitterly. "And

also because it would be easier to keep track of me in the Tomkins house."

"I don't believe you are guilty of this," Beede said. "But we cannot take chances. And if Mrs. Shelton suspects you of the crime, you're none too safe in this house in my absence."

"I see," Randolph said, after a moment. "Well, certainly for my sake, I should be moved."

"When I return, we can move you back here."

"Of course," Randolph said. "When you return." He favored Beede with a smile that said he knew Beede was lying. Beede left the room, feeling dirty.

Chapter 22

Beede rode hard and fast the following morning, propelled by a sense of urgency he had not previously felt. There were answers to be had, he thought, and the peddler held many, if not all, of them.

Was the peddler also the murderer? An accomplice? A witness? In any event, it seemed clear that he knew more than he had told. It brought back memories of the days immediately preceding the battle in New Orleans, when he and Seth tried in vain to anticipate their future.

"They ain't really soldiers," Seth said. "Mostly Kaintucks and coloreds against thousands of British regulars, and they outnumber us two to one—maybe more. It's gonna be a short fight, and we'll have to make our money quick and get out of here."

"We beat British regulars at Yorktown," Beede said.

Seth cocked an eye at him. "When did you get to be such a military expert?" he said. "We don't have the French to pull our asses out of the fire this time. The Frogs plumb gave up on this part of the world."

"There's a chance our boys can win this thing," Beede said stubbornly.

"Not a chance in hell," Seth said. "Our only hope is to be out of here before the redcoats march into the city. Course, once they're here, they'll all die of the French pox, but that won't do us no good."

Beede ate a midday meal in the saddle. He walked, to give the horse a respite from his weight. He rode some more, sometimes in his eagerness pushing the horse more than had been his intention. There were answers to be had, and the answers, he felt sure, were near at hand.

He began his search at the mill. Kerrigan was not at home, so he went in search of the overseer.

"A peddler?" Coolidge said doubtfully. "We have our share, of course, but I don't remember them by name or by sight. I don't buy from them, as a rule. I suppose you depend on them for necessities, up in the hinterlands, but down here we have established merchants with shops and stores."

"Blond fellow. Rather tall. Rather thin. He probably isn't peddling because we have his goods locked up in Warrensboro."

"Is this peddler the man Mrs. Webb mentioned when you questioned her?" Coolidge asked. He turned away from Beede as he spoke and busied himself with some papers on his desk.

"I believe so. He found the girl's body, and we had

been holding him until our investigations were complete."

"Don't know why you bothered us down here. You had your man all along. I wasted a lot of time going with you to old Mrs. Webb's place, seems to me."

"The peddler may indeed be our man," Beede said patiently. "In fact, it is beginning to appear more likely. But we want to be certain, and we must question him again in order to do so."

"I ain't seen him. Didn't even know he existed until Mrs. Webb mentioned him. I'm still not sure that he does; Mrs. Webb gets confused about things, like my being a suitor for her girl."

"I see," said Beede. "Well, I suppose I must talk to her again. Perhaps she has seen him since he left our custody."

Coolidge pointed to the window. "You'll want to wait until tomorrow," he said. "It's getting a mite dark out there. The sun goes down early these days."

"I suspect I can borrow a lantern from the tavern where I'm staying. I want this matter settled as soon as possible," Beede said. And he took his leave of Coolidge.

By the time he set out across the bridge with his borrowed lantern, the last daylight had vanished. Beede feared that he would not remember the way to old Mrs. Webb's farmhouse, and so he chose to walk rather than ride on the assumption that landmarks would be more familiar to him on foot. Leaving his horse at the inn, he set out across the river. Below him in the darkness, the angry water rushed by, the frothing rapids reflecting what little ambient light remained.

The house was not difficult to find. He knocked on

the door and heard shuffling footsteps approach, followed by a hesitant voice.

"Who is it?"

"It is I, Mrs. Webb. Josiah Beede from Warrensboro. I came to see you last week to inquire about Sharon Cudahy."

A pause.

"Is *he* with you?"

"You mean Mr. Coolidge? No, I've come alone."

He heard the string latch being lifted—he could have entered without an invitation if he had been so inclined—and the wizened head appeared before him. She glanced around, apparently to ensure for herself that he spoke the truth about Coolidge, and then opened the door for him to enter.

Once again, they went into the parlor. He chose the straight-back Hitchcock chair, leaving the rocker for her, and she sat with a heavy sigh.

"What is it that you want this time, sir? I doubt I can help you, but I'll certainly try."

"I'm looking for a man who I believe has come this way," he said carefully. "I believe that he may have been the peddler who used to visit Miss Cudahy when she was your tenant."

"Is he a suspect in your investigation?"

"No more so than anyone else," he replied. "Although he disappeared from our midst in unusual circumstances. But there are questions I must ask of him, which may go far toward resolving this puzzle."

"I cannot believe Mr. Sanborn capable of the crime you described to me," she said. "He was always the gentleman."

"Then you have seen him?"

"Oh, no," she said hastily. "Not for many weeks. I mean only that he was kind and courteous to Sharon at a time when others were not."

"Do you know where I might look for him? It's very important that I find him."

There was a creak of floorboards in the next room. Mrs. Webb heard it as well as he, for she hurried her response as if to distract his attention from it.

"I don't know where he might be. Would you care to leave a message in the event I might see him?"

He paused, as if considering the question, but there was no more creaking. Whoever was hiding in the house—and he felt certain he knew who it was—had been frightened enough to keep perfectly still.

"Why, yes," he said. "If Mr. Sanborn were to pass this way, you could tell him that I am not interested, at this juncture, in capturing him. I'm not at all convinced of his guilt and in fact am rather doubtful. Nevertheless, there are some questions to which I feel sure he has the answers, and I would appreciate the opportunity to speak with him."

"Does he have your assurance that he will not be harmed?"

"He does."

"Or arrested?"

"If I am satisfied with his answers, as I feel confident I will be, I will not arrest him nor will I send others to do so."

"I don't believe that would be sufficient assurance for him."

"Nonetheless, it is the best I can give," Beede said. "But tell him for me that his information may lead to the capture of the true murderer."

She nodded. "I can make no promises," she said. "But if I see him, I will certainly pass along your message."

Beede felt certain it had been passed along already. He stood to go.

"There is one more message you might pass along to him," he said. "Tell him that Randolph bears no grudge against him for the accident that disabled him. He is in no danger and should soon be able to walk and contribute to the farm again."

Chapter 23

Would he follow?

Beede dared not look behind him as he left the house and walked back toward the bridge and to the tavern across the river where he planned to spend the night. He believed he had planted a seed of... what?... doubt... or at least curiosity in the peddler's mind. But there would be no way to know for certain until, or unless, he made contact.

At the bridge he took advantage of the shadows of the structure to glance over his shoulder and thought he caught a glimpse of something, or someone, who melted into the shadows almost immediately. It was a fleeting sensation at best, but it gave Beede heart to continue.

The stubby candle in his borrowed lantern flickered in the autumn wind, even with the lantern door shut. He doubted that the light would last long enough to get him across the bridge, but he began the crossing, all the same.

Sure enough, the flickering light flared in a gust of wind and then went out. Beede halted his progress to give his eyes a chance to adjust to the darkness. There was no moon and few clouds; the darkness was nearly absolute.

Was that hulking shape ahead of him moving in his direction? Hard to tell in the pitch black, but he thought perhaps that it was.

In a moment, his suspicions were confirmed. The hulk materialized in the body of a man, a large man armed with a sort of stave. The man was moving fast now, and he was moving in Beede's direction.

He caught an impression of the stave being swung, and he put up his lantern hand to ward off the blow. The stave struck his forearm and caused a sharp pain to radiate upward toward his shoulder. Then he saw the weapon was slicing downward again, with an aim that would take him in the head.

Instinctively, he dodged and threw his hands over his head, the now-dark lantern clattering to the bridge surface. The blow missed his head but fell with great force on his shoulder and back. He groaned in agony and almost collapsed, holding himself up by sheer force of will. He knew if he went down, it would be all over. He forced his body into motion—it took considerable effort—and dodged a few feet away from his assailant, who immediately closed the gap between them and raised the stave again.

Beede moved inside the man's swing, lowered his head, and charged the big man like a maddened bull. He hit the man in the abdomen and heard the rush of air from his lungs. The man staggered backward, clearly stunned, but he did not fall. Beede quickly scooped up the tin lantern from where he had dropped it and swung it in a wide arc that caught his assailant behind the ear. The lantern was still hot from the newly extinguished candle, and Beede heard the satisfying sizzle of singed hair and his opponent's cry of pain.

But he had gained only a momentary advantage. The big man recovered quickly and came charging back, dropping the stave in order to grapple at close quarters.

This was what Beede had feared most. Beede was a tall man, but his assailant was bigger and undoubtedly stronger. In close, Beede knew his options would be limited, and brute strength would most likely win out. He moved to avoid the charge, but the other man was quick as well as strong, and his countermove backed Beede to the bridge railing.

Instantly, the man had his massive hands around Beede's throat and was bending him back over the railing. Beede tried to gain leverage to break the man's hold, but the grip was too strong. He felt himself slipping away. It would, he knew, soon be over. He wondered whether he would be strangled to death or simply tossed off the bridge into the raging water below.

But then another shape appeared suddenly out of the darkness, wielding the stave that his opponent had dropped. Beede's attacker howled as the blows began to rain down on him, and he loosened his grip on Beede. Beede broke away from his attacker and struggled to his feet.

His rescuer was holding his own against the bigger man, but it could not last. As Beede watched the struggle, his assailant snatched the stave away and began beating in retaliation. The smaller man countered by tackling his opponent around the waist and driving him back against the railing.

The big man, unfazed, lifted the smaller man above his head as if he were a sack of meal. He roared in anger and turned to toss his adversary into the torrent below.

It was time to act. Gathering his strength, Beede rushed his assailant and grappled with him. The man fought back, but he was hampered by his human burden. Beede beat at his assailant's arms in an effort to break his hold on the smaller man.

The wooden railing cracked and broke beneath their weight. All three men plummeted into the water below.

Chapter 24

"Get down, damn it! You'll get yourself killed!"

Josiah heard his brother's shout and wanted to obey, but he was unable to move. He stood on the makeshift rampart, watching in mortal terror as rank after rank of red-jacketed British regulars marched inexorably toward the little band of Americans behind the hastily assembled breastwork of cotton bales. So many. So disciplined and determined. He stood frozen to the spot as the troops marched ever onward.

"Damn it, Josiah!" Seth's arm shot up from where he huddled in safety, snatched the tail of his brother's coat, and tugged. Josiah was aware of it, but he felt powerless in the face of the coming onslaught.

Where did they come from? Where were the ships capable of carrying so many men and arms—the pride of the king's army—across an ocean to this godforsaken swampland? And artillery, too.

"Josiah, I'll drag you down if I have to! You're going to get us both killed!"

He sensed that Seth was now standing alongside. The thought of his brother endangering his own safety out of concern for his broke the spell. He could hear the bullets now, whizzing overhead. The British hadn't got the range yet; they were still firing high. He turned to point that out to Seth and realized suddenly that Seth would not understand.

His brother stood staring vacantly at the blood pumping from his chest. Josiah hadn't heard the shot that had opened his brother's chest.

"Oh, my God. Seth!"

Seth's hand grabbed spasmodically at Josiah's sleeve, then began slipping down and away. Josiah knelt quickly and helped to lower him to the ground, realizing with a sickening feeling that it had been his own cowardice that had done this.

"Seth, oh my God. Hang on!"

He knew it was useless as soon as he said it. He felt himself falling away, as if a pit had opened and was swallowing him whole. He was falling, falling ...

The impact with the water took his breath away.

The force of his fall drove him downward, and his feet touched the riverbed almost immediately. He pushed off from the bottom, but the weight of his heavy clothing hampered his ascent. He paddled frantically, but the rise to the surface went slowly.

He broke the surface with a gasp and sucked in as much air as he could before he began to sink again. He snatched at a nearby rock, but it broke loose in his hand.

Then the current caught him. He felt himself being dragged inescapably toward the falls. He fought frantically, but the current was too strong. In a second, he was pulled to the lip of the falls, and then over it. Once more, he hit bottom, this time much harder than before, but then the current spat him out and slammed him into a tree.

A tree in midstream. It struck him as curious. But before he could even process what that meant, the current plucked him away again and threw him against another tree.

He clutched it in desperation. Then, with first one hand and then the other, he rid himself of his heavy cloak. It would do little to keep him warm now that it was thoroughly soaked, and its weight was dragging him to places he did not desire to go.

A dark shape swept downstream toward him. He reached out with his free hand. He recognized the face of the peddler. Sanborn was breathing, snoring, in fact, but unconscious. He must have been the third man in the struggle on the bridge.

And the other? Beede had not seen his face, but he thought, from the man's bulk and strength, that it had surely been Noah Coolidge, the factory overseer.

A larger shape—Coolidge's?—now came sweeping down the river. Beede started to go after it, but it was too far away. To rescue Coolidge would mean abandoning Sanborn and probably giving up his own chances for survival, as well.

And survival was now the main order of business. He knew he was growing dangerously cold, and he thought the same was probably true of Sanborn. If he could somehow drag the peddler's body and his own to shore, they might yet live.

The tree he was clutching was one of a small cluster of trees growing in midstream. Not elder statesmen but no longer saplings, they had been there long enough and become established enough to withstand the river current. If he could work his way from tree to tree, he might reach a point near the riverbank where the current was less violent.

Dragging Sanborn's limp body behind him, he grasped the next tree in line and pulled himself to it. Then the next and the next. He eventually reached a point where the current's roar was less noisy and where the water seemed to be rushing more slowly. They were still some distance from shore, but he thought perhaps he could cover the distance safely from this point.

He had not reckoned on how weak he had become. The cold had sapped his strength and slowed his thinking. On his second stroke away from the thicket, the river seized him again, nearly snatching the peddler from his grasp. He fought as hard as he could, but the river carried him several yards farther downstream before depositing him and his human burden in a small cove where the water swirled and eddied around him but did not seem eager to rejoin the main current.

The riverbank was steep at this point, and the water was too deep for him to stand. In order to hoist the peddler onto shore it was necessary for him to sink to the river bottom and push upward from beneath. It was a time-consuming and energy-sapping task, but he succeeded after several attempts and began the equally arduous task of pulling himself out.

That done, he collapsed on the riverbank, mindless of the cold but aware that he and his young charge must soon find warmth and sleep if they were to live through the night. At present, however, he could do no more and, against his will, he closed his eyes and slept.

Chapter 25

Ghostly hands lifted him from his resting place, and ghostly voices conversed all around him. He knew that he had died and wondered if the helpful hands belonged to angels or demons. He could not bring himself to open his eyes.

He thought perhaps that they were demons. In heaven, there would be no pain, there would be no need to feel. But his head throbbed, and his arms and legs ached. In hell, pain would be the sole purpose. Well, it was no more than he deserved.

His mind replayed once again, as it had so often before, the events that had sealed his fate for eternity: the panicked flight from the parapet, leaving his brother to bleed to death in his absence; the shame and remorse that overcame him; the stumbling return to his appointed place, only to find that Seth had left him for the last time; the blind rage that caused him to pick up the rifle of the blond Kentuckian to his left, now lying

lifeless beside him, to strip the man's cartridge bag, to
load the gun hastily, to fire at the approaching enemy,
to reload and fire again, to reload and fire again, to reload and fire again, hardly bothering to aim and not
daring to look at the carnage he was wreaking.

*"Son, there's no need to keep firing. They skedad-
dled."*

*The tall, thin man who stood beside him laid a hand
on his shoulder. "You are a fighting demon, boy. I admire that. I was almost afraid to stop you for fear
you'd shoot me, too."*

"I killed my brother," Josiah said.

*"This your brother, lying here? Well, I don't think
you killed him—not unless you've been on the other
side of the battle line, firing back here at him. If you'd
shot him, he'd have powder burns around that wound.
He was shot from a distance. By one of them."*

*"General, they're surely on the run," said a voice
behind them. "Want to chase 'em?"*

*"Send out a party just to see that they don't double
back," the man beside him said. "I don't reckon they
will; they were pretty much broken there. But keep an
eye out for some of that artillery they brought with
'em. I'll bet some of it's still bogged down in the
swamp. We could put it to good use."*

Then back to Josiah.

"What's your name, boy? How old are you?"

"Fifteen. Josiah Beede, sir."

*"New Englander, huh? Nobody but a certified New
England Yankee would saddle a youngun with a name
like that. Where's your ma and pa, your family?"*

"Don't have any family, General." Not strictly true,
he knew, but as near to truth as made no difference.
His brother, who was now head of the household,
wouldn't take him back after what had happened here.

"No family. Well, son, you could use some family, I'd say, and it looks like I'm elected. I'll send you back to my Rachel, back in Tennessee. She'll be all the family you're likely to need."

He was growing warmer. So it was hell he was bound for. Strangely, the warmth was not painful, so far. He knew that the flames were coming, however, and he steeled himself for the agonies that would follow. He opened his eyes.

He was in a bed, softer and more comfortable than his own bed at home. A fire roared in a fireplace across the room. This was a strange hell, indeed.

"Good morning," said Kerrigan. "Glad to see that you're still with us."

"I'm alive?" he said wonderingly.

"Yes, indeed, sir, though it was touch and go there for a day or two. We found you lying by the riverbank when one of my mill girls was out for her morning constitutional. You must have been there all night. My Maddie is not only a cooking maid but a miracle worker, as well. She's been feeding you hot broth on a three-hour schedule since we found you last Saturday. On my instructions, of course."

"What day is this?" Beede asked.

Kerrigan made a show of stopping to think about that, counting the days on his fingers.

"Well, let's see. This is Wednesday. We found you in the wee hours of Saturday. So it must have been the third of December. You missed Sabbath meeting this week, I fear."

Nearly a week, then. And yet, he lived.

"There was another man. . . ."

"Yes, the peddler," Kerrigan said. "Some of my servants recognized him; apparently they had purchased some small items from him at one time or another. I hadn't the room nor sufficient servants to take care of you both, so I called upon a neighbor to put him up. His wife is nursing him back to health, much as we are doing for you."

"He must not be allowed to leave before seeing me," Beede said. "I believe he has answers that will assist me in my investigation."

"Ah, yes, the murder investigation. Is that why you're in town again, so soon after your previous visit? I had wondered."

"It is important that I speak to him as soon as he is able to see me," Beede said. He struggled to sit up.

"And as soon as you're able to see him, I might add. Which is not the case at this moment."

Kerrigan moved to the bedside and gently but firmly forced Beede back into a prone position.

"Sleep some more, Mr. Beede," he said, not unkindly. "I've not brought you this far only to have you die in my house."

Beede sank back into the pillows, lacking the strength to protest and soon fell asleep. When he awakened, he was alone. The fire had been banked, and the curtains had been drawn. With some effort, he swung his feet out of the bed onto a woolen rug and stood. For a moment, he was uncertain whether his legs would support him after so many days in bed. Indeed, it appeared at first that they would not, but by holding to various strategic parts of the bed frame, he was able to work his way around it and to the window.

Night. The moon was nearly full, and he could see the pale glow it cast upon the frothing water of the river. One corner of the mill was visible, and Beede stared at it as if hoping that it would reveal Sharon Cudahy's secret. He returned to bed after a while, feeling no wiser than before.

Kerrigan returned in the morning.

"Good. You're up and about. A sign that you're on the mend. It was fortunate that the night was not colder; you might have suffered frostbite in addition to suffering from the cold."

"I am grateful to you, sir. I believe you saved my life."

"I daresay I did, at that. Gratitude is unnecessary, however; I did it for selfish reasons. We Democrats must stick together if we are to continue to hold New Hampshire for the party."

Beede detested the man, but he could not confess to it. Kerrigan had indeed acted unselfishly and generously, and with no apparent objective of personal gain. That the same man who worked young New England farm girls to the bone would open the hospitality of his house to a man he had met only twice seemed wholly out of character, and yet he had done precisely that.

"I am grateful, in any event," Beede said. "But I fear I must take my leave, collect the peddler, and return with him to Warrensboro. My business there must be attended to."

Kerrigan shrugged. "As you wish," he said. "If you feel strong enough to make the journey, I've no desire to put obstacles in your way. I'll take you to the peddler tomorrow morning."

Chapter 26

"It appears that you and your peddler fell from the bridge above the mill," Kerrigan said, as they walked. "We found the railing broken at one spot. Is that about the size of it?"

"Yes. We were fighting."

"You were fighting, and in your struggle you fell from the bridge and almost died from exposure," said Kerrigan. "And now you're concerned about his welfare. I must say, Mr. Beede, that you are either an extraordinary man, a true Christian, or else you are utterly devoid of backbone."

"No, no, that's not it at all. We were fighting a third man, not each other. In fact, the peddler probably saved my life by entering the fight on my behalf."

"I see," Kerrigan said. "And the other man?"

"Lost," said Beede. "That, at least, is what I believe. I saw him float past me, swept downstream, but I was not near enough to save him."

"Noah Coolidge," said Kerrigan.

"Yes," Beede admitted. "I believe so. It was dark, and I could not see his face."

"I'm certain of it," Kerrigan said. "We found his body a short way downstream. He was not the sort of man who would choose to take a swim in the Merrimack River at the end of November. The constable had already surmised that he had fallen through the broken bridge railing. When we found you and the peddler, it seemed clear that there was some sort of connection."

Kerrigan stopped at the door of a neat but unimposing house.

"Thomas Standish is a merchant with whom I trade frequently," Kerrigan said. "He was happy to take the young peddler into his care, particularly when I pointed out to him that I would be extremely grateful to him if he did so."

He mounted the one step to the door and made as if to knock. Instead, he turned again to Beede.

"Do you have any idea why Noah Coolidge would attack you? You hardly knew the man. Or did you know him better than I thought?"

"I made acquaintance only through you on my last visit," Beede said. "But perhaps I did know more about him. I visited with Sharon Cudahy's former landlady during that trip, and she intimated, in his presence, that Coolidge had paid considerable attention to Miss Cudahy. I was on my way back from a second visit with the landlady when I was set upon by Coolidge. He must have feared that I had learned something that would further damage his reputation."

"I see," said Kerrigan. "Well, you have robbed me of a competent overseer."

"I regret your loss."

The irony was lost on Kerrigan. "It saves me the trouble of dismissing him. Coolidge was a married

man with a small daughter. I couldn't have my employee carrying on with the girls who work under him,
especially if he were married. His actions would re-
flect on my reputation in the community. I had heard
stories about him before, and I was already planning to
send him packing."

"What will happen to his wife and daughter?"

"They're living in the house I provided for them,"
he said. "They'll have to move out, of course. After
that, it's not my concern."

"Rather hard on them, don't you think?"

He shrugged again. "When a man agrees to a contract, he must abide by its terms. Coolidge's employment agreement specified that he was to avoid
becoming involved with another employee. He failed
to do so. The onus is on him, not me."

He knocked on the door.

Sanborn seemed unsurprised to see him when
Beede was ushered into his room. The room, like
the house, was less imposing than Kerrigan's but more
comfortable. The peddler was sitting in a chair, reading a book, and he smiled when he saw Beede.

"This is the first opportunity I've had in many years
to sit and read," he said, as Beede sat opposite him. "I
must thank you for this unexpected leisure."

"Thank me?" Beede said. Of all the things he had
expected the peddler to say, this was not among them.

"If you had not come visiting at Mrs. Webb's that
evening, I would not have followed you across the
bridge, or fought with your assailant, or fallen into the
river, or have been rescued and brought here to be
nursed to health by this warm and generous family. It
is all your doing, in a roundabout way."

"I'm happy that you are pleased with the outcome,"

Beede said. "In recompense for my services, perhaps you'll see fit to answer a few questions."

"You did say, didn't you, that I'm no longer under suspicion? I believe I heard you say that at Mrs. Webb's house."

"You're under no suspicion from me," Beede said. "I can't vouch for the others involved in this investigation, but your answers may put their concerns to rest."

"In which case, my goods would be returned to me?"

"Yes. If the answers are helpful."

"Very well," he said. "Ask your questions."

A young woman appeared in the doorway.

"Oh, excuse me, Albert," she said with a blush. "I didn't realize you had a visitor. I came only to collect your dishes from dinner."

"You're not intruding, Sally," Sanborn said with a smile. "I'd like you to meet an acquaintance of mine. Miss Sally Standish, may I present Mr. Josiah Beede. Mr. Beede is none other than the famous boy hero of the Battle of New Orleans, who caught the eye of General Jackson during that conflict."

The girl's face lit up. "Oh, Mr. Beede. I've heard so much about you! I'm so happy to make your acquaintance. The stories of your heroism are—"

"Greatly exaggerated, I fear," Beede said. "But it's very kind of you to recognize me. The events of New Orleans must have taken place before your birth."

"Oh, not at all, sir. Although I must admit I was quite small. But even if I had not heard of you—and I have—Albert has talked about you at some length. He's been telling me of his attempts to assist you with your murder investigation."

"Yes, Albert was—my houseguest for a while. I'm

pleased to see that you're taking such good care of him."

"Oh, my family thinks quite highly of Albert," she said, coloring again. "And I'm so pleased to meet you."

"Albert and Sally?" he said when the girl had left the room.

It was Sanborn's turn to blush. "Our relationship—yours and mine—has paid off handsomely for me, tenuous though it may have been. And young girls are so impressionable."

"If she was born before the Battle of New Orleans, she has to be at least twenty-one," Beede said. "She's not a child anymore; indeed, she's older than you are, and she's clearly taken with you, Albert. Congratulations."

"And I with her," Sanborn said. "Well, ask me what you will. I'll be as forthcoming as I can."

He had accompanied Sharon Cudahy on her journey north, he said, because he did not want to leave her to the vagaries of fate. She had a notion that she could make it to Quebec, where other Catholics could be found. It was French and not Irish, but that was a lesser consideration in her mind. She would have gone anywhere to get away from these lecherous, hard-hearted Yankees who justified their own transgressions with pious moralisms while enthusiastically attacking the failings of others.

"She trusted me, I think, because she could talk to me," Sanborn said. "We would take long walks on Sunday afternoons and talk about many things. We talked as I walked her home from the mill each evening. We would talk as I stayed for supper at Mrs. Webb's house."

"When did you leave her?"

"It was early September. The weather was just beginning to change, and the leaves were turning. I didn't want to leave her because I knew the cold weather was coming. But I had to go south, and she was determined to go north. I kissed her when we parted; it was the only time."

"How did you come to meet her?"

"I'm a peddler, remember. I sold her something. A comb. A lead comb. Had to be lead."

"Why did it have to be lead?"

Sanborn shook his head in amusement. "Old wives' tale," he said. "I can't imagine where she heard it, or maybe it's common in Ireland, also. Young ladies with red hair buy lead combs in the belief that using them to comb their hair will turn their hair black—or at least dark."

"Why would she want to darken her hair?" Beede said. "Her hair made her stand out and attract young men."

"It's my belief that she hoped to be a little *less* attractive to men," Sanborn replied. "If the stories I've heard about her are true, she had enough difficulty keeping the men away, with no need to bring them in. They came to her whether she willed it or not."

"The blue dress that she was wearing when we found her was not the garb of a shrinking violet," Beede said. "I should have thought from her dress that she enjoyed the company and attention of men."

"So she did. At least I flatter myself that she enjoyed my company. But there was a darker side to all that masculine attention, also. I myself saw that when I was with her. Men would turn on the street and follow her with their eyes. Those who were more forward would actually approach her and attempt to make conversation with her, with or without an introduction.

She began allowing me to accompany her home to Mrs. Webb's house each evening, if only to discourage would-be suitors from accosting her. Even I could see that it might be a nuisance over time."

Something that had been worrying Beede suddenly fell into place, but he quelled his excitement for the moment.

"Did she not see you as a potential suitor?" Beede asked.

Sanborn sighed. "Alas, no. I would have been flattered if she had, but I am impoverished and unsettled, and of the wrong religion, besides. At one time I had allowed myself to hope, but it became clear to me that I would never measure up to her standards."

"And what were her standards?"

"Well, Catholic, above all else. Otherwise, I was young enough but not wealthy enough. And I think she had had enough of rural life. She wanted a city."

Beede came to a sudden decision.

"Mr. Sanborn, I would like for you to return with me to Warrensboro."

Sanborn started to object, but Beede raised his hand to forestall the objection.

"I mean you no harm," he said. "When we are done there, I will not prevent you from leaving. Indeed, if I am correct in my deductions, there will be no need to stop you, for you will have been vindicated."

The peddler thought for a long moment before responding.

"I want this matter cleared up," he said. "And I suppose I can trust you. But for my peace of mind, I'll tell Sally and her father where I'm going. It this is a trap of some sort, I want to have someone who can help spring me."

They talked together uninterrupted until long after darkness had fallen. A domestic servant entered to light the candles, but their feeble glow did little to disperse the gloom. At length, Thomas Standish, the father of pretty Sally, entered. Sanborn made the introductions, and Standish seemed genuinely honored to have Beede as a guest.

"I beg your pardon, Mr. Beede," said Standish. "There is a gentleman downstairs who wishes to speak to you."

"Very well. Who is it?" Beede asked, quite surprised that he should have a visitor there at the Standish house.

Standish shook his head. "I believe it will be better if you learned that from him."

The man who awaited him in the front parlor of the Standish home was a small, balding man dressed in garments that had been fashionable nearly a generation ago, which he wore in a careless fashion as if he gave little thought to appearance. The man stood as Beede entered the room and extended his hand.

"Mr. Beede, I presume? I'm so pleased to meet you. I am Elisha Townsend. I had called upon you at Mr. Kerrigan's house but was told you were visiting here. I hope I'm not intruding."

"Not at all, sir. How may I assist you?"

"I am the coroner here, and I would ask you some questions concerning the death of Noah Coolidge, if I may. Mr. Coolidge is . . . was the overseer at the—"

"I'm aware of who Mr. Coolidge was," Beede said. "What would you ask of me?"

Townsend peered at Beede over the top of his rimless spectacles. He was a man whose features clustered closely together in the center of his face, as if huddling there for warmth.

"I would be most grateful for anything you could tell me about the manner of his death," he said. "I understand you were there."

"In a manner of speaking, yes, but I'm afraid there isn't much I can tell. Mr. Coolidge attacked me on the bridge. In the act of defending myself against him, I fell against the bridge railing. We fell into the river below."

"Yes, that corresponds with what Mr. Kerrigan has already told me," Townsend said. "However, I was hoping that you could tell me more."

"About what?"

"Well, is there anything you can tell me about how he died?"

"I did not see him after we fell into the water," Beede said. "I saw a human form sweep past me on the river as I clung to a pole sapling in fear for my life. From its size, I concluded that it must have been Coolidge, but I was not close enough to tell."

"I see," Townsend said, thoughtfully. "And you did not see him after that?"

"I did not."

The little man pondered for a moment.

"And so you could not confirm even that he died in the river."

"That is correct, now that you put it that way," Beede said. "Am I now a suspect in his death?"

"Oh, no, sir," the little man said hastily. "Not, that is, unless you and Mr. Kerrigan have concocted this story between you, which I do not believe. Still, it is a puzzle."

"I thought he had drowned. I believe Mr. Kerrigan said as much."

"I also thought so, sir," said Townsend, nodding in agreement. "Indeed, we all believed it in the beginning. But as coroner, it falls to me to direct the autopsy."

"And the autopsy did not confirm that conclusion?"

"No, sir. There has been, as yet, no formal autopsy.

I was forced to revise my conclusion after merely a cursory examination. There were curious anomalies, sir. Curious anomalies."

"Of what sort?"

"If you would come with me, it will be easier for me to show you."

Chapter 27

"I did not see this until I had cleaned away the hair and the debris around his face," the coroner said. "But you can see that he did not drown, as I had thought. The bruising and bleeding here, around his temple—that all occurred before he died."

Beede looked where the little man pointed.

"If he had drowned, he would not have bled so profusely," Beede said. "Is that your point?"

"Precisely! When the heart stops, so does the blood. And if that were not sufficient, I found very little water in his lungs. No, this man was deliberately murdered."

Beede peered closer at the body, noting particularly the cuts and abrasions about the face.

"I see what looks like wood splinters embedded in the head. Could they have been acquired during his struggle? Or while he was battered by the river?"

"These injuries were inflicted before his death," Townsend said. "Possibly by the river. In any event, they were not serious enough to kill him, I don't believe. The murder was actually much more subtle."

"He was a big man," Beede said. "It would take a strong person to kill him."

"Not if he were unconscious," Townsend said. "And considering what he had been through, it is quite likely that he was. Keep in mind that we found him on the riverbank, not in the water. If he had pulled himself out of the water and fallen unconscious on the riverbank, he might not have been able to resist an attack. In that event, almost anyone could have had the strength to perform the task."

The coroner had taken Beede to a house, probably Townsend's own, where the body lay naked on a table. He had been covered with a sheet, which Townsend unceremoniously stripped away upon their arrival. Like most New England houses, with the conspicuous exception of Kerrigan's, Townsend's house was only marginally warmer than the outdoors. Even so, Coolidge's corpse was beginning to swell as the gases formed inside his body. The odor, unenhanced by aromatic herbs of the sort usually employed to render bodies less offensive to mourners, was almost more than Beede could bear. Townsend, by contrast, seemed to have no problem with the smell and stood chatting easily, as if it were a perfectly normal aroma, like that of brewing coffee.

"And here," Townsend said, "is one of the curious anomalies." He turned the corpse's head to the side and directed Beede's attention to the man's left nostril.

"I have cleaned it up a bit so that I could see more clearly what had occurred. But as you can see even now, he was stabbed. It is definitely a puncture wound, and it goes quite deep."

"Strange place to stab a man," Beede said, feeling a bit more nauseous than he had before.

"Not at all, sir!" Townsend exclaimed. "One rarely sees it, of course, because we are so very protective of our heads. We seem to know instinctively that it is a place of great frailty. But if one were unconscious and unable to resist, this would be a particularly vulnerable place. A single thrust might penetrate all the way to the brain."

"Instant death," Beede said.

"Quite so," said Townsend with what Beede considered a singularly inappropriate smile. "If one were seeking a way to kill a man and an opportunity such as this arose, it would be difficult to find its superior."

"So your assumption is that Coolidge pulled himself out of the river and then collapsed on the bank, perhaps from exhaustion."

"I believe so. It is likely that he fell facedown on the earth, but he was found lying on his back. Either he rolled over in his unconscious state or he was turned over by his murderer; it would not have been difficult."

"Would there not have been considerable bleeding from such a stab wound?" Beede asked. "I'd think that the presence of so much blood would have indicated murder immediately."

"Not so much blood as you might think," Townsend said. "Death would have come so quickly that there would have been little opportunity for bleeding. And what blood did appear drained to his throat. He was found lying on his back, you recall."

"What was the weapon, do you think?"

"I'm undecided," Townsend said. "Something sharp, of course, like a knife. But knives rarely are equipped with blades as thin as the one that caused this wound. An awl, perhaps. A sailmaker's needle. An ice pick."

"Surely no one would stroll the streets of the village in the early morning carrying such a weapon."

"One would hardly think so. And it is even more difficult to believe that this was a premeditated crime. Who could have expected to find Noah Coolidge's body thrown up on the bank like a beached whale in the hours before sunrise? Indeed, who would expect to find anyone's body here at that hour? And yet the evidence of murder seems to me irrefutable."

"Did Mr. Coolidge have enemies?"

"It's been my experience, Mr. Beede, that all men have enemies," Townsend said. "Noah Coolidge probably had more than most. He was brusque and ill-mannered, and he was not averse to throwing his not inconsiderable weight around to achieve his ends. I know he was not popular among many of the girls at the mill. I didn't care for the man, myself."

"Why was that?"

Townsend frowned. "I have been called to the mill on a number of occasions to deal with unfortunate accidents there. It has been my impression that Mr. Coolidge was not especially sympathetic to the concerns of the girls who worked around the victims of such accidents. He seemed to take such things personally, as if the poor girl had gotten herself killed deliberately in order to hold up production."

He pulled the sheet carefully over Coolidge's body once more and went to wash his hands in the nearby basin.

"Did Coolidge ever abuse the girls in his charge?" Beede asked.

"I've no knowledge of it," Townsend said. "But then, I *wouldn't* have knowledge of it. I'm not a physician. I'm simply the coroner; Mr. Kerrigan has a physician of his own who is called in to assist when injuries occur."

"Of the dead girls you've examined, were there signs of abuse?"

"You mean beating? No, sir. Nothing like that. Whatever may go on over there, it's a cotton mill, not a cotton plantation. Of course . . ."

"Of course, what?"

"Well, the girls aren't whipped, I don't believe. And they are free to leave, of course. But if they leave before their term of employment is up, they'll not obtain employment elsewhere, so they aren't as free as they might otherwise be. In some ways, sir, it *is* actually quite similar to slavery."

Who would have had reason to kill Noah Coolidge, and why? The question plagued Beede long after he had taken his leave of the coroner and begun the walk back toward Kerrigan's house. Was Coolidge's death connected in some way to that of Sharon Cudahy? He found it difficult to believe that it was not. Two such violent deaths of people connected to each other in such an intimate fashion—it was impossible for Beede to separate them in his mind. In New Orleans, where human life was daily rendered cheap by passion and disease, it might have been feasible. In Washington City, where congressmen had been known to attack each other physically over personal or political differences, it was barely possible. But in New England!

On the other hand, the two deaths had occurred many miles apart—nearly a day's journey on foot. Who might have had both the freedom and the ability to travel between Manchester and Warrensboro, and at the right time?

And what possible motive might connect the two? If, as he supposed, Coolidge had taken advantage of his position in order to obtain sexual favors from Sharon Cudahy, he then might have had reason to murder her to protect his reputation. But since he was also a victim, that scenario seemed unlikely. Further, Coolidge seemed to have done little—perhaps nothing—to cover up his relationship with the murdered girl.

That point also bothered Beede. Why had Coolidge *not* attempted to hide his relationship with Sharon Cudahy? It would hardly have raised his standing in the community to be exposed as an adulterer, regardless of its potential effect on his standing with his employer. Yet Coolidge had acted as if he lived in sublime indifference to gossip and scandal. Did he not value his reputation more than that? It might be useful, Beede thought, to speak to Coolidge's widow.

Lost in thought, he directed his steps toward the river. For a considerable time he stood on the bank, looking at the scene before him. There was the Kerrigan mill, thumping and grinding, tearing apart cotton bales and transforming them into cotton thread and cloth. There was the bridge, the wooden railing still broken where he and his assailant had struggled and fallen into the water. And there below were the rapids, which swept everything downstream to Nashua, and Lowell, and the sea.

Strange, he thought, how the river had changed so dramatically in his own lifetime. As a youth, he would have known it merely as a pleasant stream, well suited for peaceful fishing from the riverbank. The falls would have been thought of, if at all, as an obstacle to navigation. And now, after only two short decades, they were on the verge of becoming the hub of a new form of human endeavor. No longer merely man's adversary, they were becoming his servant. He suspected that he would never be able to see the river in the same light again.

And if the river could be harnessed to spin thread and to make cloth, he had no doubt that it could be used for other purposes as well. He had no idea what they might be, but he imagined that the power produced by falling water could be adapted to a multitude of uses. Perhaps the efforts of a handful of industrious and enterprising men could alleviate much of the backbreaking labor that presently consumed mankind and offer them an opportunity to further develop their imaginations and their compassion.

And, no doubt, their greed, also. Beede had a sense that greed played more than a minor role in the gruesome death of Noah Coolidge. Not greed for money, perhaps—not avarice, necessarily—but an overwhelming desire to possess something that belonged to another or to prevent another from acquiring it.

The place where he had finally contrived to pull himself and the peddler from the water must, he realized, be close at hand. He set out in search of it.

It was, he discovered, several hundred feet farther yet. He saw the dry grasses, still recovering their posture from having been beaten down, and he noticed the pathway that his rescuers must have followed in their efforts to reach him. He followed the path to its origin and found himself behind the tavern where he and Deborah Tomkins had sat awaiting the stagecoach to Concord.

To his left he saw an orderly row of two-story brick buildings: boardinghouses for some of the female operatives, as they were called. In one of those houses, he assumed, lived Alice Patterson.

The houses faced away from him, toward the street, but he noticed that a number of windows looked out upon the river. Could someone in one of those houses have witnessed the events of that evening when he went into the river? It might be useful to make inquiries among the mill girls themselves. Perhaps someone there saw Noah Coolidge pull himself from the stream. Perhaps she even bore witness to his murder.

Chapter 28

The first order of business, he decided, was the wife of Noah Coolidge, painful as that would be. He obtained her address from Kerrigan and called upon her the following morning.

She lived with her daughter in a small brick cottage that resembled in many respects the larger buildings that housed the mill girls. He assumed the buildings had all been erected according to one or two simple plans, probably at about the same time. They were largely devoid of decoration, although the presence of lilac bushes around the Coolidge house offered a promise of springtime color that the boardinghouses lacked.

The door was answered by a neatly dressed child of perhaps five or six years, who immediately made her manners with a quick curtsy, even before Beede could speak. She then stood waiting expectantly for Beede to state his business. Beede remembered, in his childhood, doffing his cap and bowing from the waist whenever he came into the presence of an adult, or indeed when an adult passed on horseback or in a carriage, but it was a practice that seemed to have fallen into disuse in recent years. Seeing the gesture of respect practiced here by such a young child gave him momentary pause.

"Good morning," he said. "I am Josiah Beede, from Warrensboro, and I wish to speak to Mrs. Coolidge. Are you her daughter?"

"Her name is Patsy," said a voice behind the girl. "Come inside, Mr. Beede. I know who you are."

The woman who spoke was tall and slender and very young, he thought. The ravages of time had not yet begun their work in earnest, for her face was firm and largely without wrinkles. She wore her auburn hair in a bun, covered with a delicate black veil. It was the only concession to the formalities of mourning that Beede could see.

She stood aside and ushered him into the house while the girl stood close at her legs.

"I am Elizabeth Coolidge," she said. "I assume you have come to pay your respects to Noah's survivors."

"Yes," he said. "But I have questions, also, that I would ask you. I realize these matters may be painful to you, but it would be helpful in my effort to determine who murdered your husband."

"Who, other than you, you mean?" she said, her voice cold.

"I don't believe I'm under suspicion," he said. "I was unconscious on the riverbank myself that night. I believe Mr. Kerrigan and his domestic staff can confirm this."

She favored him with a brief nod of agreement. "Yes, I had heard so. It appears that no one could have killed my husband, and yet, someone did."

"Yes."

"It was cold-blooded murder, sir, and no one seems concerned to find the person who did it."

"I am, Mrs. Coolidge. It is the reason I've come to see you."

She looked at him skeptically.

"And why would you be concerned about our troubles, sir?"

"I believe your husband's murder is related to another murder that occurred in my village a few weeks ago. I would like to ask you some questions that might help clarify these events in my mind."

He waited. She made no response for a moment. Finally, she stood aside and opened a door that led into a small parlor. Beede entered ahead of her, and she closed the door noiselessly behind him, motioning him to a seat as she did so. She sat herself on a bench across the room.

"I am at your disposal, sir," she said. "If you can help me bring my husband's murderer to justice, you will have my full and fervent cooperation."

They talked for some time, but Beede came away no wiser than before. Of one thing, Elizabeth Coolidge seemed certain: Her husband had not been unfaithful to her, despite the mounting evidence to the contrary. She seemed so thoroughly convinced on this point that Beede began to wonder if he had misunderstood the information he had received from Mrs. Webb, Sharon Cudahy's landlady. But what had been the purpose of those Sunday trysts, if not infidelity?

"Mr. Coolidge was a good and faithful husband," Mrs. Coolidge said hotly when he raised the issue with her. "I do not know what his purpose may have been in visiting the Irish girl so frequently, but I am quite persuaded that his intentions were neither lustful nor romantic. I have never had occasion to doubt his devotion to his wife or his family."

"Well-meaning men, nevertheless, often succumb to temptation," Beede said, thinking involuntarily of Randolph as he did so.

"I am well aware of that, Mr. Beede," she replied. "But it would have meant the end of his livelihood to indulge himself in such a manner. To Noah, his occupation was the most important thing of all."

"There is reason to suspect—" Beede began before Mrs. Coolidge interrupted.

"I know what people suspect, Mr. Beede," she said. "It was the talk of the community for many months before that wretched girl left us. None of the talk was true. I am assured of that."

"By whom are you so assured?"

"By my own Noah Coolidge, sir."

"And you believed him?"

"You did not know my Noah, Mr. Beede. If you had, you would never have doubted him."

Beede left the Coolidge house more confused than he had entered. He remained unconvinced of the overseer's innocence, but he found himself with new doubts. He told himself that wives often were unaware of their husbands' dalliances, but he was impressed with Elizabeth Coolidge's absolute certainty.

But if Coolidge was not having his way with Sharon Cudahy during those Sunday afternoon visits, what was he doing instead? For he did come for her at her boardinghouse and leave with her for hours on end. Beede could think of no explanation other than that some illicit relationship had existed between the overseer and the mill girl.

The boardinghouses stood in neat rows, lining both sides of the street. Beede made his way there slowly,

knowing that the girls would be in the mills until long
after dark.

He contented himself in the meantime by calling
on the girls' landladies, a chore that turned out to be
less formidable than he had imagined. He found them
to be a varied assortment, with little in common besides a vaguely matronly appearance and an eagerness to entertain visitors that bordered on anxiety. At
each house he visited, he was received, made welcome in the front parlor, served a cup of vile-tasting
coffee and a plate of cream cakes, and a full helping
of gossip.

He heard *only* gossip, and little of it served his purpose. Yes, they knew of the girl in question. Yes, they
knew her by sight. No, they knew little about her other
than that she was Irish, and Catholic, and that it was
said that she was carrying on with the overseer, that
Mr. Coolidge, and wasn't it terrible the way he treated
that poor Mrs. Coolidge. No, they didn't know Mrs.
Coolidge except to speak to on the street. Well, she
was a bit standoffish, wasn't she, probably due to the
fact that the Coolidges hailed from over to Kenne-
bunk. It was well known that folks from Maine kept to
themselves.

Beede remained at the last boardinghouse on his list
until long after sunset, when the girls began trickling
in from the mill. One by one, the girls were drawn into
the discussion. They, too, remembered Sharon Cudahy, some fondly, some less so.

"I would say hello to her, of course, but I can't say
I really knew her," said a small, thin young lady whose
apparent frailty was belied by a hard-lined face. "I
walked with her once or twice on our way back to the
boardinghouses. I'm not certain which house she lived
in. We would say our good-byes at the front door here,

and she would continue walking down the street toward the river."

"She didn't live around here," said a blonde girl, whose ringlets framed a round, pink face. She had been introduced to him, but Beede had already forgotten her name. "She was a papist, you know, and Mr. Coolidge put her up in a house across the river. Sometimes that young peddler would walk her home, I think."

"Well, Mr. Coolidge *would* have to separate her from the rest of us," said her companion. "It wouldn't do to put a *Catholic* in amongst us."

"Did she have friends?" Beede asked.

"Well, of course," said the blonde girl. "She was quite pleasant, actually. She spoke funny, though. I suppose it was because she was Irish."

"I would like to talk to some of her friends," Beede said. "I must know more about the girl, I think, if we are ever to find her murderer and make sense of her death."

"I don't know that anybody was closer to her than anyone else," said the blonde girl. "On account of her living over to the other side."

"Well, there was Alice Patterson," said the other. "They seemed close until the last month or so."

"They had their falling-out," said the blonde girl. "That last two or three weeks—just before Sharon disappeared—they seemed to quit speaking."

"Did they, now? I didn't hear about that," said the girl's companion.

"Oh, yes," said the blonde. "You wouldn't hear of it, I suppose, up there in the carding room, but they maintained a certain chilly distance in those last few days."

"Why did they grow apart?" Beede asked.

"I don't know the answer to that," said the blonde

girl. "Perhaps no one knows, excepting Alice. If I were required to guess, I'd say it involved a gentleman."

"Mr. Coolidge?"

The girl shook her head. "I don't believe so, but I cannot be certain. Most of us talk freely about our gentleman friends, but Sharon never did. Nor did Alice. Perhaps she feared that someone would attempt to win away the affections of her beau, if his name were known to us."

"And Sharon?"

"I, for one, cannot imagine anyone competing successfully with Sharon," she said.

So there had been a falling-out between the two friends, Beede mused as he walked back to Kerrigan's house, where he was to spend the night. It was interesting that Alice Patterson had said nothing about her differences with Sharon Cudahy.

Was it, as the girls had suggested, a falling-out over a suitor? And, if so, who might that suitor have been? Alice had talked at length with Mrs. Shelton about someone named Peter Taylor, but he had had the impression that the boy in question lived near her home in East Sandwich, not among the denizens of this southern New Hampshire mill town. Had he imagined this?

Beede could see that life in the mills, with its opportunities for girls to become self-sufficient, could well change a young woman's outlook. The opportunities stemming from such a life would, without doubt, include more than simple economic freedom. There would be lectures to attend, books to read, new people to meet, and new affections to develop. Could "Peter Taylor" have been merely a ruse, so strangers such as

Mrs. Shelton and he would not know her true interests in someone here?

It was a matter that would have to be taken up with Alice when next he saw her. It could wait, however, for in the meantime, there was more important information to acquire.

He turned his steps toward the mill itself, in search of the young Scotsman, Coolidge's assistant, Richard Hamilton.

The mill yard gate was locked, so Beede began a systematic canvass of the taverns. It was a time-consuming process, as he had no idea where Hamilton might typically go for drink and conviviality. It was unlikely that he was a temperance man, Beede thought. He knew the movement was making itself felt on both sides of the ocean, but Hamilton was a recent arrival from a land that excelled in the making of whiskey.

It was late in the evening when he finally tracked the young man to a decrepit ordinary on the outskirts of the village. Hamilton sat alone in a nearly deserted taproom, nursing a tankard. He was deep in his cups.

"Drinking alone?"

Hamilton looked up with a sour expression. "They left me," he said. "My companions have deserted me in my hour of need and left me here to drink alone."

"What is it that you need?" Beede asked.

"Well, that should be obvious. I need another toddy." He drained the last of the liquid from his tankard and looked directly at Beede for the first time.

"I know you," he said.

"Yes."

"You visited Mr. Coolidge not long before his

death, did you not? You were asking about one of the mill girls."

"Sharon Cudahy."

"She passed on, I hear. So sad, for someone to die so young."

"Her parting from this world required human assistance," Beede said. "She was strangled."

Hamilton nodded, as if it were only what he would have expected. "I didn't know her, really, but I could see how she could have inspired such passions. She was a striking young woman. Even on the weaving-room floor, she stood out like a rose among thistles. But if she's dead, why are you inquiring about her?"

"Ah, well. I should like to explain that to you," Beede said, "in return for some information you might be able to provide."

"In that case, please join me, Mr. . . ."

"Beede. Josiah Beede."

"Please join me, Mr. Beede. And I believe it's your round." He held up his tankard significantly.

"I am glad of some company," Hamilton said, after Beede had seen to it that the young man was properly fortified. "I fear that a prolonged evening without pleasing conversation would leave me morose to the point of suicide."

"Truly?"

Hamilton nodded. "I have come upon some distressing news, and it has caused me to question my decision to emigrate to this country."

"I understand that many Englishmen have occasion to question such decisions after they arrive," Beede said sympathetically. "I suppose it's because this is such a vast continent and that much of it is so wild, still."

Hamilton drew himself up in indignation. "I, sir, am a Scotsman, not an Englishman. And as for wilderness, I have seen nothing on this continent so far that can compare with the highlands of my own country. No, I am troubled by professional concerns. I learned today that Kerrigan Mills will soon cease operations, and I will be without a livelihood."

"So I understand," Beede said. "Mr. Kerrigan informed me of this during my previous visit."

"Would that he had informed the rest of us," Hamilton said bitterly. "His employees do not know of this decision. I learned it only by accident from one of the men who are building the new village across the river. Apparently, it's common knowledge over there."

"Are you certain that the employees do not know? I have reason to believe that at least one of the mill girls has some general knowledge of this," Beede said, thinking of the conversation Deborah Tomkins had had with Alice Patterson.

"Then she must have some source of information that is unavailable to the rest of us," Hamilton said. "None of the employees with whom I have talked had any idea that their future here was so limited."

"I am surprised. Perhaps she learned about it from Mr. Coolidge."

Hamilton shook his head. "Mr. Coolidge was likewise unaware," he said. "I am certain of that. Only last week he was telling me that he hoped to acquire a part interest in the mill in the near future. I gather Mr. Kerrigan had encouraged him in this belief."

"Strange," Beede said. "What will you do if the mill closes?"

Hamilton shrugged and again drained his tankard.

"I suppose I shall cross the river and seek employment there," he said. "I am an accomplished mechanic, and I am quick with sums, and I have many years' experience with cotton weaving and spinning. I should have little difficulty getting on. It's just the uncertainty of the thing that rubs me the wrong way."

Beede rose to order a refill of Hamilton's tankard, but the young man motioned to him to remain.

"It's my round," he said. He picked up his tankard and Beede's and weaved his way to the cage where the publican was holding court.

Beede sat and considered this information. Why, he wondered, had Kerrigan not told his employees what their future held in store? Presumably, he feared losing his workforce too soon, which would leave him unable to continue running his mill long before he was prepared to close its doors. But if that were the case, how had Alice Patterson learned of it? And once she had learned of it, why did she remain rather than seek employment elsewhere?

Perhaps she had only deduced that the mill was soon to close? But, if that were the case, what clues had there been that such a future awaited them all? And why had not others also made the same deduction and reached the same conclusion?

Had he underestimated her intelligence? Was she, perhaps, more perceptive than he had assumed? It would not be the first time he had misjudged another human being, nor, he suspected, would it be the last.

On the other hand, if she had deduced correctly, why had she not said something to her friends, who worked alongside her at the looms each day? In Beede's experience, information was one of the most valuable commodities in the exchange between people, and a piece of information of such great import would have been nearly impossible for most human beings to resist passing along. She might, of course, be unsure of its reliability, but he doubted that she would be overscrupulous about such considerations. And even if she were, why wouldn't she apply the same scruples to Deborah Tomkins, who she had not met prior to Alice's visit to Warrensboro and who she was not likely ever to meet again?

"To continued employment," Hamilton said after returning to the table with their drinks. He raised his tankard, and the two men clicked their full containers together.

"Tell me, Mr. Hamilton," Beede said after they had drunk. "Do the mills in England and Scotland employ children as they do here? I find that aspect of the industry depressing."

"Aye, and even younger," Hamilton said. "It is one of the reasons I came to America. In Scotland I saw children working the looms and spinning jennies who were barely able to see the shuttles, let alone reach them."

"Do they work the same long hours?"

"Aye, and they're liable to feel the overseer's whip if they make a mistake, or if their attention wanders. Conditions here are altogether better, in my opinion."

"Do the overseers ever take advantage of their charges?"

Hamilton looked up, startled. "You mean violating them?" he said. "I have seen it happen. Not here, fortunately. Not yet, in any event."

"I had heard," Beede said, "that it *had* happened here. At Kerrigan Mills."

"Here? Have you heard names?"

"Two," Beede said. "Sharon Cudahy. Noah Coolidge."

To Beede's astonishment, Hamilton broke into laughter.

"Noah?" he said. "Of all people, not Noah!"

"I have heard otherwise."

Hamilton shook his head vigorously. "You have been misinformed, Mr. Beede," he said. "I worked with the man every day for six months. We talked but little about matters unrelated to business, but I would lay an oath that he was as chaste as a maiden, at least as far as the mill girls were concerned. He was more devoted to his family than any man I have ever known."

"Miss Cudahy's landlady says Mr. Coolidge often called upon Miss Cudahy on Sundays and that they would disappear for hours."

"Perhaps so," Hamilton said. "But I'm certain that nothing untoward occurred during those visits, no matter where they might have gone. Noah Coolidge may have admired Miss Cudahy, as I did myself, but it would have gone no farther than that. I'd stake my life on it."

Beede pondered this information, if such it was. If true, it forced him to reconsider a number of assumptions he had begun to accept as fact, and it raised new questions that he could not, at present, even begin to express. But all his questioning so far had tended to confirm what Richard Hamilton was now saying to him.

He looked up, puzzled, and tried to form a question that might put the matter into perspective. He saw Hamilton looking at him expectantly.

"I believe it's your round, again," the clerk said, offering his tankard.

•   •   •

He returned to Kerrigan's shortly before midnight, disconsolate and more than a little inebriated. The house was dark save for a single candle in the foyer that almost guttered out in the blast of wind from the open front door. He took the candle and made his way upstairs to his room, but as he passed his host's room, the door opened. Kerrigan stood before him in his nightshirt.

"Ah, there you are, sir," Kerrigan said. "I had feared that I would miss you if I did not see you again tonight. It is your intention, is it not, to return to Warrensboro on the morning coach?"

"That is correct."

"Then I am gratified that I was still awake when you came in. A letter arrived for you today, while you were out. It is from Warrensboro, I note. I had anticipated seeing you before now, for I thought that it might be important. Nevertheless, I am happy to be able to present it to you."

"I wonder how anyone in Warrensboro knew where I was," Beede said.

"I can answer that. They know because I told them. I thought that someone should be made aware of the events that have transpired, and so I wrote a letter to the Warrensboro postmaster. I assumed that he would deliver it to someone with an interest in your whereabouts. I'm pleased to see that my surmise was correct."

He reached inside his room and lifted the letter from a small table. Beede thought he had seen the small, neat handwriting with which the letter was addressed, but he could not think where. It was, he thought, a feminine hand.

Beede took the letter to his room and read it by candlelight. It was from Deborah Tomkins:

Dear Mr. Beede,

We learned today that you were assaulted during your investigations in the Amoskeag region, but that you are recovering nicely. Please accept our prayers and concern for your well-being. Be aware that you are in all our thoughts. I'm certain that I speak for everyone here.

I had not intended to trouble you with my thoughts while you are recovering from your injuries, but I have concluded that my information might be useful to you. I recalled today a bit of a conversation that I had engaged in with one of the girls in the boardinghouse where I stayed while we sojourned at the Kerrigan Mills. Whether it has meaning, I know not, but it seemed odd to me, and I thought you might also find it so.

During my visit to Manchester I made the acquaintance of several of the girls who were employed in the mills. Staying together in the same boardinghouse as we did, sharing the same room, in fact, we had occasion to discuss many matters of mutual interest in the hours before bed. I became quite close to one girl in particular, whose name is Martha, and we have continued to correspond since my return to Warrensboro.

I believe I told you that I thought Alice might have been romantically interested in Albert Sanborn, the peddler. I suggested as much to Martha not long before I left the boardinghouse. She said that she had heard nothing to this effect but agreed to ask discreetly among the other girls.

*I received a letter from her today, and she is
most emphatic in her insistence that no one in
her acquaintance has ever heard even the
slightest rumor concerning Alice, at least as far
as her interest in Mr. Sanborn. She did,
however, say that she and her friends have
grown suspicious that Alice has become
engaged in some sort of activity of an unusual
and perhaps illicit nature. She has, for one
thing, become extraordinarily secretive, and
this, as you are well aware, is most unlike her
usual temperament.*

*Normally, I do not abide gossip,
particularly when it concerns relationships—
putative or real—with young men. However, I
feel certain that Alice is "romantically
involved" with someone, and I cannot help
feeling it would be helpful to know who that
someone might be. Why it might be helpful I
cannot say, but my intuition tells me that it
will give us some insight into the
circumstances of the tragic events with which
we are now concerned.*

The rest of the letter concerned events in the town
and the state of affairs on his farm, which Beede
skimmed quickly. He paused a moment at the close:
"Your friend, Deborah Tomkins," pleased to think that
she regarded him in a friendly manner.

Beede refolded the letter thoughtfully and placed
it in an inside pocket. He could think of no reason
why the identity of Alice Patterson's suitor, or even
the object of her secret admiration, might have a
bearing on the solution to the murder of Noah
Coolidge or Sharon Cudahy. He had come to respect
Deborah's intuitive grasp of her circumstances, how-

ever, and he was inclined to pay attention to her fore-
bodings.

But what did it mean, and why did it matter? There
seemed little doubt that Sharon Cudahy had been
killed in a fit of anger and lust. What could Alice Patterson have done to alter that? As for Noah Coolidge,
there seemed to be even less that she might have done
to affect *that* outcome.

Chapter 29

The coach to Concord and Warrensboro left early the following morning. Beede saw to it that Albert Sanborn was aboard and then followed close behind on his horse. He did not believe Sanborn would attempt to desert him, but there was no sense in tempting fate.

They stopped in Concord to change and water the horses. Beede led Sanborn to a tavern, where they discussed the day's business.

"You're certain that your plan will work?" Sanborn said. "I don't fancy my chances of escape again, if it does not."

"There are no certainties in life, Mr. Sanborn, but I believe this will work. Once I had thought about the evidence, the solution to Miss Cudahy's slaying seemed clear."

"Pity you didn't think about the evidence sooner,"

Sanborn said, dryly. "It would have saved me no end of anxiety."

"I agree. But I did not, and there is no turning back the clock. There are no second chances."

The coach was ready to depart, and the two men hastened to join it. As he followed the coach on horseback, Beede found himself wondering again about the strange behavior of Noah Coolidge. That night on the bridge over the Merrimack, when Coolidge had attacked him, made no sense. Neither did Coolidge's subsequent murder. What had caused Coolidge to act as he had that night?

He had assumed that Coolidge was protecting his reputation from accusations that he had taken advantage of Sharon Cudahy. After talking to mill girls and landladies, and most particularly to Richard Hamilton, he had come slowly and reluctantly to the conclusion that Coolidge was innocent of the charge and that few people, other than Mrs. Webb, believed otherwise.

But if he were innocent, what prompted him to react in such a violent manner? The logical answer was that Coolidge was attempting to protect someone. But if not himself, who might it be?

Sharon Cudahy? It was too late for that.

Hamilton? Kerrigan? Neither professed to know the girl personally. Hamilton, in fact, had hardly been at the mill long enough to establish an acquaintance with her before she left in such haste.

And why did she leave so quickly and stealthily? Deborah Tomkins believed Sharon was pregnant and seeking a way to rid herself of the unwanted child. But whose child might it have been?

He had more questions than answers and still had more questions than answers when they arrived in

Warrensboro. He put the questions aside for the time being in order to deal with the business at hand.

They stopped first at Stephen Huff's house. Although initially dubious, Huff listened to Beede's explanation.

"I fear it sounds all too likely," he said reluctantly. "And I suppose we should move on this information immediately."

"I doubt that the murderer will escape us if we do not move quickly," Beede said. "However, I see no reason to wait. It's best that we go ahead."

They walked together to the house, and Beede knocked on the door. It opened presently, and Jacob Wolf stood facing them expectantly.

"Josiah."

"Hello, Jacob. May we come in?"

Wolf retreated wearily, holding the door open wider to allow the two men to enter. He was unprepared for the third man who came in behind them.

"You remember Albert Sanborn, I believe?" Beede said.

"The young peddler," Wolf said dully.

"That's correct," Beede said. "As you may know, Albert has been living with me for several weeks while Constable Huff and I have been investigating the death of Sharon Cudahy.

"I know," Wolf said. "Free boarding for a suspected murderer doesn't seem appropriate, somehow."

"Ah, well, Albert is no longer a suspect," Beede said. "We're all but certain we have identified the murderer, and we expect to apprehend him very soon."

"Very soon," Huff repeated. "Just a few small matters to clear up."

"In the meantime," said Beede, "young Albert has

decided that he enjoys farm work after all, and he is hoping to find sufficient acreage nearby on which to establish himself."

"I've managed to save a considerable sum from my profits," Sanborn said. "I believe that I can make a substantial payment for the right property."

"I happened to mention to Albert that you had been thinking of selling your land," Beede said. "He asked if he could come inspect the property immediately, and I said I felt sure you wouldn't mind."

"Indeed not," said Wolf, brightening considerably. "Be my guest, young sir, and inspect whatever you like. I'll be happy to show you around."

"I thought that he might begin by inspecting the house itself," Beede said. "Is that acceptable to you?"

"Certainly," Wolf said. "Look wherever you like. I'll be here to answer any questions you may have."

"Go on, Albert," said Beede. "Inspect the house. Mr. Wolf has given his permission."

The young peddler nodded and went off. Wolf watched him go, then turned expectantly to the two men remaining.

"So you are about to arrest someone for the murder of the young girl," he said. "This is certainly good news. Can you tell me who the culprit is?"

"Oh, yes, I think we can tell you," said Beede. "It will be common knowledge by tomorrow, and I know you won't give the murderer advance warning and allow him to escape."

"Indeed not."

"But it might be easier," Beede said, "to explain how we came upon the solution to the mystery."

"I am curious."

"Well," said Beede, "the solution occurred to me after our Thanksgiving dinner."

"*After* dinner?"

"Long after, actually, but the solution was presented to me at that time. I simply didn't recognize it until some time later. You see, while preparing our Thanksgiving dinner, Mrs. Shelton had occasion, of course, to kill a chicken."

"And what does this have to do with the murder of Sharon Cudahy?"

"I'm coming to that. When Randolph and I inspected the place where the girl's body was found, we came across a few small white beads. They looked like this one."

Beede took a bead from his pocket and held one out to Wolf in his hand. Wolf inspected it at close range.

"I believe I've seen one of these before," he said.

"I'm quite certain you're right," Beede said. "Randolph and I had seen them before, also, many years ago. It's a rosary bead, and worshipers in the Catholic faith use them to help them remember their prayers. I was married to a young French girl from New Orleans, and she used a rosary with beads much like these."

"You're saying that this bead belonged to the murdered girl?"

"Precisely," said Beede. "But then we found another bead precisely like this one in the gizzard of our Thanksgiving chicken. And I began to wonder how it might have gotten there."

"Chickens often pick up stones and swallow them to help them digest their food," Wolf said, musing. "They don't have teeth, you know."

"Exactly what I thought," Beede said. "But our chicken hadn't been near the place where we found the girl."

"Perhaps she picked up the bead in your farmyard," Wolf said. "That would imply that the girl had been murdered on your land."

"Or yours," Beede said.

"Mine?"

"Perhaps you'll remember this chicken," Beede said. "It wandered into your farmyard last week and mingled with your own fowl. You returned it to me on Monday. At the time of the murder, it was in your yard, not mine."

"But you have no way of knowing where the chicken picked up the bead," Wolf said. "Why must it have come from my yard? Is it not more likely that it came from yours?"

"I thought about that," Beede admitted. "But I think it unlikely that something so attractive—to a chicken—would have remained in the yard very long. If it had been in my yard all those days, another bird would have gobbled it up long before."

"Even if the chicken picked up the bead somewhere other than your yard," Wolf said, "it need not have come from mine. Perhaps she picked it up on the road. I don't know where she wandered before she came to me."

"I thought of that, also," Beede said. "And I felt that we needed another test before we accused you of murder. That's why I asked young Albert to accompany us."

"You said Albert was inspecting the house and that he was interested in purchasing the farm from me," said Wolf, his eyes narrowing with suspicion.

"Yes, I did," Beede said. "And that is what he is doing as we speak, although I'm not certain he has saved enough money just yet to purchase a farm as grand as yours. While he was inspecting your house, I asked him to look for something that might be familiar to him."

"Familiar to him?"

"And I see he has returned. How did you fare, Albert? Did you find what you were seeking?"

"Indeed I did, sir," said the youth as he entered the room. "It was in the bed chamber, where it might be expected."

He held the object aloft in a triumphant pose.

"This, gentlemen, is the lead comb I sold to Sharon Cudahy only months ago."

Chapter 30

"I loved her," Wolf said. "She gave me new life. Seeing her in my house, hearing her singing softly to herself as she worked on the spinning wheel. There was music here, where there had not been music before."

Wolf was standing by the mantel, some time later. The appearance of the lead comb had seemed to destroy him utterly. He had cried broken sobs for nearly half an hour before he could be sufficiently calmed. Now he seemed compelled to tell the story.

"She came to me in the summer. She appeared at my door during an afternoon rain, and she was shivering and dripping. I brought her into my house and gave her some tea. She was about Lavinia's size, so I showed her where Livvy's old clothing was kept. And then she slept all day and all night."

"And when she awakened?" Beede prompted.

"I was sitting by the window when I felt her touch

on my shoulder," Wolf said, after a sigh. "I turned, and she was standing there in Lavinia's favorite dress. For a moment I could not speak. It was as if my Livvy had returned to me."

"Did she speak? Thank you for your kindness?"

"She thanked me for my kindness," Wolf said. "But she did not speak."

"How, then?" Beede asked, although he had an inkling of what the answer might be.

"She took my hand," Wolf replied, "and led me to her bed."

Wolf looked around at the barren house. "I was a lover after all these years. It seemed miraculous. And I believed that she felt for me as I did for her. I have since come to believe that she took me to bed out of gratitude for my care. And there are limits to gratitude."

He had been standing with his back to the fire. Now he turned to face it, turning away from the small party of accusers. He stared into the flames and spoke more softly than before. "When Lavinia died, I ceased caring about my surroundings," he said. "Sharon changed that. For that gift alone, I would have given her anything within my power to give. But what she wanted was my soul."

"Are you saying that Sharon Cudahy was a witch?" asked Huff. He glanced at an equally bewildered Beede.

"She was a papist," Wolf said hotly. "Are they not witches, one and all? Do they not seek to seduce us with their wiles and cause us to follow false gods?"

Beede thought briefly of Adrienne, who was Catholic to her core. Religion had certainly played a part in the friction between them.

"How did Sharon Cudahy seduce you to false gods?" Huff asked.

"She used her own unborn child," Wolf said with evident bitterness. "Our loving had put her in a family way. When she told me the news, I was overjoyed. Here, at last, was the child I had always wanted, which Lavinia had been unable to bear. I offered her marriage. I asked no dowry. I had land already, and I was able to support her and our child in substance, if not comfort."

"And she refused?"

"She did not merely refuse; she laughed at me. If she ever were to marry, she said, it would be to a much younger man. A Catholic man and, if possible, an Irish man.

"'But the baby,' I said. 'The baby will need a father, and a means of support. I can offer you that. And if I am old, well, that means your life with me will be short. And when I am gone, you can find your younger man, and you can offer him land as a dowry.'"

"But she still refused you?"

"'New England land,' she said. 'Who wants New England land? And who will want me when I am worn out at a young age from keeping house and raising a child on this slovenly farm?'"

"She must have made you very angry," Beede said.

"No, Josiah," said Wolf. "Her words hurt me deeply, but I was too downhearted to respond in anger. It was what she said next that caused me to respond in blind anger.

"She said, 'I should be going now. And do not worry that the child will be a burden to you. The child will be disposed of quietly. It will not be the first time, and I fear it will not be the last.'"

Wolf turned away from the men and walked slowly to the window.

"I was consumed with rage," he said. "I caught hold of her and dragged her to the bed. She screamed and struggled. I'm aware that I'm old, and my strength is not what it once was, but on that afternoon I had the strength of many men. When I was done with her, she lay still and I found that my hands were around her neck. Her eyes—those eyes—stared blankly at me. I closed them, and she did not object."

"She was dead," Beede said. It was a statement, not a question.

"I killed her," Wolf said. "I believe she deserved to die. Perhaps she wanted to die. But she had no right to kill her child. No right at all. After I realized that she was dead, I determined to bury her behind my house. But I discovered that I could not do so. Each time I passed her grave I would think of what I had done. Instead, I carried her as far as I could and laid her in the grass. I believed that she would not be found so quickly as so few tend to use that road."

There was silence for a moment.

"Jacob," Beede said quietly, "I have lived close to you for two years. I have seen you in your barnyard, and I've worked with you in your fields. How is it that I never saw this girl before her death?"

Wolf shrugged. "It was the way she wanted it," he said. "She begged me not to tell anyone about her. When visitors came, which they seldom did, she would shrink back into the shadows where she could not be seen. She was very helpful to me in the house, but she would not set foot outside it."

"What was it that she feared so much?"

"I do not know," Wolf said. "I asked her several times. She would say only that someone would be searching for her."

Huff approached Wolf from behind. "Jacob," he said, "I must arrest you for the murder of Sharon Cudahy. Will you come quietly with me?"

"I'll come," Wolf said. "My life is over."

Chapter 31

Beede was working alone in the barn a few days after the arrest of Jacob Wolf when a shadow fell upon him. Glancing toward the door, he saw with some surprise the figure of Randolph.

Uncomfortable greetings were followed by a few minutes of equally uncomfortable but inconsequential conversation. Beede felt that he should make some move to ease the tension between them, but he could not bring the proper words to mind.

"It is good to see you again," Beede said finally.

Randolph opened his mouth as if to speak, but he did not do so. Instead he hobbled into the barn and stood leaning on his crutches, facing Beede.

"I had forgotten how unpleasant it could be to work alone," Beede said, immediately regretting his words. Randolph had, after all, worked alone frequently while Beede had been away, following the court circuit.

Randolph cleared his throat.

"Perhaps you recall, sir, that our agreement was that I would work for you and learn to farm, and that when I knew enough and had saved enough, I would be free to leave."

"You have my permission to leave at any time," Beede replied. "It was never my intention to hold you against your will."

"I never thought that you would, sir. My remarks were mere preamble. You may know that Jacob Wolf's will leaves all his possessions to me. Unusual, I would have thought, but I am nonetheless grateful for it. His possessions, of course, include his farm."

"I was unaware of that, but I'm happy for your good fortune."

"Thank you, sir. I have seen and inspected his farm more carefully since he notified me of my inheritance, and time alone will tell whether it will be good fortune or ill. Nevertheless, it will enable me to become independent, and the money I saved to buy property can be devoted instead to securing my wife's freedom."

"I'm happy for that, also. I have some money that I intended to give you when you left my employ. That sum, though not large, might also be helpful."

"Again, thank you. But I'm afraid I've been diverted from my purpose in visiting you today."

"And that is?"

"My good fortune, as you term it, means that we will be neighbors. I feel that cordial relations among neighbors are essential to survival in these regions, and I would wish that whatever strains may exist between us could be eliminated. To that end, I would like to apologize for my actions and my feelings toward you."

"No apologies are necessary," Beede said, feeling his shame acutely. "I have been consumed with guilt ever since I left you in the hands of the constable and Squire Tomkins. It is I who should apologize to you."

"The fabled New England conscience," Randolph said with an ironic smile.

"It is an instrument of both good and ill," said Beede. "Often at the same time."

"Perhaps so. In any event, I hope that we can be friendly neighbors. I feel sure that I will be in need of your advice and assistance as I begin my new life."

"You shall have it. And my highest esteem, as well—although the labor of my back may prove to be of greater value to you."

"Perhaps," said Randolph. "We shall see."

"In any event, please feel free to call upon me at any time."

"Thank you, sir."

"And if we are to be neighbors, I think we should be on a less formal basis. Please call me Josiah, as Jacob did."

Randolph smiled. "I fear I am not inclined to do that just yet," he said. "In time, perhaps, I can bring myself to that point."

"Of course," Beede said, crestfallen. "I look forward to that day."

Randolph made his farewells and turned to leave. After a moment's hesitation, however, he turned back to face Beede again.

"If you would be so kind, Mr. Beede, there is a question that has been bothering me ever since I was removed to Squire Tomkins's house. Would you tell me what led to the suspicion that I might have killed the girl?"

"Certainly," Beede said. "It was the rosary bead, the one that Mrs. Shelton found in our Thanksgiving chicken. She speculated that the chicken had gobbled it up in our barnyard, proving that the girl had been here. Since I was away at the time, she concluded that you were the only one who could have brought the girl here."

Randolph frowned. "Strange," he said. "Do you have the bead still?"

"I do."

"May I see it?"

Beede found the bead in his bedchamber, brought it downstairs, and handed it to Randolph. "I did not realize until later that the chicken in question was the one that had wandered into Jacob's barnyard at the time of the murder," Beede said. "Jacob himself returned her to me. It was one of the clues that led eventually to his confession."

Randolph, to Beede's surprise, was laughing.

"I'm afraid you have been misled," Randolph said. "It's an interesting theory, I admit, and I'm grateful that it took the burden of suspicion from me, but it cannot be true."

"And why not?"

"Because this bead has never seen the inside of a chicken," Randolph said, greatly amused. "I have killed more than a few chickens in my life, and opened more than my share of gizzards. The stones in a gizzard are always worn smooth and featureless. If this had been inside your hen for more than a day or two, it would no longer be recognizable as a rosary bead. Indeed, it would most likely be little more than an unidentifiable mound of grit. This bead is hardly altered at all."

He returned the object to Beede's hand and opened the door.

"But Jacob confessed to killing Miss Cudahy."

"So I understand," Randolph said. "Clearly he was

misled as you were. Perhaps his guilt overcame his reason."

"But Mrs. Shelton told me the bead was found in the hen's gizzard."

"Were you there when the gizzard was opened?" Randolph asked. "If you were not present, then you have only her word that she found the bead there."

Beede considered this and realized with a start that Randolph was correct. "I hadn't thought of that. I must speak to Mrs. Shelton about this matter," he said.

"You have taught me much about farming, Mr. Beede, but there are, apparently, some matters that are still foreign to you," Randolph said with a wry chuckle. "Perhaps I will be of more value to you than I thought."

Armed with this information, Beede confronted Mrs. Shelton. To his surprise, she readily admitted that she had found the bead in the house and not in the Thanksgiving chicken, as she had claimed. To his further surprise, she was not at all apologetic.

"You had been blinded by loyalty, Mr. Beede," she said. "You were unwilling to consider the possibility that your precious Randolph might be involved in this awful murder. It was my duty to open your eyes to reality."

"It was your duty to plant evidence pointing to an innocent man?"

She regarded him with a sorrowful expression. "Come, now, Mr. Beede. How was I to know he was not the man you sought? It stood to reason that he was involved. How could it have been anyone else?"

"But it *was* someone else," he said. "Jacob Wolf confessed to the murder."

"I did not know that he was guilty when I told you about the bead I discovered—"

"That you *claimed* to have discovered—"

"That I claimed to have discovered," she admitted. "I invented a small falsehood in order to point you in the correct direction. The bead must have fallen from your pocket, for I found it on the hearthstone one morning after you had left for the fields. It seemed the answer to my prayers."

"And do you tell me, even now, that you do not regret your actions?"

"I regret that my efforts misled you temporarily," she said, "but I must point out that, were it not for me, you might never have come upon the solution to your mystery."

"Nevertheless," he said, "I believe you owe Mr. Randolph an apology for casting suspicion on him."

"He shall not receive it," she said, bristling. "I do not regret my actions in any way. Indeed, I am not certain, even now, that he is not the true villain in this affair. Perhaps he acquired some knowledge of the black arts during his time in New Orleans. Perhaps he clouded Mr. Wolf's mind in order to divert suspicion from himself. Does that not seem more plausible than that an upstanding man such as Jacob Wolf might be guilty of such a heinous crime? Yes, I'm certain that that must be the answer; I don't know why it didn't occur to me before!"

Beede was at a loss for words. For a moment, he could do nothing but stare at the woman in amazement.

"You are dismissed from my service," he said when he had composed himself. "I must go to Manchester tomorrow on a personal matter. When I return, I do not expect to find you on my property."

"You may be assured of it, sir," she said. "I would not remain any longer in this house of negroism."

What did it mean? Was Wolf *not* guilty of the crime after all? Beede thought long and hard about this revelation and, in the end, could conclude only that Wolf was, indeed, guilty. He had admitted as much, and his story of the circumstances of the crime fit everything he knew to be true. It seemed unlikely to the point of absurdity that Wolf might not be the guilty party, even if part of the evidence against him was falsified.

On the other hand, there was the matter of the murder of Noah Coolidge. His death certainly could not have been Wolf's doing, for Wolf had not the means of transporting himself to Manchester to kill a man and to return.

Did that mean that the two murders were unrelated?

But coincidence was even harder to swallow than conspiracy. Whatever had happened, Beede believed that the two incidents were related in some way that he did not yet understand. Perhaps he would never understand.

Months went by. Wolf was tried for murder in what was more a formality than a trial, Wolf having admitted to the crime. Trials were usually major sources of entertainment in New England villages, but surprisingly few spectators were present for the trial of Jacob Wolf. Beede, who had offered his legal services to his neighbor (but was turned down), was one of the few residents of Warrensboro who made the journey to Concord for the proceedings. He supposed that his neighbors were preoccupied with their own affairs.

Many, he thought, felt too close to Wolf to take pleasure from his humiliation. In any event, the trial was over almost as soon as it had begun, and Wolf was returned to jail to await the hangman.

Life went on. The first day of the new year was traditionally the day for settling accounts and paying outstanding debts. As was often the case, Beede received payment for his services in eggs, butchered beef, promises of assistance with planting in the spring, and a small amount of cash. He noticed, however, that the amount of cash received was increasing each year. A cash economy seemed to be catching on, however slowly, in upcountry New England.

On the fourth of March, his election having been duly certified by the college of electors, Martin Van Buren formally took the oath of office in Washington City. Beede realized he could not attend the inauguration and sent his regrets. With a shortage of reliable hired help, he was loath to leave the farm for so long a time so close to the planting season.

In truth, he felt little desire to return. The events of the preceding months had further weaned him from his previous life. He found himself thinking less and less of Washington, and he rarely dreamed of Adrienne and New Orleans.

His involvement in the murder investigation seemed to have created a place for him in the life of the community that years of living among them could not have accomplished. He searched his soul and found that his feelings for the community had changed, as well. He had always felt affection for the town and its people, but they had not truly been *his* town and *his* people—not until now.

For the first time, he found himself thinking of marriage. Clearly, it would be a way of committing himself to the town in an unequivocal way. Clearly, too, it would be an act that the town would recognize as appropriate and good. By marrying—a local girl, of course—he would be establishing roots in this rocky soil and declaring publicly that he had cast his lot with them.

But he saw just as clearly that he could not marry Mercy Gray. However much she might excite him, he could not conceive of a life spent with her. She was too young, in too many ways, and he was likely to make her as unhappy as she would make him. The thought of listening to her playing her fiddle for a lifetime filled him with unspeakable dread. And since she was likely to be the only woman in Warrensboro who would actually wish for a proposal of marriage from him, marriage was probably a forlorn hope.

Perhaps, he thought ruefully, there would be a likely widow in some future year, who would look favorably on him. Although that assumed that he would benefit from the death of some man whose friendship he valued. In this respect, his future promised to be unpleasant.

Jacob Wolf was hanged for the murder of Sharon Cudahy on an unusually balmy Wednesday in April. Beede, though no great aficionado of executions, made a point of attending, though it was held nearly thirty miles away. He had admired Wolf and looked upon him as a friend as well as a neighbor, but his crime could not be countenanced. Beede felt he had a duty to the poor girl who had died so horribly at his neighbor's hand. Perversely, he felt he also had a duty to his neighbor to be present at the end as Wolf had so often been present for him. This sense of duty, both to the murderer and to his victim, seemed illogical when he thought seriously about it—the rational lawyer's mind at work—but his Calvinist soul won out.

He was not alone. Indeed, most of the town of Warrensboro and of the surrounding settlements made the long trek by horse, by oxcart, dog cart, and on foot. Like other executions he had seen, the hanging of Jacob Wolf took on a festive tone. The spectators brought elaborate picnic dinners, and entire families, including children barely old enough to walk, took advantage of the holiday.

Beede stood on the fringes of the bustling, jostling crowd and watched the activity. There were vendors selling food and drink. Printers hawked freshly printed broadsides that told the story of the "old man's folly" in ballad and prose. A local militia provided music with fifes and drums.

Beede knew many of the spectators, for much of New Hampshire's legal establishment was present. Another court season had only recently concluded, and many lawyers had chosen not to return home until after the execution.

Beede watched it all with a sense of unease, knowing there was little that he could do to alter the carnival atmosphere that prevailed at public executions. Reformers had been working to forbid public executions for some years, but they had met with mixed success. For people who spent much of the year tied to their lonely villages, a public hanging was too exciting an opportunity to miss. Irate citizens had been known to mount an all-night vigil at the local jail to ensure that condemned criminals did not commit suicide in their cells and thereby cheat the public of its spectacle.

The event attracted other old acquaintances. As he

stood watching the throng milling expectantly about, Beede heard a familiar voice at his side.

"I wondered if I might see you here, Mr. Beede," said Kerrigan. "I hoped that I would. I fancy that you are not much enamored of these occasions."

"Jacob Wolf was my friend and neighbor," Beede said. "I came to visit him in his cell and be with him in his final hours."

"And how is the condemned man holding up?"

"How could anyone hold up under such circumstances? He is not a happy man, but I doubt he has been a happy man for many years. He is resigned to his fate, and I believe he feels it is merited. I don't doubt that he regrets his crime."

"So would I, if I knew the hangman were waiting," Kerrigan said with a laugh. "Will you accompany him to the gallows?"

"No, he did not desire that I do so. But I intend to be in a position where he can see me and know that I am there."

They talked quietly for a few minutes about the events that had transpired since they had last met. Kerrigan said that young Sanborn, the peddler, had taken a position in Thomas Standish's retail establishment and was doing well. There was talk of marriage, he said, with Standish's young daughter, Sally.

"I'm happy to hear that he is prospering," Beede said. "I'm afraid his experiences in Warrensboro were not happy ones."

"And speaking of marriage," Kerrigan said, "I am considering that step, myself."

"Please accept my congratulations, sir," Beede said. "Have I met your future bride?"

"Oh, yes," said Kerrigan. "She is Miss Alice Patterson, the young lady you so gallantly returned to us."

"I would not have expected that," Beede said. "I

would rather have thought you would marry a Southern girl and return to the South when your lease expires."

"Oh, well, I may yet return to the South in a few years. In the meantime, however, I intend to find employment nearby and wait."

"Wait for what?"

"For Miss Patterson's father to die," Kerrigan said. "He is old, and he is wealthy, at least in terms of land, and Alice stands to inherit a significant portion of his estate. That land, when sold, will contribute substantially to my portion when I begin looking for land in the western cotton states. Land in Arkansas can be had for next to nothing. I could probably buy substantial acreage today, but it amuses me to think of the proceeds from the sale of a New England farm contributing to the sale of land in the slave states."

"And do you have no feeling for Miss Patterson?"

"Of course I do," Kerrigan said. "She is a delightful young lady who will acquit herself well as the domestic head of my household. She can be as imperious as a duchess when she chooses, and she understands the importance of appearances. She is not uncommonly attractive, I admit, but she is ever so enthusiastic, and she is, in addition, becoming quite skillful in certain marital arts, if you catch my meaning."

The crowd noises began to die down, and Beede saw that the prisoner was being escorted to the gallows. He took his leave of Kerrigan.

"Are you returning home after the execution?" Kerrigan called after him. "If possible, might you turn aside and call on Miss Patterson in Manchester? I'm certain that she would want to tell you of our impending wedding. I have business in Boston, I'm afraid, or I would accompany you."

"I should be happy to call upon her at her boardinghouse," Beede said.

"Oh, she isn't at the boardinghouse, now," Kerrigan replied. "I moved her to my house, which is much more comfortable than the workers' quarters. Her mother has joined her so that they may plan for the future. I daresay they are planning a wedding of major proportions—certainly larger than anything seen previously in East Sandwich."

Beede made his way to the front of the crowd, jostling some irate spectators out of the way in his haste. As he stood waiting, he puzzled over Kerrigan's news. In his mind, Beede had begun to think of Kerrigan as a man wholly devoted to enterprise. He was startled to hear the man talk so candidly about matters of the bedroom.

He reminded himself that no man was impervious to desire. But why Alice Patterson? Kerrigan had admitted that she was no beauty, but that was understating the case. She was, to be charitable, plain, and Kerrigan was a man of substance and property. Surely there were other young women, even in the mills, who were fairer of face and possessed of more pleasing disposition.

Beede remembered Deborah Tomkins's observation during their previous sojourn in Manchester. She had marveled that Kerrigan had remembered Alice Patterson and not Sharon Cudahy, and she had thought that he had been disingenuous.

Perhaps she was correct. Mrs. Webb, Sharon Cudahy's landlady, had suspected Noah Coolidge of taking Sharon away on Sunday afternoons for his own pleasure. Richard Hamilton had scoffed at that notion. Perhaps, instead, Coolidge had taken Sharon to see

Kerrigan, the one man he obeyed implicitly and depended upon for his livelihood.

That explanation had the ring of truth, he thought, but it did not explain why Kerrigan would then turn to Alice Patterson as Sharon Cudahy's successor. Even less did it explain why he would choose to marry her. Alice must have some qualities that were not immediately apparent.

But if Beede's speculations were correct, one conclusion was inescapable: If Sharon Cudahy had believed herself to be expectant when she left Kerrigan Mills, Kerrigan himself must have been the father. And if Kerrigan was the father, he did have reason to wish the girl dead, if not to do the deed himself.

On the other hand, Sharon Cudahy's murder was an act of passion, and Beede thought Kerrigan would be more careful than that.

The murder still bore the unmistakable stamp of Jacob Wolf. Much as he wished it to be otherwise, he had no doubts that the man on the gallows was, indeed, Sharon Cudahy's murderer.

There was no minister on the gallows. Beede assumed that Wolf had declined Pastor Gray's offer of spiritual solace. Wolf had been unhappy at the minister's refusal to preside at Sharon's funeral and continued to hold a grudge against the man.

Wolf was asked if he had any final words. He shook his head. The noose was tightened around his neck, the hood was placed over his head, and the trapdoor was sprung. Wolf's body dropped, and Beede heard the snap of his neck. The body dangled at the end of the rope, but there was no life remaining.

"Over a little too quickly for my tastes," Beede heard a spectator say.

"It surprised me, too," his companion said. "They fed him too well. If they'd starved him a little, he would have been lighter, and his neck wouldn't have broken. Would have made for a better show."

The two men moved away, unaware that Beede remained rooted to the spot, seething with barely contained fury.

Chapter 32

He found Alice Patterson, as Kerrigan had said, living in Kerrigan's house. The maid who answered his knock upon his return to Manchester recognized him immediately and escorted him, smiling, to the parlor. There, Alice sat knitting quietly, accompanied by an older woman whom Alice introduced as her mother.

"Mr. Kerrigan told me of your betrothal," Beede said. "Please accept my best wishes for the future."

"Thank you, Mr. Beede," she said. "It is good to see you again. And please accept my gratitude for your part in my good fortune."

"I don't believe I played such a role," he said. "But I thank you, in any event."

She smiled, as the knitting needles continued to click. She was quite accomplished with them, he thought, and seemed never to be without them.

"Are you working still on the stockings for your

brother?" he asked. "I recall that you were knitting them on our journey from Warrensboro."

She shook her head. "I was forced to put them aside for a while. I'm working now on a shawl for myself. The weather is growing warmer daily, but winter will soon be with us again."

The clicking continued without a pause, and Beede found himself staring at her hands, so skillful and sure in their motions, and at the thin steel needles with which she worked. She followed his gaze and smiled.

"You seem fascinated with my knitting needles, Mr. Beede," she said. "Have you not seen them before?"

"Of course," he said. "But they look different, somehow. May I inspect them more closely?"

"Certainly," she said, handing the knitting to him. He took the needles and studied them carefully, noticing her knowing smile as he did so.

A chill coursed through him, despite the roaring fire in the fireplace, as an unsettling thought took hold. The point of one needle was clean and bright. The point of the other was tarnished. "Have you had these needles for some time?" he asked.

"Yes, I have been a confirmed knitter since I was a small child," she said. "Although, now that I think of it, one needle is newer than the other. I had to replace one when it was bent beyond repair."

"Only one needle was bent?" he said.

"Yes. Curious, is it not?"

"It had not occurred to me before," he said. "But instruments such as these could be dangerous, even lethal, if used for some immoral purpose."

"Yes," she said. "I suppose they could."

"I am wondering," he said, "whether it might be that one of the needles was bent beyond repair when you used it to puncture something."

"One moment, if you please, Mr. Beede, before you

continue," she said. She turned to her mother, who was engrossed in a stitching project of her own. "Mother, would you mind asking cook to prepare coffee for our guest? I'm certain he could take some refreshment after his journey."

When her mother had left the room, Alice turned back to Beede. "Please go on, Mr. Beede. You were saying . . ."

"I was saying," he said, "that your needle might have been ruined when it was used to puncture something."

"How interesting," she said. "And where might this have occurred? And how? They've not been out of my possession."

"As for their not having been out of your possession, I'm perfectly prepared to believe it," he said. "And as for where, I would venture to say, on the riverbank . . . perhaps in the left nostril of a large man, who was lying unconscious at the time."

Alice Patterson laughed.

"Are you suggesting that I killed Mr. Coolidge? Yes. I killed him. Your conclusion is correct."

"You admit it?" Beede was shocked by her open confession, not to mention her clear lack of remorse.

"Oh, yes. It was much simpler than I had imagined it would be. I like to walk along the river in the morning, briefly, before going to the mill. On that morning, I happened to come upon Mr. Coolidge. He was not conscious and so was unable to put up a resistance. The opportunity could not have been more fortuitous."

"How did you kill him?" Beede asked.

"It was quite simple, really," she said. "I had my bag with me, and my knitting needles are always in my bag. I merely placed a knitting needle in his nostril and shoved it in as far as it would go. A little pressure with the heel of my hand, and it slid in quite nicely. Indeed, the most difficult part was turning him onto his back. He was quite a large man, you recall."

"How did you know that such a method would be successful?"

"I didn't know," she said with a smile that chilled him as much as his plunge into the river. "An opportunity presented itself, which I knew would not be offered again. I had the knitting needles at hand, and his nostril seemed best suited to my aims. I could have stabbed him in the throat, I suppose, but I feared that there would have been far more bleeding from such a wound. I felt it was in my interest to disguise the cause of death, if possible."

Beede felt a wave of nausea pass through him. He waited until it subsided before speaking.

"May I ask why you killed him? Were you wreaking revenge upon him for having taken advantage of Sharon Cudahy?"

"Mr. Coolidge did not take advantage of Sharon," she said.

"Did you not learn this until after you had killed him?"

"Oh, no," she said. "I have known that for quite some time. Indeed, I never suspected that he had done so. Sharon was not the sort of girl to be coerced by a man, even so formidable a man as Noah Coolidge. She would bestow her favors as it suited her, and only as it suited her."

"Then you do not believe that Coolidge forced himself upon her."

"Noah Coolidge?" She laughed again. "He would have been grateful for any such favors, had she seen fit to grant them. But to take his advantage against her wishes? He would not have been as bold as that. Moreover, he was indebted to another."

"And who might that be?"

"Why, Mr. Kerrigan, of course. Mr. Kerrigan held the key to Mr. Coolidge's livelihood. Mr. Coolidge would have done whatever Mr. Kerrigan asked of him, for Mr. Kerrigan was his employer."

"Are you saying that Mr. Kerrigan assaulted Miss Cudahy?"

"Well, it was hardly an assault," she said, laughing. "Sharon understood the value of establishing a close, personal relationship with her employer."

"So it was not coercion that moved her to consent to his demands?"

"No, sir. If coercion was involved in the matter, it was Sharon who employed it. She understood her power over men and what it could bring her. I learned much from her."

Beede was silent as he pondered ramifications of the girl's words.

"Yes, Mr. Beede," she said, comprehending the meaning of his silence. "I did not go searching for Sharon Cudahy strictly from concern and affection. I considered her my friend, but there are limits to friendship, and it had become clear to me that she had to be removed."

"Why? What had she done to you?"

"She had *done* nothing," Alice said. "But she was an obstacle in my path, and I knew it was essential that she continue running away—or at least that she not decide to return to Kerrigan Mills. Fortunately, your Mr. Wolf handled my problem nicely."

"You *intended* to murder her?"

"If it had been necessary, I suppose. I had not thought so far as that. I believe I would have settled for her assurance that she did not wish to return. In six months, when I had achieved my end, it would have made no difference in any event."

"I don't understand," he said. "Why are you telling me this?"

"Because I have achieved my end," she said, smiling. "And there is nothing that can be done about it. I am betrothed to Mr. Kerrigan, and that is an end to it."

"I *could* tell him what you have told me," Beede said. "Do you think he would be kindly disposed toward a murderer?"

"Do you believe that he does not already know?" said Alice. "I have never spoken of it to him, but I feel certain that he knows what has happened, at least in general terms. I'm not so vain as to believe he would marry me on the strength of my youth and beauty alone. I needed a stronger hold on his loyalties."

"How did he learn about this if you did not tell him?"

"Oh, that was simplicity itself. I let it be known that I had ruined a knitting needle and begged him to replace it. He is aware of the manner of Mr. Coolidge's death, and no doubt he is perceptive enough to deduce the rest."

She shook her head and took up her knitting again.

"And what evidence could you offer to anyone else that would support the theory that I killed Noah Coolidge?" she said. "Certainly you could offer nothing that would induce Mr. Kerrigan to confirm your accusation, and without his support, you would be unlikely to prevail, for I could testify in return that Mr. Kerrigan had impregnated Sharon. In fact, I could testify that he had also impregnated *me*. That would destroy his reputation and weaken his influence in the community."

Outside, snow had begun to fall. If he hoped to return to Warrensboro before the roads became impassable, it would be necessary to leave soon.

"Why, then, did you kill Noah Coolidge?" he asked, finally.

"For insurance, sir. It was necessary to maintain secrecy about Mr. Kerrigan's relationship with Sharon. If it became known, Mr. Kerrigan's reputation in the community would be harmed, perhaps irreparably, and he would cease to be of value to me," she replied. "But the secret could not be maintained if two people knew about it. Mr. Coolidge could not be trusted not to use this information for his own personal gain, rather than for mine. And it is much neater this way, don't you think?"

"After your marriage," Beede said, "do you believe Mr. Kerrigan will be faithful to you?"

"For a while. After all, he knows, or suspects, what happened to Mr. Coolidge, and he must realize that a similar fate could also befall him. But in the long run, I don't care to hold him in enforced fidelity. Indeed, a certain amount of shame on his part might place him more completely under my influence. We shall see, I suppose."

Beede sat in stunned silence. Alice Patterson watched him for a moment. Finally she rose and extended her hand to him.

"I'm afraid I must leave you now, sir," she said. "I'm sure you can find your way out. I'm sorry you cannot stay for coffee."

He rose, still in shock.

"Please try to come to terms with this, sir," she said. "It should not be so very difficult for you. We women are the weaker sex, as you men are always telling us. We must be certain that we are provided for, and we must do whatever is needed to gain that certainty."

Then, as she turned to leave: "I hope you will come to Sandwich for the wedding in the fall. I'm certain that I speak for Mr. Kerrigan as well as myself when I say we would consider you an honored guest."

Alice Patterson, Beede thought as he left the Kerrigan house, was no frail vessel. Indeed, she might well have evaded an arrest for murder, and he could not see a means of forcing her out from behind the protective wall she had so cleverly built.

As a Yankee, Beede had no doubts about man's sinful nature, and he took it to be an article of faith that men and women—and children—could convince themselves of the righteousness of any act they might be inclined to commit. Nevertheless, the flagrant nature of this crime shocked and angered him.

The murder weapon, the knitting needle, lay at the bottom of the Merrimack, if Alice were to be believed. It seemed unlikely that it could be recovered easily, if at all, and without corroboration from another source, it would be merely a random object like so many others people had thrown away. The blood that had clung to it would have been washed away, and the needle itself would have begun to corrode.

Without corroborating evidence, in fact, it would be impossible to link the needle to Alice, even if it were found. Kerrigan could provide circumstantial evidence, for Alice had asked him to replace it, but he would have no reason to cooperate with Beede. He would, in fact, have good cause to muddy the waters further, since connecting the needle to his betrothed might also connect him to Sharon Cudahy.

Perhaps he should speak to someone and pass along what he had learned from Alice. Mr. Townsend, the coroner, might be interested in the information, he thought. But what use could the information be put to, once he had acquired it? He would have nothing more than the secondhand testimony of a stranger, which would be denied by everyone involved.

He walked toward the falls. He stood for a long time watching the rushing water as it plunged over the precipice. Not since that January day in New Orleans when he had seen the British approaching, rank upon scarlet-clad rank, had he felt as powerless as he felt at this moment.

He watched as the water shoved aside all opposition in its rush to the ocean, and he felt feeble and alone. The Kerrigans of the world were determined to have their way, and there would always be people like Alice Patterson around to aid and abet them.

Well, it would be his calling to fight them. He would return to his upcountry farm, but he would continue to seek opportunities to oppose those who would have their way regardless of the needs of others.

He was in a position to do so. He was a lawyer. He had no great need for money. And he had no doubts that the challenges would arise, for bullies and exploiters were everywhere in the world. From his small place in New England, he would do his part.

And if it were not enough?

Well, he told himself, he would be able to say, on his deathbed, that he had not given in. If he could not save the world, he might, at least, be able to save his soul.

And as he thought about it, he realized suddenly that he was not altogether without options, after all. Alice Patterson might never appear in a court of law, but there were other courts, other juries, that might serve almost as well. If she could not be brought to justice for murder, she might at least be deprived of the respectability she had hoped that that murder would acquire for her.

Coolidge had been murdered in order to protect Alice and her chosen husband from ostracism and ridicule. It stood to reason, then, that the good opinion of the community was of great importance to her. The best he could do, then, would be to see to it that the good opinion of the community was denied her. And one person in Manchester would have both the position and the motivation to ensure that this would be the case.

He walked away with new resolution. On the way to his destination, he thought about what he would say and the arguments he would present. And on the way, the river roared its defiance.

It took a while to find the house where they had moved after being evicted from the mill housing. He was met at the door by the same neatly dressed child—Patsy, was it?—as before. This time, after making her hurried curtsy, she hurried off and returned with her mother in tow.

"Mr. Beede."

"Good morning, Mrs. Coolidge. I'm on my way home to Warrensboro, and I thought that I should stop and inform you of the progress of my investigation before I left."

"Have you identified the murderer of my Noah?"

"I believe I have," he said. "If you can spare me a moment, I'd like to tell you what I have learned . . . and what you might be able to do about it."

She studied him intently for a moment, then stood aside for him to enter.

Chapter 33

It was after morning meeting on the Sunday following his return to Warrensboro that Beede again encountered Deborah Tomkins. The day had turned unaccountably warm for April, and Beede had stood watching as the worshipers hurried to their homes for dinner before returning for the evening meeting. Beede felt no such pressure; he knew he faced a cold, solitary meal of bread, cheese, and cider, and he was in no hurry to rush home to it. Far better to stand here in the sunshine for a few minutes and enjoy the fleeting pleasures of the waning winter. The time for planting would arrive soon enough, and then there would be few moments such as this.

"I always enjoy the changing of the seasons," he heard a female voice saying. He turned with a start to see her at his side, quietly standing as if she belonged there and had been at his side forever.

"So do I, Miss Tomkins," he said, making conversation. "Indeed, the longer I remain on this earth, the greater the pleasure I extract from days such as this one."

"Come, Mr. Beede. You're hardly ancient."

He stifled a laugh, not wishing to appear impolite. "I'll be thirty-six years old in August, Miss Tomkins."

"As old as that?" There was a note of amusement in her voice, and he glanced quickly to see whether she was laughing at him. Her face was composed, but there was a twinkle, he thought, in her eyes.

"I was eighteen on October twenty-third," she said at last. "It seems only yesterday that I played with hoops on the common, but it was not yesterday. I have a doll with which I once played happily for hours, but it has languished for many years. I'm afraid that my interests have changed."

A strange conversation this was! Beede thought.

"You will soon be a young woman," he said, since that seemed to be what he was expected to say. He was puzzled by this turn, for Deborah Tomkins had not seemed to him to require flattery or coquetry, as had so many of the young Southern girls he had known.

She responded with a firm shake of the head.

"No, Mr. Beede, I will not *soon* be a young woman," she said. "I am a young woman now. Already I have had suitors. John Potter visited my father only last week. They met behind closed doors, in the sitting room, but I know that he asked my father's permission to call upon me because Mr. Potter himself told me so. My father has not informed me yet, but I know that permission was granted."

"John Potter is a good man," he said. Potter was a landholder of some importance in the west village, perhaps five miles away, a shrewd man with a bargain and a conscientious husbandman.

"John Potter *is* a good man," she acknowledged,

"but he is also an ignorant man. He can barely write his name. He would not be the husband I envisioned."

"I am certain there will be other suitors."

She shrugged. "I will have my share," she said.

She had been staring, as had he, at a plum thicket on a hill beyond the green. Now she turned and faced him directly.

"I had hoped," she said, "that you would be among them."

Once, at Chalmette, a shell had exploded barely fifty yards from where he was standing. He had not seen it coming, and the sudden explosion had startled him out of his wits. That shock was nothing compared to this. After all these years, to be pursued by two women, both of whom were younger than Adrienne had been when he had married her. It was inconceivable.

"Miss Tomkins, I am flattered," he said after a moment. "I hope you will not be offended if I point out to you that there is a vast difference in our ages."

"Vast but not insurmountable," she said, nodding. "We are eighteen years apart. My father is twenty years older than my mother, and they seem content."

"I was married before," he said. "It is not a pleasant memory."

"So I am given to understand," she said. "Women discuss such things, you know, and you have been the subject of more such discussions than you may be able to believe. It is widely thought that you were a brute, who beat your wife unmercifully until death seemed to her a comforting refuge."

He had not expected that, either. He, who had believed himself unshakable, had been shocked to his core twice in less than a minute by a girl half his age. What other shocks might lie in store for him?

"I never beat her," he said, surprised at the defensiveness he heard in his voice. "Not once in our five years together did I lay a hand to her."

"I never thought that you had," she said firmly. "And for the matter of that, there are many ways that a man and woman may hurt each other, some of which are at least as painful as beatings. I have seen the manner in which Mr. and Mrs. Huff live, in a never-ending war of wills. I think I would rather be beaten."

"Surely not."

"I don't know," she said. "Perhaps not. Life's a gamble for all of us; more so for a woman. We make the best choices we can, based on whatever knowledge we can muster at the time, and then work to make the most we can make of them, once we've chosen."

The rest of the Tomkins household had gone ahead and had almost reached the front door of the big house at the far end of the common. Beede wondered what sort of speculation was buzzing through their heads. They must have seen their eldest daughter linger behind at the door to the meetinghouse to converse with the lawyer, the outsider. He studied the gaggle of young Tomkins females, the stocky frame of Israel Tomkins in his bottle green Sunday coat and wide-brimmed hat, the stockier frame of Sarah Putnam Tomkins bobbing beside him. The Tomkinses stared resolutely ahead, as if the absence of their eldest daughter had not yet caught their attention.

"You must know," he said at last, "that your father and I are not close. I doubt he would approve of a match between us."

"My father is not a fool," she said, dismissing his concerns with a wave of her hand. "He fears you as a rival for influence in the community. As a son-in-law, you would no longer be a rival. You might even, on occasion, be an ally."

He watched silently as Israel Tomkins opened the

front door to the big house and shepherded his flock inside. For a brief moment, he thought he saw Tomkins looking in his direction, but it was too fleeting an instant for him to be sure.

Could it be that Tomkins knew what his daughter was now saying? Was this meeting planned, or at least tacitly consented to, by the old man? Had Tomkins already approved such a match, and was he even now encouraging it?

Beede turned to Deborah, intending to ask her that question, and discovered that there was a tear in her eye.

"This is not easy for me, Mr. Beede, but you are making it much more difficult than I had hoped," she said. "As you say, I will have suitors. I need not, and will not, throw myself at you. But a woman must do what she can to fend for herself in this world. I have seen this for myself, and I am determined to make the best marriage I can."

"I cannot believe I am the best you can do," he said feebly, for his heart was no longer in it.

"I do not know. Perhaps you are not. But you are the best I have seen to this date, and the time for a decision is near."

"But . . ."

"And if you were truthful with yourself, you would see that I can offer much to you. I will not talk to you of my father's land, for I do not believe it would sway your decision. Nevertheless, I believe I am not without appeal. I am able to read and write. I am quick with sums. I am skilled in all the crafts a wife should know. I am pretty, I believe. Perhaps you fancy that you think of me still as a child. Well, sir, you are wrong. I have noticed how your manner toward me has altered recently. Clearly, your heart understands what your mind may not have encompassed."

"Miss Tomkins, I am astonished."

"So it would seem."

She gathered her crimson cloak tighter around her.

"I must go now," she said. "My family will be concerned about me. I only stayed after to assist Mrs. Marston with the candles. I will not ask you outright, Mr. Beede, for I fear to hear your answer. I will only say that I hope you will call upon me in the near future. I feel certain that my family would make you welcome."

She stepped through the columns and began walking across the common toward her house, leaving Beede to stare after her in amazement.

She was wrong, he told himself. She was a child still. She had no need to marry for many years. The day in which young women were wed early and bred like mares had passed. Young women were waiting longer before marriage, well into their twenties. The times had changed. And yet, she was very nearly a woman, after all, and a remarkably attractive and self-possessed woman at that. And though she could not see his eyes upon her departing back, he thought perhaps she could feel them, for her walk at once seemed to become straight, proud and, yes, womanly.

Afterword

Visitors who drive through Manchester—New Hampshire's largest city—on their way to the state's lakes and mountains are often amazed by the massive riverfront facade of the Amoskeag Company. Though it remains impressive—not to mention depressing—even today, it was once much more so. At its peak the Amoskeag complex stretched nearly a mile along the eastern bank of the Merrimack River and nearly a half mile on the western bank, and it employed more people than any other textile manufacturing plant in the world.

Today, seeing these skeletal buildings surrounded by an increasingly prosperous city, it may be difficult to imagine the extent to which Manchester lived out nearly its first full century as a company town. It may be equally difficult to imagine this land as it was before it became Manchester. The industrial revolution, of which the Amoskeag companies were a conspicuous symbol, altered the landscape and economy of New England more than any other event, the Civil War not excepted.

In order to facilitate my story, I have fictionalized a number of elements. There is not now, nor has there ever been, a town named Warrensboro, New Hampshire. There was not a Kerrigan Cotton Mill, nor a John Kerrigan, nor for that matter, an overseer named Noah Coolidge. All the characters in my story, with the obvious exceptions of Andrew and Rachel Jackson and Martin Van Buren, are fictitious. There are anachronisms, also, which I have left in place because they seemed important to the story I was telling.

A number of people provided important assistance during the writing of this book. Francine Bradley, an extension agent with the avian sciences department at the University of California, Davis campus, was extremely helpful on the subject of chickens, gizzards, and rosary beads. Several people who I met on a forensic sciences E-mail list contributed useful information concerning murder techniques. Eileen O'Brien, curator of library collections at the Manchester Historic Association, led me through early records of the city of Manchester, both before and after its conversion from farming community to major world manufacturing center.

There were others, too, whose assistance was invaluable. Most of all, I must thank R. Stuart Wallace of Plymouth, New Hampshire, a freelance consultant on New Hampshire history and adjunct professor both at Plymouth State College and the University of New Hampshire's Plymouth campus. Dr. Wallace read the entire manuscript and offered important suggestions. I must also thank the members of the Washington Independent Writers history writing small group, for wise and sympathetic counsel. My agent, Jenny Bent, and my editor at Berkley, Martha Bushko, were extremely supportive and even kind. Ann McMillan, author of a remarkable series of Civil War era mysteries, read the completed manuscript, and I was heartened by her enthusiasm.

Any errors of fact in this book are, of course, my own responsibility. I am grateful to those who prevented me from making further, more egregious mistakes.